EAST
RIVER
TRUST

EAST RIVER TRUST

D.S. COOPER

For Betsy-Bob

ON THE JOB

Urban travel guides love to point out that Brooklyn would be the fourth largest city in America if it were not one of the five boroughs of New York City. Brooklyn has Coney Island, Nathan's Famous, Brighton Beach and Prospect Park. The Dodgers and the Brooklyn Navy Yard are long gone, but two-and-a-half-million inhabitants remain.

There are ninety-one ethnic groups and hundreds of churches, temples and mosques in Brooklyn. There are twenty-three NYPD precincts.

The Seven-Six in Red Hook is one of the smaller precincts. It is a modern house with a blue-tile facade and a phalanx of Radio Motor Patrol units parked halfway onto the sidewalk out front, but it still has the extra large American flag and the traditional green lamps on either side of the front entrance.

Red Hook is the neighborhood of *On the Waterfront*. There are hundreds of two-floor houses and six-story apartment buildings, and a deli or restaurant or barroom on nearly every corner. Trucks come and go from the Marine Terminal at all hours of the day and night. The Manhattan skyline looms beyond Buttermilk Channel and Governor's Island.

Ted Lamont was already a veteran cop when he stood on the roof of the Seven-Six Precinct and watched the second plane fly into the South Tower across the harbor in Manhattan.

"Son of a bitch," he had muttered several times at the sight that morning, before he drove across the Brooklyn Bridge to help.

Eleven years later, almost to the day, Lieutenant Ted Lamont was close to retirement when he arrived to work the third watch at the Seven-Six. Ted wore dungarees and a crew-neck sweatshirt. His black laced boots had soles that were good for running and for sure footing in a pinch. The eight members of his unit worked in plain-clothes. They carried their weapons in the open and wore their shields on chains around their necks. Their job was to keep a low profile on the street and stop crimes in progress.

Ted Lamont and his crew were very good at grabbing bad guys in the act.

He would be riding with Murph. The black guys usually rode to-gether, in another car. And the same with Rodriguez and Sanchez. In Brooklyn, an unmarked car with mixed race occupants might as well have a neon sign on the roof that said *cops*.

They took portable radios from the bank of chargers in the mus-ter room. They wore red wristbands, the color of the day. So that any cop in the city would know that the hand reaching into a scuffle to assist with an arrest—or holding a gun—was on the job. They carried 9mm Glock semiautomatic pistols and handcuffs. They didn't carry spare ammunition, since any hostile encounter would be close and over in moments. Ted had been shot at, but never hit.

His right shoulder hurt like hell.

"Any luck selling the house yet?" Murph asked as they climbed in-to their unmarked unit, a green minivan.

"It's only been on the market a month. I'm not going to give it away."

Ted didn't really want to sell the house in Queens where his kids had grown up. But he didn't want to spend his retirement in the city, either.

"Is the house out on the island ready?"

"Sure. Bev and I are there every weekend."

Ted and Beverly had fixed up a retirement nest in Lindenhurst, with a dock for his boat outside their back door, on a canal off Great South Bay.

"When do you haul the boat out of the water?"

"I leave it in until the stripers are gone. End of October, usually."

"You've got it made, Teddy."

"Come out sometime. We'll go fishing."

"Maybe next year."

Never happen, Ted silently mused. *Murph will never drive halfway out on Long Island to go fishing.*

They cruised the neighborhoods. It was dark. Atlantic Street had four lanes and wide sidewalks with trees and small shops and restaurants and bars. Then Court Street and Smith Street. It was a slow night.

Some nights, they rolled up on bar fights that had spilled outside to the sidewalk. If the combatants were fairly matched and the spectators were behaving, they usually let them tire each other out before they made the easy arrests. If a man was getting rough with a woman or a minor, Lieutenant Ted Lamont would probably get another police brutality complaint entered into his personnel jacket, along with all the others.

But not this night. They drove over to Columbia Street at Van Vorhees Park, where they could see cars getting on and off the Brooklyn-Queens Expressway. They parked their vehicle and waited.

"Hello," Murph said, when a Toyota with four kids drove by.

"I don't think so," Ted said. "But what the hell. There's nothing else going on."

Criminals act a certain way when they are at work. You could see it in the walk, and the looks, in the prison yard at Rikers Island. You could see it when they are selling drugs on the corner. You could see it in the way they drove into a neighborhood with nefarious intents.

Ted wasn't feeling it, but he followed the Toyota anyway, just to shut Murph up.

The Toyota entered in side streets and stopped in front of a single-family house. Ted and Murph double-parked a few doors down and waited.

"Crap," Murph groused. "I hope this isn't a home invasion."

Murph, you knucklehead, Ted thought. *You need to get your street radar adjusted. These are just kids out for fun on a Saturday night.*

"Let's take a look," Ted decided, as he drove the minivan in front of the house and stopped alongside the Toyota. They took a good look at the boys and ignored the car behind them when it honked for their minivan to get out of the way.

"These kids look all right," Ted said.

Three girls came out of the house and piled into the car. Everybody was smiling, except for one of the boys.

"Somebody's not getting laid tonight," Ted laughed as he drove away.

"There can't be seven seatbelts in a Toyota Camry. We could stop 'em and take a closer look."

"They're okay," Ted laughed.

What the hell, Murph. We don't need to look for excuses to toss kids out of a car. Until they repeal stop-and-frisk, we can always find real bad guys. Be patient.

The radios had been unusually quiet. Until some cop on the frequency spoke to everyone listening.

"We might as well go home," the radio voice said. "This place is dead tonight."

"Who said the city never sleeps?" some other cop quipped on his radio.

Murph had another bright idea.

"Since there's nothing going on, why don't we head back over to Court Street?"

"Jeez, Murph. Really? Again?"

Murph shrugged.

Ted didn't like it, but he drove over to Court Street anyway and parked the minivan on a side street, facing the intersection.

"Nice," Murph said. "She's home, looks like."

"Jeez, buddy. Can't you keep it in your pants until you get off duty?"

"We can't all be Saint Teddy," Murph said as he got out of the minivan with his portable radio. "I'll be right back."

Ted shut off the motor and shifted around in the driver's seat. The window on his side was rolled halfway down. He had his portable radio in his lap. His right shoulder ached. The blade in back. His fingers tingled and the joint didn't seem to move smoothly as of late. He didn't have the strength he used to have.

"In strict medical terms, your shoulder is shit," Doc Kaplan had told him. He was the best kind of doctor—a Jewish one—so he was probably right.

Ted wondered what the MRI results would show. He didn't particularly want surgery or medical retirement. And who knew if the damage was from wrestling perps down to the street or swinging a hammer getting the retirement nest ready. Or casting a fishing rod too hard. But whatever…

There was another car parked between him and the intersection. So he had nice cover to watch from as people crossed and walked along Court Street. They picked their restaurant or decided to stop in the bar for another one for the road. A couple stepped together to kiss across the intersection and another couple was exchanging heated words.

Jeez, that's Mary Love over there in the way-too-short shorts. She's working this block again. If she doesn't land a John before Murph is done, we'll have to toss her. And what is that other young kid doing out by himself at this hour?

Ted Lamont sat in the unmarked minivan on a side street near Atlantic Avenue in Brooklyn with his portable radio in his lap, enjoying the greatest show on Earth.

———

Across the East River in Manhattan, another Lamont was standing alongside a car on the Lower East Side, trying not to arrest the driver. The car had made an illegal U-turn on Canal Street. The driver had taken a long time to find his license and registration. His very pregnant wife was in the passenger seat and there was a kid in the back seat.

Sean Lamont looked like a younger version of Ted. So much so, that he had grown tired of older cops commenting on the fact. He was twenty-six years old, a Marine Corps veteran, and married. He had been a cop for almost two years.

Officer Lamont could smell beer on the driver.

"Get out of the car please, sir."

Sean's partner was on the curb side of the car. Erik Ramos, six years on the job. They were working a Radio Motor Patrol in Manhattan South. A U-turn was going to turn into a DUI arrest.

Police Officer Sean Lamont watched the driver's hands when he opened the car door. He knew that this was often the point where bad things might happen. He didn't want to look at the kid in the back seat. But one glance told him that the kid was terrified. Big-eyed.

The cops looked imposing. The lights on the roof of their car swept the streets and their faces with blue beams. Radios crackled. They wore uniform caps and carried big 9mm Glock pistols on their sides.

Damn it! Sean thought. *I didn't take this job to scare the crap out of kids. The guy driving this car is a spring-loaded knucklehead for putting me in this situation.*

"I know I screwed up," the driver told the cops at the back of the car. "Just do what you have to do, and let my wife and kids go home. Please. She can drive. She just doesn't want to."

The driver was making good eye contact with the cops. He was steady on his feet. Wasn't talking too much. Maybe he wasn't that bad.

"Where are you coming from?" Police Officer Lamont wanted to know.

"My sister-in-law's house in Williamsburg. I had a few beers. I know I screwed up. But, please. If I lose my license, I lose my job."

Police Officer Erik Ramos had heard all this a hundred times.

"You should have thought of that before you got behind the wheel, mister."

"Your license says you live in Baldwin," Police Officer Sean Lamont said.

"I know. I know. I didn't even want to come to Manhattan. The wife was arguing and the kids were whining. I made a wrong turn. I just wanted to get out of here."

Sean went to the side of the car.

"Are you okay to drive, ma'am?"

The woman looked disgusted with the whole situation.

"I'd rather not," she said, holding her swollen abdomen. "Not in this condition."

"Okay. Can you call someone for a ride? We'll have to tow the car."

"What a prick! You'd make us walk home? Me at seven months?"

Sean Lamont was developing real empathy for the driver standing at the back of the car.

"You can drive, ma'am. Or we can have it towed. Those are your choices."

"Since you're going to be a jerk about it, I'll drive. And turn off those damn lights! Why are you making a federal case out of a stupid U-turn?"

The woman got behind the wheel. Sean took the man by the arm and sat him in the passenger seat.

"Good luck, sir."

"Thanks, Officer. You're okay."

"No sweat," Sean said, winking at the kid in the back seat. "You folks have a nice night."

When the officers got back into their car, Eric Ramos took the wheel.

"What the hell was that?" Erik wanted to know as they pulled back into the traffic.

"He wasn't that bad," Sean said, "and his driving record was clean when we called it in."

"He was drinking and driving with his pregnant wife and kid in the car. You know he'll do it again."

"Maybe," Sean shrugged. "But my old man told me to never embarrass a man in front of his kids. He said it just makes us the bad guys."

"That doesn't mean you give a free ride to everyone with a child. Next time that guy gets behind the wheel drunk, that kid might get killed. How would your old man feel about that?"

"I don't know," Sean shrugged.

Seems like everything I do is wrong, Sean Lamont thought. *Maybe I'm not cut out for this job. Why do I want to be a cop, anyway?*

Erik Ramos turned them onto Mulberry Street. North of Canal it was Chinatown, to the south, Little Italy. They hadn't gone half a block when their portable radios spoke.

"All units, be advised, ten double-zero in the Seven-Six."

"Damn it," Erik said. "Officer down."

"That sucks," Sean agreed.

Erik Ramos almost said, *Is your old man on the job tonight?* But he checked himself before the words came out. Sean didn't need to be reminded that his father was probably working anti-crime patrol in the Seven-Six at that very moment.

From Van Cortland Park in the Bronx to the Outerbridge Crossing in Staten Island to Saint Albans in Queens, the five thousand or so cops on duty had all heard the call. One of their own was down. Everybody knew somebody in the Seven-Six. The NYPD held its breath.

Sean pulled out his cell phone. He expected his father to call at any moment. *I'm okay.* But then again, the old man might be very busy at the moment. He'd be in the thick of it, for sure.

Police Officer Sean Lamont did the only thing he could do. He kept his eyes on the sidewalk and his mind on the job.

Mulberry Street was Old New York. The horse-drawn delivery wagons, street vendor carts and throngs of recent arrivals from Ellis Island were gone. The narrow streets and fire escapes on brick facades remained.

"That guy," Sean said, pointing to a shabby-looking character walking against the flow of pedestrians. He was ferreting through trash cans and holding something close in front of his torso.

Erik Ramos stopped the car and Sean jumped out. The man turned and tried to disappear into the walking crowd.

He tried to fall down and feign injury when Sean grabbed his arm.

"Why me? I didn't do nothing. Leave me alone. Let me go!"

Sean held the man up and dragged him over to the RMP. He was scrawny and had a shabby beard. His body stank and his breath was acrid. The pedestrian traffic on the sidewalk parted around them without taking much notice.

"Shame on you, Jimmy," Erik Ramos said. "Don't you know by now that panhandling is against the law?"

"That's my money!"

"Right," Erik said, dumping the coins from the cup the man had been holding onto the hood of the police car.

"What's this?" Sean wanted to know as he held the man against the car and emptied his pockets onto the trunk. "This wallet belongs to a woman. So just relax, you're taking a ride with us."

"I didn't do nothing wrong! I found that! Stop hurting me!"

"Shut up," Police Officer Lamont said as he snapped his handcuffs onto the man and eased him into the car. "Watch your head."

"What's your name?" Sean asked the perp after he had him seated in the car.

"Jimmy."

"Does Jimmy have a last name?"

"He calls himself Jimmy the Finder," Erik offered. "You'll get to know him well on this beat."

"Okay, then. Relax, Mister Finder," Sean laughed. "No one is going to hurt you. We're going to take you over to the First Precinct and sort this out. Maybe you could even talk to a social worker for me. Okay?"

Erik Ramos looked around on the sidewalk with his flashlight to make sure the perp had not thrown down anything else. Sometimes they found knives or a razor blade. Or guns. You just never knew.

When both cops were back in the car, the call came on their portable radios.

"Car nineteen, Command Five, what is your location?"

Erik Ramos spoke into his portable radio.

"800 Mulberry."

"Hold your position," the radio said.

"Jeez, what the hell would the deputy chief want?" Sean wondered out loud.

"Hell if I know. Unless some citizen dropped a dime on us for police brutality."

"For this guy?" Sean shrugged. "We're just going to take him to the house and process him. Before we kick him back out the door. Right?"

"That's the drill. As soon as we're done with him, he can crawl back into his rathole or cardboard box or whatever. He'll never show for court. But he won't bother anyone else on Mulberry tonight."

An unmarked SUV came around the corner in a rush and stopped behind their patrol unit, blue lights flashing in the windshield. The commander of Manhattan South stepped down and came around to Sean Lamont's door.

Deputy Chief Sy Levinson was a bear of a man. Balding. His long-sleeved, white uniform shirt was crisp and creased and there were three stars on top of his gold shield. Ordinarily, the patrol officers only saw the commander of Manhattan South when he was standing out in front of a group of cops at some critical incident, close to the action and ready to make the decisions.

After speeding to their location, he moved reluctantly for the last few steps. He looked washed-out. Stone-faced.

By then, Sean and Erik both knew why he was there.

"How bad is it?" Sean asked, matter-of-factly.

"As bad as it gets, Lamont. I'm sorry."

"No."

People kept moving on the sidewalk, paying little attention to the cops double-parked on Mulberry Street, having a casual chat—as it looked like. Except for one woman who stepped close to Deputy Chief Levinson and said, "Excuse me."

The cops ignored the woman standing outside their world.

"Where is he?" Sean asked.

"They took him straight to Long Island College Hospital. Not the best ER, but it was only four blocks. Anyway, it's no good, Sean. They're just going through the motions. It's no damn good."

"Excuse me, sir!" the lady on the sidewalk insisted.

The deputy chief turned around and snapped, "What do you want?"

"Which way is Sofia's?"

"Go half a block that way," he waved. "Sofia's is on the right."

Sy Levinson leaned back into the car.

"It's no damn good going to the hospital, Sean. It's too late. Is your mother at the house in Queens?"

"I think so. She's probably home right now."

The lady stepped off the sidewalk with another question. She spoke to Deputy Chief Sy Levinson's back.

"Is Casa Bella better?"

The deputy chief turned and said, "Get back on the sidewalk, ma'am."

Then he turned back to his officers.

"You better get over there forthwith," Levinson said. "I'll make sure they hold the chaplain off until you are at your mother's house."

Erik Ramos was already dragging the panhandling vagrant out of the back seat. Ordinarily, only the cop who put handcuffs on would take them off. But Erik pressed the man against the car and used his key to open Sean Lamont's handcuffs.

"This is your lucky day," he said as he pushed the grubby man away. "Get lost."

"False arrest!" the man said, turning back and yelling at the cops. "I'm going to sue!"

"Really!" the woman on the sidewalk involved herself in the scene.

"You heard my officer," Deputy Chief Levinson ignored the woman and spoke to the man. "Get lost. Move on."

When the burly veteran cop in the white shirt said it like he meant it, Jimmy the Finder stopped arguing and disappeared into the crowd.

"Lady," the deputy chief added, "I already told you to get back on the sidewalk once."

Sy Levinson leaned back to the patrol car.

"You know how I feel about your old man, Sean. Damn it, this is no good. You guys should be in Queens by now. Get going."

Sean Lamont was at a loss for words. Shock was setting in.

Erik Ramos yelped the siren and screeched the car away into the traffic with the lights flashing. They skidded around the corner towards the Queensboro Bridge.

The lady looking for the restaurant cleared her throat and said something which she thought was important to the deputy chief as he climbed back into his SUV.

"I must say, sir. I can't approve of the way you go about your job."

"Ma'am," Sy Levinson said out the window as he closed the door and put the SUV in gear. "You have no idea what my job is."

———

Beverly Lamont was enjoying a quiet night at home in Queens. The narrow two-story house was halfway down a quiet side street near Queens College, with roses and azaleas in front and a one-car garage in back. There was a real estate broker's *For Sale* sign on the postage stamp of a front lawn.

She was watching a PBS mystery on Channel 13, with the cat snoozing on the sofa next to her and her notebook computer open on her lap. Beverly was a buyer for Bloomingdale's. So when she did her own shopping online, she carefully sought quality over price. This was especially true now that she and Ted were moving to the smaller house out on the island. They had too much stuff already, and she was determined to populate their retirement home with only the best.

It helped that her commission from Bloomingdale's was considerably more generous than the salary of a city cop.

The cat left her lap and jumped up at the front window. Intently watching outside. Tip of the tail flicking side to side like a J-hook.

"What is so interesting on our street, Smoky?"

When she went to the window, Beverly saw two police cars sitting at the corner. Ready to move in.

None of my business, Beverly thought, turning away from the window. *If the neighbor's kid is about to get arrested for dealing pot or stealing cars or something, I don't want any part of that drama.*

Deflecting police business away from her home was all part of being a cop's wife.

No, Ted can't fix your parking or speeding tickets. If your neighbor is making too much noise or their kids are smoking dope outside your kitchen window, he'll say to call the precinct and let the cops on duty deal with it.

Then there were the neighbors and friends who wanted to talk to Ted about guns.

Guns. Guns. Guns. That's what civilians wanted to talk to Ted about, in her house. Which she had always worked to maintain as a sanctuary from the streets.

When pressed to show his gun, which was well hidden but readily accessible in their bedroom, Ted would take out his old nightstick instead. An ash baton with a leather lanyard. He had left it in a corner near the piano in their living room after the last day he walked a beat on the Lower East Side.

"Actually, I hate guns," Ted would say. "This stick has solved more problems than any gun."

That usually ended the gun talk with curious civilians.

Cops like to stay with their own kind, Beverly knew.

That had been part of the reason for the tough times. Drinking with the guys. Working odd hours. Poker night at their house, in the basement. Coming home bruised and bitter after a battle. Never talking about the job in their home.

Ironically, 9/11 had been the beginning of the change. Sy Levinson had been one of the last cops out of the North Tower. Some cops Ted knew well never got out.

Many of his friends had retired as soon as the department would let them go.

After a month-long tear, Ted had given up drinking. Typically for him, for no particular reason that he wanted to share. He never had the time or patience for an AA meeting. He just stopped. Lost some weight. Spent more time with Sean, who was fifteen and in high school. And Rebecca, who was eleven and needed her father.

Matt had been twenty, a college dropout living at home, and had barely noticed the change in his father.

Ted bought the new boat after 9/11. Bigger than his old outboard. His pride and joy. Mostly open, with no real cabin. A Jersey Skiff, he called it. Made of wood, which seemed to be much more trouble that it was worth. But Ted loved the boat and maintaining it gave him something to do with his hands.

Buying the house on the canal on the south shore of Long Island had been a major concession.

Beverly was an elegant woman. Definitely not a strong swimmer. She did not like the water, especially saltwater. Her hair was coiffed. Her makeup was understated, but had to be perfect. She avoided wind and strong sunlight.

But if Ted wanted a dock for the boat outside their back door, he deserved that much.

Only recently, he had started talking about the job. When they were working together to fix up the new house, he started sharing things he had not before. As if with retirement in sight, it was time to reflect on the past.

When they were alone in the new house, spattered with paint and plaster, they made love whenever and wherever the mood struck them. On perfectly calm nights, they took the boat out into the middle of the bay and let it drift while they lay on the planks between the wooden sides and looked up at the stars.

It hadn't always been that nice being married to Ted Lamont.

Beverly did not know why Ted had never become a ranking officer, like Sy Levinson. Or a detective, like Dexter Birmingham. Or why he hadn't retired early, like most of his friends. Why he stayed on street patrol was a mystery.

Unless it was just that Ted could never give up a fight.

She sometimes thought that it might have been better if Ted had been wounded in a gun battle and forced to retire, like his pal Jake Morrow. Jake had moved to North Carolina, where his city pension went a lot further and opened a used car lot.

What was important was that, somehow, he was finally retiring and the kids had moved out—sort of, except for Matt—and they were still together.

When there was a knock at the door, there were two radio patrol units in front of the house. She certainly didn't expect to see Sean standing there. In uniform. She had seldom seen her middle child in his patrol uniform, and she had never seen that look on his face.

Sean caught her when she fell to her knees.

———

When a cop dies on the job, a parade of top brass pays the city's respects to the family. So chauffeured limousines for the deputy mayor, the chief of police, and the Queens borough president were soon stopping in front of the Lamont home.

The neighbors brought food and milled through the living room paying their respects. They lingered with each other in the dining room and kitchen on the first floor speaking softly ... *poor Beverly ... so close to retirement ... such a nice family* ... and then went home.

A contingent of cops was standing on the sidewalk near their RMP units. The neighbors sent their kids over with coffee and food for all of them.

Sean had already taken off his Glock and duty belt and put them on the top shelf in the master bedroom closet where his father used to keep his.

He sat next to his mother on the sofa. His older brother Matthew had come home from his job as a waiter at the restaurant and sat on her other side. Matt was five years older. Quiet and even more distant than usual. Rebecca, the youngest, had come home from Hofstra University. She was crying and too distraught to see people. So Aunt Jean, who wasn't really their aunt but their mother's friend from the old neighborhood, took her upstairs to her bedroom.

Deputy Chief Sy Levinson was there by then. He stood behind the sofa, between Sean and Beverly.

"Too bad Giuliani isn't still mayor," Sy whispered in Sean's ear when the third assistant deputy mayor arrived, in place of the mayor. "Rudy would be here himself, no matter what."

Sean got up when his brother's best friend from the neighborhood arrived. Nick Shellaine was closer to Matt's age, but he had drifted away from the older brother to become more Sean's pal at some point when they were kids. Sean hadn't seen him much in recent years. Sean had been in the Marines and Nick had been cloistered at the seminary in Yonkers. The last time was when Nick was ordained as a priest at St. Patrick's.

He still had the dark red hair, but the freckles were fading.

"Hey," Sean said, "it's Father Nick."

"Hello Sean. Sorry for your loss. Your dad was a great man. I always loved him."

"Thanks, Nick. Although he was never too sure about you."

Lamont was a clan name from Scotland. But there weren't many Scots in the neighborhood, so Sean and Matt had hung out with the Irish kids. Close enough.

"I always took his advice to heart," Nick Shellaine said. "And I appreciated his harshest attention as fair guidance."

"Jeez, Father Nick. Are you going to talk like a priest all the time now?"

"You're not a Roman Catholic, Sean. You don't have to call me Father. Just Nick will do."

"Yeah. But Father Nick has a ring to it. I can't resist."

They went into the back of the house.

"It's weird seeing the neighborhood's troublemaker in that collar," Sean said as they walked through the dining room. The table was heaped with food.

"Not as weird as seeing the biggest juvenile delinquent in Queens in a police uniform."

"I was just bad," Sean pointed out. "You were a sneaky little bastard. Where did you get assigned?"

"Saint Mary's. Not far from your precinct. I'll light a candle for you on occasion."

"Knock yourself out, Sneaky Nick."

The Lamonts had been Presbyterian but had joined the nearby Episcopal Church when they came to Queens. The church had, over time, become little more than a function hall in their lives. A place for Boy Scout meetings and weddings and funerals. Beverly and Rebecca might go to services at Easter and Christmas. But none of the men had been in quite a while.

"Hey, Helen," Sean said as they entered the kitchen. "Look who's here."

Sean's wife barely acknowledged Nick Shellaine and went back to cleaning dishes.

"Really. At least you have one friend who's not carrying a gun."

"Forgive Helen, Father Nick. She's pissed. She wants me to take a job in Suffolk County. It would be a big pay raise, and get us out of the city."

Nick looked surprised.

"Could you get a job on the Suffolk County Police?"

"I aced the test, and they offered. And Nassau County, too."

"Why don't you go?"

"Because he's a damn Lamont," Helen interjected. "The city is in his blood."

"Tell Father Nick something he doesn't already know, Helen."

"Listen, Nick," Helen said. "Sean won't ever leave the city. I wish we could get away from here. I wish he would give up police work altogether and get a real job. But, no. My husband won't be happy until it's me sitting on the sofa greeting the cops and politicians."

"We'll pray for that to never happen."

"Where are you going?" Sean asked as she threw down the dish towel and left the kitchen, choking on a wave of emotion.

"Upstairs. To be with Becca."

She stopped on the back stairs and turned back to them.

"Sean..."

Her eyes said that she was sorry.

"Right," Sean nodded.

The two young men walked into the dining room. The house and rooms seemed to fill with people and then empty in waves. Sean accepted kind words as they moved through the dining room before he nudged Nick into a quiet corner.

"Sorry about that, Nick. I wish Helen wouldn't make my old man's funeral all about herself."

"I could talk to her, Sean. Try out some of the counseling skills I learned in the seminary."

"Good luck. You're on your own with that, pal."

When the dining room filled again, they made their way back into the living room and found another quiet spot.

I can't believe he's gone, Sean thought. His chair. His penchant for English driving caps. His Old Spice aftershave. His silly quips, heard a million times is these rooms. *Don't cut off your nose to spite your face. No ifs, ands, and buts.* The way he would stand at the sidelines at Little League games and yell, *Sean! Do something!*

Father Nick's words brought Sean back to the moment.

"You could use some counseling yourself, Sean."

"Thanks. I'm fine."

"Outwardly, you appear to be remarkably calm."

"I can't believe it," Sean shrugged. "Not yet. It'll hit me later, I guess."

"I hope I can be there for you."

Sean didn't commit to Sneaky Nick's offer.

"Listen, Nick. Dad's funeral is going to be a big deal. Will you say a few words?"

"I don't know if I can do that, Sean. I'd need permission from the archbishop."

"No kidding? We came to your ordination. Saint Patrick's didn't fall down."

"It's complicated, Sean. I'm the newest priest in the Archdiocese. I feel like I'm on thin ice already and participating in a Protestant service is a big no-no. They might ship me off to do missionary work if I'm not careful."

They both looked at the front door when Dexter Birmingham arrived with his wife. A svelte woman, in a tight dress which fit her perfectly. They looked like they might have come straight from a cocktail party on the Upper West Side. Joyce Birmingham sat next to Beverly on the sofa, in the spot Sean had vacated.

Dexter himself was no slacker in the fashion department. Tall and urbane. A trim beard and a gold earring. A beret on his shaved ebony head.

He dropped to one knee in front of Beverly and took her hand.

Sean couldn't hear, but he knew that Dex was saying the right words. Soft spoken. Articulate, with a common touch. A voice as smooth as a tenor sax, which he could also play. Dexter Birmingham was always feeling the beat of life. Loving every moment, even the sad ones.

He was the coolest man Sean had ever known.

Dex didn't waste words when he left Beverly and strode straight to Sean.

"Damn, Sean," Dexter Birmingham said, and gave him a big old bear hug.

"Thanks for being here, Dex."

"Of course, man. Of course. How are you holding up?"

"We're all just going through the motions. This is Father Nick. He was Matt's pal growing up."

"Yeah. Yeah, man. I remember," Dex smiled broadly. "You were the smug little bitch with the freckles and red hair."

"Nice to see you, too, Detective Birmingham."

"Dex is retired," Sean offered to Nick. "He's won Cop Lotto."

"Oh?" Nick wondered.

"Not quite," Dex laughed. "My new gig is with the *Law and Order* television series. They call me a technical advisor. But all I do is hang out with the talent so they might pick up some of my charming New York cop lingo and demeanor."

"Why don't they just put you in front of the camera?"

"Are you kidding. Look at me," Dex smiled and spread his arms. "I'm too beautiful to be a TV cop. Nobody would believe it."

Sean saw Erik Ramos come in the front door. He had been out front with the other cops, talking and making some phone calls.

Sean waved him over.

"Erik, this is the famous Detective Dexter Birmingham, NYPD, retired."

"Hi," Erik offered. "I've heard the name. Don't you show actors how to be like real cops?"

"Hey, I'm all Hollywood now," Dex said. "Ted Lamont was the real thing, to the end. A cop's cop."

"For sure," Erik nodded.

"Erik, what did you find out?" Sean wanted to know.

"One of my classmates from the academy was in the first unit to roll up. When you get a chance."

"Just tell me."

"Is there a quiet place?"

"Let's go down in the basement."

"Yeah, man," Dex agreed with the younger cops.

Deputy Chief Sy Levinson appeared as the group turned towards the back of the house and the basement stairs.

"What do you know, Erik?"

Erik was surprised to hear the deputy chief use his first name. Roughly the equivalent of a buck private being addressed by a general.

"I just talked to a friend in the Seven-Six who was on the job, sir."

"Erik was just about to go to the basement and fill us in," Sean offered.

"Count me in," Sy Levinson said.

"You must know more than us, sir," Erik Ramos suggested.

"I've heard the party line from the brass," Deputy Chief Sy Levinson said. "If you know what the cops on the street are saying, I'm all ears."

"Okay," Sean nodded and turned to Nick Shellaine. "Father Nick, I'll be right back."

"I'll go with you."

"I don't think so. You wouldn't understand. Try some of that counseling crap on Helen and my sister. I'll be right back."

"Oh, I see. It's a cop thing."

"Yeah. I don't listen in when you talk to saints, either."

The four cops clomped down the narrow stairs to the basement. The ceiling was low and the floor joists above were exposed. Dexter Birmingham had to bow his head to get under an iron drainpipe. But he knew when to duck since he'd been down there often when he, Ted, Sy Levinson and Jake Morrow used to play poker in the basement.

Ted Lamont had never quite finished remodeling the basement. It had been in a state of partial completion forever, as far as Sean could remember. But he had it divided into three sections with Sheetrock interior walls. The space with the card table and bar was at the bottom of the stairs.

The room was rich with cop memorabilia, from the days when RMP units were green and white Plymouths, and officers still walked a beat. A vintage call box was mounted on a wall. There were faded photos of cops in double-breasted tunics and a die-cast scale model of a Paddy Wagon.

"This place looks the same," Dex patted a wall.

"Nobody comes down here anymore, except Matt and his friends," Sean said. "They get stoned when Mom isn't home."

Bracketed by the older cops, Erik and Sean faced each other.

"Let's have it," Sean said, with his arms folded across his chest.

"He was in an unmarked car, near Atlantic Avenue," Erik said. "Parked, with the motor off."

"Okay."

"It was a handgun. At close range."

"It always is," Dex Birmingham muttered.

"Who was he riding with?"

"A guy named Murph. Sixteen years on the job."

Sy Levinson nodded.

"Yeah," Dex said. "We know him."

"Did Murph get any shots off?" Levinson asked.

Erik Ramos hesitated and looked at the two senior cops on his flanks. Dex Birmingham was retired, but he was still a legend, with a lot of stroke in the service. And—*for Christ's sake*—Deputy Chief Sy Levinson was the commander of Manhattan South. There wasn't much higher brass than that.

"Just say it," Sy Levinson said.

"Okay. This is just what I heard, mind you … Murph wasn't in the car."

"Damn it," Sean muttered. "Where the hell was he?"

"Word is, he was in some whore's apartment. Getting a quickie."

"Sweet Jesus." Dex sighed.

"What about evidence?" Sy Levinson asked. "Did they find shell casings?"

"Nothing," Erik said. "The perp must have used a revolver."

"None? How many shots did Ted get off?"

"None. His piece was still in the holster."

"What?" Sy Levinson was incredulous. "I'm having a hard time with that."

"Yeah, man," Dex chimed in. "Ted Lamont was old school. He would have had his piece in his hand if anyone who wasn't completely kosher came anywhere near the car."

Sean was mad as hell. Fists clenched at his side.

Sy Levinson was just as mad. He spun around and punched the drywall. The house seemed to shake when his fist landed.

"We'll get the son of a bitch," Sy said when he turned back to Sean. "I promise you that."

"We always do," Dex Birmingham offered. "Believe it, Sean."

"I know." Sean bowed his head. It was all starting to seem real. It had actually happened.

"Anyway," Erik said. "That's all I know. I've got to get our car back to Manhattan South. Sorry, Sean."

"Wait," Sean said, head still bowed. "You didn't say where he was hit."

"Aw, I don't know, Sean."

"Yes, you do," Sean looked up and in Erik's eye. "I'm going to hear it anyway. It might as well come from you."

The young cop's voice almost faltered when he looked at Sean.

"It was a head shot. Sorry."

"Front or back?" Sean said, rather matter-of-factly.

"They said it looked like someone pressed a gun into his neck."

There were probably only a few seconds where nothing was said in the huddle. It only seemed like an eternity.

"Thanks, Erik. I need to be with my mother now."

The cops went upstairs. The group dispersed and mingled around the house. Sy Levinson went to the living room to be with Beverly. Dex Birmingham went upstairs with Joyce to talk to Rebecca.

So this is my role, Sean thought as he walked through the dining room, accepting condolences and regaining the composure that had seen him through the ordeal of his father's death so far. *I'm the tough cop now. So this is what that "all the world's a stage" crap is about.*

Sean found Father Nick in the living room.

"That was different," Father Nick said after Sean appeared at his side.

"Huh?"

Sean was still regaining his footing. Nick might be an old friend and a priest, but only a cop would understand. You had to be in the fight to know the utter bitterness of losing.

"You've changed, Sean. We never used to have secrets."

"You know we can't reveal details of an investigation, Nick."

"Investigation? That was more like a meeting of the United Nations."

"What?"

"You know, I never thought I'd see Sean Lamont leave his friends upstairs and go into the basement with a Latino, a Black and a Jew."

Sean looked around the living room of the house he had grown up in. Rich with memories. His mother and older brother were on the sofa. On some evenings—not all that long ago—Sneaky Nick used to sit there watching Walt Disney with them.

Sean leaned closer to Father Nick and spoke softly.

"I've changed? When we were kids getting in fights in this neighborhood, you would have said a Rican, a Spook, and a Hebe."

Father Nick Shellaine looked around. Concerned that someone might have overheard their words.

"Sean, please. I didn't mean it that way. I forgot myself. All the emotion of this moment. The memories … when we were kids … I'm a priest now, for God's sake."

"That's good. Because we're not kids anymore. And all I saw down in the basement was cops."

AN INSPECTOR'S FUNERAL

The day of the funeral was clear and calm. Perfectly still. Beverly's dress was black only at first glance, darkest indigo in sunlight, and she was attending to some last-minute straightening up around the house. Rebecca and Aunt Jean were helping in the kitchen.

Matt was upstairs getting dressed when Sean and Helen arrived. Sean in his dress uniform tunic.

"Go upstairs and tell Matt to get a move on, Sean."

Helen stayed with Beverly.

"How was your night, Helen?"

"Sean wouldn't let me sleep. He tossed and turned all night."

"Of course."

"And ... he hasn't cried. Not at all. That's not normal."

"He will. Later. It will hit him all at once."

"It's weird. He's so quiet. It ... scares me."

"Lamont men can be stoic to a fault. But everybody grieves the same way, eventually."

"It's not normal."

Helen went to the kitchen when Sean came downstairs, without Matt.

"He's almost ready, Mom. Worse than a girl."

"You and your father were quick to get out the door because you had to get to roll call on time. Matt doesn't have that problem."

"I guess."

"How was your night, dear?"

"Helen wouldn't let me sleep. She cried all night."

"Let her get it out. Everybody grieves the same way, eventually."

Sean lifted the lace and the candy bowl so his mother could dust underneath it.

"Mom, I just looked for Dad's .38 upstairs. It wasn't there."

The snub-nosed Smith & Wesson .38 had been Ted's off-duty piece for as long as Sean could remember. Much easier to carry in civilian clothes than a bulky NYPD-issued Glock semi-automatic.

"Did you look in the nightstand?"

Sean had known about the hidden niche under the drawer in the nightstand all his life, too. He used to risk a beating to secretly hold the .38 when no one was watching. The slim walnut grips had fit his little boy hands perfectly, in moments of exquisite fascination.

"It wasn't there."

"On the shelf in the closet?"

"Nothing, Mom."

Helen finished dusting. Sean put the lace and candy bowl down. They moved to the piano.

"I'm sure that it will turn up," Beverly said, dusting the piano. "Somewhere."

"I was thinking that you should keep it here, Mom. I'll take Dad's old M1 carbine. But you should hang on to the revolver."

"No more talk of guns in my house, please. I don't need one."

"Just in case. I'd feel better if you had some protection, living in the city. That snub-nosed .38 should stay with you."

"Sean, I won't be living in the city. I'm going to sell the house."

"Which one?"

"This one. The one with the *For Sale* sign out front."

"Oh. I thought you might want to sell the new house."

"Why would I do that? Your father and I just finished fixing it up. It's nearly perfect."

"Well, do you still want to move out on the island? You don't really like the water. I mean, now that Dad…"

"We had a good offer on this house. Not quite our asking price, but the market is down. So..."

"I never thought you'd really sell this place. All of your friends are here. All of our memories."

"That's been the plan, all along. It's time to move on."

"I always thought you might hold off until Helen and I could afford to buy this house."

"Sean, the upkeep on this old house is extraordinary. Anyway, you won't want to live here. Not when you're working way out in Suffolk County."

"All the memories..."

"You can buy a newer house and make your own memories. There are lots of nice new housing developments on the island."

"It sounds like everybody has made up their minds about a job in Suffolk County. Except me."

"Or Nassau. If you have to be a cop, get out of the city, Sean."

He shrugged and looked out the bay window. He'd been fourteen when he helped his dad build the extension on the front of the house. It seemed like a long time ago.

"Do it for me, Sean," Beverly said, at his side. "If not for Helen. Get out of here."

"Queens isn't much different than some Podunk town on Long Island as far as I can tell. Houses and tree-lined streets. It's just closer to all the good stuff."

"On a clear day we can glimpse the Manhattan skyline from our upstairs windows. That's too close, Sean."

It was true. And on summer evenings in their backyard he, Matt, Rebecca, and Sneaky Nick had often seen the loom of the downtown lights in the night sky. *Aurora Gotham.*

"This is what I know, Mom. This is home."

———

The limousine arrived for the family. Beverly sat in the back seat, flanked by Rebecca and Matt. Sean and Helen occupied the rear-facing jump seats.

There were about a hundred cops standing motionless outside the funeral home. The street had been blocked off, and a dozen NYPD motorcycles leaned on their kickstands in a perfect line, with motor patrol officers in tall boots, gantlets and blue helmets standing alongside.

Silence.

Deputy Chief Sy Levinson and Dexter Birmingham were waiting just inside the stained-glass double doors with hugs for Beverly. Both of them were in uniform, even though Dex was a retired detective.

Like all the cops in the city that day, they wore black ribbons across their shields.

And Jake Morrow. A big, red-faced man, with emotive gestures, wore a dark gray suit with his shield and awards on the collar. The Medal of Valor and the Combat Cross.

"Sean, I'm sorry." He touched Sean's shoulder. "I drove up from North Carolina as soon as I heard. What a kick in the nuts."

Jake had lived near them in Queens before his divorce, with two daughters. He was the family friend who would take Sean to the Bronx Zoo or the games at Yankee Stadium. Or to watch the ponies race at Aqueduct. When they went somewhere, he always slipped Sean a five or a sawbuck. "A man should always have a little money in his pocket, Sean." And he never paid the tolls on the Triborough Bridge. "Suckers!" Jake would laugh as the bell went off and he sped away in his old Cadillac, with an open beer in his hand.

"Thanks for coming, Jake."

"Sorry, I couldn't get into my old uniform," the big man patted his ample gut. "It must have shrunk in the closet after I retired."

Jake still walked with a slight limp from the gun battle that had ended his career. An awkward gait. As if his left knee didn't want to bend.

The funeral director hustled about his domain seeing to all the arrangements, even though there was really nothing for him to do. The cops knew the script, moment by moment, all too well.

Sy Levinson stayed with the family when Sean, Dex Birmingham, and Jake Morrow stood by the casket. Dex was discreetly carrying Ted's nightstick.

The casket had been closed.

"I want to take a last look at him," Sean said.

"You don't have to," Dex Birmingham spoke, like the reed of a tenor saxophone.

"I have to," Sean said. "I have to know this is really happening."

"Okay, son," Dex said as he signaled for the funeral director to open the top.

Ted Lamont was laid to rest in his double-breasted dress uniform tunic. His face was covered with powder. Peaceful features. The sides of his face oddly not as symmetrical as in life. A wound on his neck mostly hidden by the high collar of his tunic and heavy makeup.

Dex Birmingham laid Ted's nightstick in the coffin, unseen by the other family members.

Sean touched his father's arm.

"Thanks, Dad."

Jake Morrow pulled Ted's leather blackjack from his pocket and handed it to Sean.

"We were going to send this with Ted, too. But maybe you should keep it. Just in case you need a little backup from your dad sometime."

Sean took the heavy leather sap from Jake. It was flat and springy, about seven inches long, and lead-weighted. The hand strap was worn and frayed. He hadn't seen it in years, but he remembered that *Jay-Pee Short Slugger* was embossed into the leather. It was the sort of backup that cops used to carry before every cell phone had a camera, as an alternative to shooting a perp.

As the funeral director closed the casket, Sean slipped the sap into his back pocket.

Beverly had decided on an American flag rather than a New York City flag. Pallbearers from Ted's unit took the casket outside. Followed by Sy Levinson, Dexter Birmingham, and Jake Morrow. Then the family.

Silence.

The rumble of the motorcycles starting as one made Beverly flinch. They peeled out in twos and the hearse followed for the slow drive to the church. The procession made two turns and traveled seven blocks, with more motorcycles and cruisers holding every intersection.

"I've never seen cops on horseback around here before," Rebecca said between sobs. "Where did they come from?"

"The police stables are in Tribeca," Sean told her.

"They galloped here all the way from Manhattan?"

"No, silly. There are some horse trailers parked around here somewhere."

All the streets near the church were cordoned off amid a sea of blue uniforms and white gloves, on both sides of the streets and up on the sidewalk. There was barely enough room for the procession to idle through.

"I sort of wish all these men would go away," Becca said in a flat monotone.

"Why is that?"

"It's a spectacle. Do you think Dad would want all this?"

She's the youngest by four years, Sean thought. *The baby. Daddy's girl. This has to be brutal for her.*

"I don't know," Sean said. "But I'm pretty sure he'd be happy to see how much backup he had on this last ride."

A color guard waited in front of the church steps. The mayor and the commissioner were in attendance, standing with their minister in full clerical garb.

The persistent echoes of the city were held at bay by the profound silence in the presence of so many souls. Sean heard someone cough, a block distant. When the limousine door closed behind them, the sound echoed down the lines of cops.

Television cameras panned on the mayor and the casket going up the steps.

Erik Ramos and his wife met Sean and Helen on the steps. Also Sy Levinson's grown daughter Miriam, who was an assistant district attorney, and Joyce Birmingham. They all sat with Beverly.

Sean didn't hear much during the service. The music was nice, but the pastor's words seemed like hollow ramblings. He hadn't known Ted Lamont.

It wasn't until they were leaving the church that Sean saw Nick Shellaine, without his clerical collar, sitting alone in the rearmost pew.

———

The procession to the Woodlawn moved quickly. A dignified pace up the Bronx River Parkway. The rites were crisp and military. Taps and three rifle volleys.

"Hey, Sean," Dex said as they walked away to their cars. "Ride with us."

"Go ahead," Beverly approved, taking Helen by the hand.

Sean climbed into the back seat of Deputy Chief Sy Levinson's smoke-gray city SUV with Jake Morrow. Dex Birmingham hopped shotgun.

"Hey, Sean-Boy," Jake tapped him as they climbed aboard. "You're getting a bald spot right on the back of your head, just like your old man's."

"Helen won't let me forget that," Sean shrugged. "It's the family curse."

They drove out of the cemetery towards Beverly's house.

"Why didn't one of you guys point out Murph to me?" Sean asked. "I don't even know who he is."

"Murph is a mess right now," Dex said. "The sight of you or your mother would have given him a full-on breakdown. Maybe later."

"That asshole got his partner killed," Jake said. "What would you want to say to him, anyway?"

"I'd just like to hear what happened. Face to face."

Dex shook his head and looked out the window.

Deputy Chief Sy Levinson drove and listened but did not speak.

"What have you guys heard?" Sean wanted to know.

Dex spoke from the front seat.

"Ted's right shoulder was dislocated, Sean. It must have been a struggle."

"It had been bothering the crap out of him."

"If Murph had been there," Jake muttered, "Teddy would have had a chance."

Sean looked at the back of Sy Levinson's seat.

Dex and Jake told a few stories from the bad old days. Reminiscences of Ted. Tales of the Stakeout Squad, which Sean had never heard. When Sy, Jake, Dex and Ted were young cops hiding in liquor stores and shops on the lower east side. Springing out from behind stacked cases of beer to halt robberies and assaults in progress. The perps' shots—if they lived long enough to get one or two off—starting streams of beer from punctured cans in the cops' barricade.

Maybe the war stories had grown grander over time, Sean thought as he looked out the side window. *Dad never spoke much about the Stakeout Squad. All that was before I was born.*

Ted Lamont was always nominated to carry the pump shotgun, Dex remembered.

And they never forgot to yell "Halt! Police!" after any gun-toting perps were dead on the floor or the sidewalk, Jake laughed.

I always knew Dad was a tough cop, Sean grimaced. *But I'm not sure I want to know that he used to sweep bad guys out of a store and onto the sidewalk with volleys from a 12-gauge.*

Then Dexter Birmingham turned around and put his arm on the backrest of his seat so he could see Sean's eyes.

"Listen, Sean. There's something we need to talk about later. A thing that only concerns those of us in this car. That includes you."

"Okay. Shoot, Dex."

"Not now. It's tough business that you'll have to finish for your father. But just let the dust settle. And trust us."

"What's the deal, Dex?"

"Just wait until after we catch the son of a bitch who killed your old man, Sean. After that, we've got to talk."

"We're family," Jake slapped Sean's knee. "Nobody else. Just remember that."

"What the hell?" Sean said. "Tell me, for Christ's sake."

"We can't, Sean. Not until the damned investigation is over. You just need to know that we are the only cops you can really trust. The only ones that matter. We have to stick together."

Jake slapped his leg again.

"Blood is thicker than water, Sean-Boy."

"This sounds complicated." Sean shook his head.

"No," Dex smiled. "It's the simplest thing you'll ever hear. Pure as can be. But you have to trust us. No matter what, we've got your back. And you've got ours."

"Okay," Sean sighed. "Am I going to want to be in on this? Whatever it is?"

"Probably not," Dex smiled sweetly. "Not at first. It will grow on you."

They arrived at Beverly's house.

When they went inside, Helen used icy silence to let Sean know that she was mad about being left to ride back with Beverly and Rebecca and Matt.

Father Nick was there, with his clerical collar back on. Sean made a round of the dining room table, heaped a plate with food, and spent some time with Rebecca, Sneaky Nick and Matt and some of the old gang from the neighborhood.

During a lull in the conversation, he pulled his older brother aside in the kitchen.

"Matt, have you seen Dad's .38 snubby?"

"No. I thought you had it."

"Nope. I was looking for it while you were in the shower this morning. And it wasn't there."

"I don't know where it is."

"I hope not, Matt. You're not a cop. You can't have a gun in the city. So if you find it, give it to me."

Matt folded his arms across his chest. Sean knew his look of disdain well.

"Thanks for reminding me that I'm not one of the chosen few, little brother. I don't know where Dad's .38 is. And I don't care. Even though I have as much right to it as you do. Maybe more, since you can get all the guns you want. And by the way, lots of people carry guns and never get caught."

"Think about that, Matt. There's a thing called the Sullivan Law in the city. If you get caught, there's nothing I can do for you. You're going to prison. End of story."

"Why don't you just arrest me now, Sean. Try it and see what happens."

Sean raised his hands in surrender and dismissal as he left the kitchen.

"Stop being an idiot, Matt. Think about it."

When he walked through the dining room to the living room, he found that Sy Levinson, Jake Morrow and Dex Birmingham—Ted's old Stakeout Squad—had left the house.

SIGNAL 10-2

The morning after the funeral, Sean opened the slider in their bedroom and stepped onto the balcony of the third-floor apartment he shared with Helen. He looked over the rooftops and windows of the nearby apartments of Forest Hills and stretched his back and shoulders. He inhaled deeply before he went back inside and took his shower to get ready for work.

Helen sat on their bed and watched him dress in civilian clothes.

"Aren't you going to help your mother today?"

"With what? She's got it all under control."

"How could she? Aren't there lawyers and insurance agents to talk to?"

"We already met with the lawyer. He's going to handle everything."

"You should be there for her."

"Matt and Becca are there today."

She stood up and hugged him and let him hold her up.

"When are you going to take time for your own feelings?"

"Right now, it's better if I stay busy, Helen."

"Don't hold it in, Sean. I can't take the silence."

"I can't force myself to feel something, Helen. It is what it is."

"You're in shock, Sean. You've got to face reality."

Sean took his service weapon from the locked box in their closet and slid it into his belt holster.

"I'm all set with reality, kitten."

She sat back down on the bed.

"There are stages of grief, Sean. You have to work through them all to be healed."

"That psycho-babble crap doesn't count with me."

"What are you going to do, put on your gun and go shoot someone?"

"That probably would make me feel better. Maybe we'll get some action today."

"Don't talk like that."

"That's what I'm feeling. Do you want to hear it, or not?"

He put on a shirt with the hanging tail barely concealing his Glock. He took the black gym bag with his duty gear from the closet and went to the kitchen.

Pulling on a robe, Helen followed.

Their two-bedroom apartment was small and modern. Helen worked as an elementary school teacher at PS 133. They shared the cleaning and the cooking and their one car.

"It's okay to cry, Sean. I miss him, too. He was the one person in your family who understood me."

"Beverly understands you."

"Not like Ted."

Her parents had divorced when she was nine, Sean reminded himself. *The old man must have filled a bigger void in her life than I imagined.*

Sean filled a glass with water from the tap and drank it in deep gulps.

"My mother told me not to marry a cop," Helen rued.

"Too late for that." He put his arm around her waist and kissed her forehead.

"Why do you have to love your other cops, too?"

"Some of them aren't so bad."

He put the strap of the gym bag over his shoulder and reached for the front door.

"Sean, you've got to make a choice."

He stopped and turned but didn't let go of the doorknob. "What?"

"Me or your cops, Sean."

"I thought we agreed never to give each other ultimatums."

"It's not like that, Sean. I just can't do this anymore."

Sean looked at the ceiling and exhaled. Then at her.

"We'll go out to eat tonight, Helen. La Botega, if you want."

"Let's stay home today, Sean."

"Listen, in a few weeks ... after all this is over ... we'll take a vacation. Okay?"

"You're hunting for the man who shot Ted, aren't you?"

"We can go anyplace you want. Jamaica or Las Vegas or Aruba."

"Please don't go to work today, Sean."

He let go of the doorknob and put his hands on her shoulders.

"Hey, kitten. I'm not hunting anyone. It doesn't work that way. The crew in Brooklyn South will find the man who shot Ted. I'll be across the River in Manhattan. But I need to be on the job today. Do you understand?"

"No. I don't understand at all."

"Let me get back on the horse my way. Okay?"

She put her head against his chest.

"We can talk about the future tonight." Sean tried to sooth her. "Okay?"

"I ... guess ... so."

"There you go. Love you, kitten."

Sean ignored the elevator and bounded down the stairs. Helen would need the car to get to work. So he walked quickly down the sidewalk for three blocks and crossed the six lanes of Queens Boulevard near the Art Deco facade of the Ridgewood Savings Bank. He got a black coffee and a bagel with cream cheese in the coffee shop on the corner. Then he went down the green iron stairs on 71st Avenue—almost hidden behind the newsstand—and stood on the platform waiting for an express train on the Blue Line.

Parking a car in Manhattan was just a big hassle, anyway.

———

Sean climbed back to street level at Fulton and Nassau in Lower Manhattan. He walked down Beekman at a quick pace until the asphalt turned into cobblestones on Front Street. The First Precinct was on the corner of Old Slip and South Street. A down-on-luck corner of Manhattan. Old brick buildings in the shadow of the soaring financial district.

Old Slip was once a place for boats to pull into Manhattan. It had long since been filled in and turned into a street. The precinct house was an elongated granite castle in the middle of Old Slip, with traffic on both sides. Only the elevated trestles of the FDR Drive separated it from the East River, almost in the shadow of the Brooklyn Bridge. South Street Seaport and the Fulton Fish Market were to the south. To the north, Chinatown, Little Italy and the Bowery.

In the cracks between the lesser skyscrapers of the financial district, the World Trade Center towers also used to peek down on Old Slip.

There were patrol cars out front, backed in over the curb. The rusticated granite facade was seasoned by decades of street pollution. Arched windows lined the first floor, like a Florentine palazzo, with smaller windows on the two upper stories. The bronze doors were flanked by two massive lanterns with green leaded glass. When the cops came and left the house, a very large American flag hung over their heads. The date over the door said 1909.

The muster room was directly inside the front doors, and a long wooden desk spanned the far wall. The officers manning the switchboard and filing reports hardly looked up when Sean crossed the room.

Eric Ramos greeted him in the locker room with a surprised smile.

"What are you doing here?"

"Nice to see you too, Police Officer Ramos."

"What about your bereavement leave?"

"I can't sit around doing nothing. Besides, who else could stand to pull a whole watch with you?"

They put on their uniforms and mustered with a platoon of cops, standing in two ranks for roll call.

Captain Sweeney went over recent crime statistics and new departmental policies. The big item of interest was a ruling that it was no longer illegal for women to expose their bare breasts in the city. The activity should be discouraged, but the women should not be arrested. This drew snickers and laughs from the cops. He ended roll call with an update on the shooting in the Seven-Six, without looking at Sean.

"An unknown shooter remains at large. Keep your eyes and ears open. Sooner or later, somebody will talk."

When they were ready to go out to their patrol car, Sean was surprised to see Jake Morrow standing in front of the holding cell near the doors, with a little girl.

"Hey, Jake."

"This is my granddaughter, Molly."

She was sitting on a pew-like bench. There were rings in the wall behind her, for prisoners in handcuffs.

"Shouldn't you be in school, young lady?"

She slid across the bench and hid behind Jake's leg. Pigtails and missing teeth. Maybe a bit too young for school.

"I'm showing her where Grandpa used to work."

"Nice."

"You know, I've been retired and living in North Carolina since before Molly was born. But I thought she should know about me and my real pals in the city. The good old days."

"In that case, I'm happy I got to meet you, Molly."

"Sorry, Sean," Jake offered. "I have to head south later today. The damn used car lot takes way too much of my time. I should sell it. I don't get up here often enough."

"Always good to see you, Jake."

The big man had his arm on Sean's shoulder. By necessity, that put his belly button too close for comfort.

"Let me know how you make out, Sean. I'll be keeping in touch with Sy and Dex, too. Anything you need ... anything ... you just give me a call."

"See ya, Jake. Bye, Molly."

Sean and Erik got into their patrol car in front of the House. They turned onto South Street. A tug boat pushing two barges heavily laden with garbage chugged down the East River, just beyond construction barriers and the shadow of FDR drive.

Their first call was for a minor burglary on the Bowery. Signal 10-21. See the woman about the broken window.

The streets were narrow and winding, more like New Amsterdam and Old New York than the perfect grid of avenues and east-west streets in Midtown. Their beat was cobblestone streets in front of tenements *cum* rent-controlled apartments.

Sean saw a priest walking towards the Bowery Mission and raised a hand for Erik to stop the car.

"Stay away from the altar boys." He surprised Father Nick out the open car window from behind. "I don't want to have to come up here and arrest you."

When he turned around, he looked like Sneaky Nick in a penguin suit.

"Bless you, Sean. How are you making out?"

"Fine. You're a bit far from Saint Mary's."

"I'm volunteering at the Mission." Father Nick pointed to the narrow five-storey brick structure in a row of similar buildings. The fire escapes from the top floors extended to the three-storey building next door, also part of the Mission.

"We always knew one of us kids would end up in there," Sean smiled. "Except on the receiving end of the soup line. Not the serving side."

"I try." Father Nick shrugged.

"Well, good. Now I know where I can find you. Take care, buddy."

Sneaky Nick waved as he and Erik pulled away.

"You know, Sean," Erik said as he drove the narrow street. "As a Catholic I resent that altar boy nonsense. You shouldn't disparage the clergy."

"We're old friends," Sean shrugged. "He knows that I love him like a brother."

Good Lord, he's my oldest friend, Sean thought. *Of people still in my life, anyway. Have I really known that priest since grade school?*

They hadn't made it far from the Bowery Mission, not quite to their 10-21, when the next call came. Signal 10-2. Return to your command.

"What the hell would they want already?" Sean wondered out loud. "We haven't even made it to our first call yet."

"It's going to be one of those days." Erik shrugged.

Maybe they found the guy, Sean thought. *They'd tell me right away, wouldn't they?*

Two right turns and threading the narrow streets brought them back to Old Slip. While Erik parked the car, Sean went up the steps under the flag and in through the doors between the big green lights.

Captain Sweeney was in the muster room, hanging a new picture on the wall of heroes. Officers from Old Slip killed in the line of duty.

"I was hoping I'd be done hanging this picture before you got back, Sean."

The eight-by-ten photograph was of Police Officer Ted Lamont. Dress tunic and uniform hat.

"Yeah. But why is that going up here? Ted was working out of the Seven-Six, in Brooklyn South."

"Blame it on Sy Levinson. The deputy chief thought that your Dad's picture belonged here. You know, he was at Old Slip for so many years. History, right? The bad old days, they say."

Sean scanned the line of timeless black-and-white pictures, going back to the turn of the century. There were officers shot in robberies and when making arrests and a motorcycle officer with his Sam Browne belt and gantlets. The portraits of two detectives killed by an escaping prisoner hung alongside each other.

"I guess it's okay," Sean shrugged. "But you didn't call me back here for this, did you?"

"I wish," Tom Sweeney nodded his head towards the stairs to the second floor and said two words.

"Internal Affairs."

Sean found two polyester detectives waiting for him in the squad room. Slightly overweight cops in ill-fitting permanent press slacks and off-the-rack sports coats.

Just my luck, Sean mused. *Frick and Frack. The toughest two guys from Internal Affairs.*

"What do you guys want?" Sean asked, before the introductions. "I already talked to the Brooklyn South Homicide Squad."

"We're working the case, too. Let's take it to an interrogation room."

"If we have to," Sean shrugged.

Good Cop—Frick—opened the interview as soon as they were sitting at the table in the room.

"Sean, I'm Dick Francis. I knew your father. Sorry for your loss. We all want to get this mess cleared up as soon as we can."

"Thanks."

Bad cop was wearing a scowl from the beginning.

"I'm Frank Capella."

Frack, Sean thought.

"Great. What do you know?"

"Not much," Frack said. "Suppose you tell us everything you know, and we'll take it from there."

"I know that my dad is dead. We buried him yesterday."

"Anything else?" Frick asked.

"I know that he was on anti-crime patrol in plainclothes with a guy named Murph. Who wasn't in the car."

"Anything else?"

"I was hoping you'd have answers, four days after. Not questions."

Bad Cop tagged in.

"Did the Brooklyn South squad tell you the shooter's location?"

"A handgun," Sean said. "At close range. I guess he was right outside the driver side window."

"Not so much. We know that the shooter was in the back seat. From the blood splatter on the headliner."

"I didn't know that."

No wonder Internal Affairs has a hard-on, Sean thought. *It had to be somebody Dad knew. Maybe it was the worst. Blue on blue.*

Sean said the first name that came to mind.

"Murph?"

"If it was Murph, he didn't use his service weapon. The shooter used a .38 revolver, which we haven't been able to secure."

"A swing gun would have left all sorts of residue," Sean suggested.

"Nobody thought to test Murph's hands for gunpowder residue that night."

Idiots! Sean thought.

"Nice work, detectives."

"Easy, Sean," Good Cop offered. "Granted, mistakes were made. But it's not our fault if there were no fingerprints. No physical evidence at all to lead to the identity of the shooter."

"I hope you have a Plan B to find this guy."

"Who said it was a guy?" Bad Cop sniggered.

"The autopsy said that my dad's right shoulder was dislocated. I don't think that happened from wrestling with a woman."

"Who have you been talking to? We haven't gone public with that report yet."

"People tell me things. Whether I want to hear them or not."

"So you admit that you're not telling us everything you know."

"You asked me what I knew. Not what I've heard. There are enough rumors going around."

"Okay. Fair enough. How about Ted's gambling habit?"

"What gambling habit was that?" Sean laughed.

"You tell us. Did he talk about gaming at all? Numbers? Maybe the ponies?"

"My old man bought one quick pick on every draw of Powerball. You tell me if that's a gambling habit."

"Drugs?"

"Get serious. That's just ridiculous."

"Is it? A heavy dose of painkillers was found in his system."

"His shoulder hurt like hell." Sean shrugged.

Good Cop weighed in.

"Sean, we all knew your father liked his whiskey, as much as any of us."

"That was a long time ago. He gave up booze after 9/11. A lot of guys did after they saw what it was doing to each other."

"Was he still going to AA meetings?"

"I don't think he ever went. He just quit when he knew it was time."

"How could he do that? That's hard to do. Everybody needs help."

"I guess you really didn't know my dad. When it was time to quit, he did."

Bad Cop took over.

"Who did he hang out with?"

"Other cops. Like most of us. The old crew from this precinct were his best friends, from back in the day."

"Did he have any dealings with criminals? Druggies? Pimps?"

"Now I'm sure that you didn't know my old man very well."

"Sean," Good Cop looked in a manila folder. "I see that your father owned two houses and a boat."

"So?"

Bad Cop tagged in.

"Waterfront property on Long Island. A dock for a yacht at the back door. On a cop's salary? He must have been some good with money."

"My mother is a buyer at Bloomingdale's. And it's an old wooden boat. A Jersey Skiff. Twenty-eight feet. Hardly a yacht."

"He didn't have a part-time job? Maybe a lucrative hobby?"

"Listen, you're wasting your time and mine fishing for dirt on my old man. While you're at it, go to hell."

The detectives looked at each other before Good Cop turned to Sean.

"Officer Lamont, the brass seem to think that you have a big future in the service. A thing like this reveals a cop's true character. You could be in line for a gold shield someday soon."

"I like my uniform. And street patrol."

"Suit yourself," Bad Cop said. "Just take a bit of advice. Don't talk to any other cops about this. Our biggest problems come from street cops trying to help. No muddying the waters. Let us do our thing. We want a nice, clean investigation."

"Good. I hope you start doing your thing soon, whatever it is. So far, all I hear is a lot of talk."

"That's all for now, Police Officer Lamont. We'll be in touch."

When Sean was almost out the door, Good Cop Frick stopped him with a question.

"One other thing, Sean. There's a .38 snubby registered in Ted's name. His off-duty piece. The crime lab needs to take a look at it."

———

Beverly sat at the dining room table in her home with a cup of coffee and stacks of papers. There was nothing to do but wait for the real estate man to arrive, so she compulsively reviewed and rearranged the manila envelopes and file folders which contained the paper trail of her life with Ted Lamont. Navy discharge papers. Birth certificates. Insurance policies, automobile registrations and pension plans.

A marriage license.

The papers had been stashed away in various places and nearly forgotten until the night when Ted did not come home. Now she had gathered and arranged every sheaf and scrap and knew each fold and tear and notation in the margin of each document intimately.

There was also a box for old pictures, which had turned up among the papers.

Becca was sitting with her legs drawn up underneath her on Ted's chair in the living room. Talking and texting on her cell phone. Friends and classmates. She had the framed picture of her father as a young cop in his double-breasted dress tunic on her lap. The one they had taken off the wall in the front hall to put on his casket.

The cat sat where it had for Ted, on the back of the armchair near her head.

Matt hadn't gone back to work at the restaurant yet, but he still kept the late hours. He was just getting up and he came downstairs for a cup of coffee two or three times and then went back to his room.

When Beverly heard a car in the driveway, she knew it was Helen before she turned around to look.

Her daughter-in-law came in the back door, through the kitchen.

"Hi, Helen. Coffee is right there. I suppose Sean went to work this morning?"

"Yes. Because he is an idiot."

"He gets it from his father. Ted only missed a handful of shifts in thirty-two years. Why aren't you at school?"

"I can't teach today. I'm a mess," Helen whined. "Sean is holding everything in."

"He gets that from his father, too."

Helen came out of the kitchen with a cup of coffee and sat across from Beverly. She could see the "Love" tattoo on the inside of the younger woman's wrist.

I just don't get why kids want to maim themselves, Beverly thought. *In my day, we smoked a little weed and wore tie-dyed shirts and thought we were cool.* Helen had a belly ring when Sean first met her. *Thank God that didn't last.*

She hoped Becca wouldn't get any ideas.

"Look at all this stuff. How do you keep it straight?" Helen said.

Beverly laid her hand on each stack in order.

"Taxes, financial records, insurance, mortgages, personal papers. It's all here."

"Okay. What's next to do?"

"The real estate agent is coming over. He should be here anytime."

"Oh. So you're still thinking of selling?"

"He's bringing a contract, Helen."

"Really? Somebody met your price?"

"Not quite. But Ted had set the selling price too high, anyway."

"Don't you want to keep the house in the family?"

"Not particularly. In our minds, Ted and I had already made the move to the island. It is time to let this house go."

"We could take over the mortgage payments. Sort of rent to buy."

"This house is paid for, Helen. We burned the mortgage a few years ago."

Becca and Matt joined them. Becca set the picture of Ted flat on the dining table. Matt sat at the far end of the table in pajama bottoms and a T-shirt.

"Maybe Matt and I could buy the house." Rebecca shrugged.

"You wouldn't be able to handle the mortgage, Becca."

"Listen," Beverly faced all of them. "I'm going to pay off the new house with most of what we get for this house. And there is insurance money. Give me a little time to sort out how much I'll need to live on, with your father's pension. Then I'll give some money to each of you. You'll find cash a lot more useful than a mortgage for this old house."

The doorbell rang.

Rebecca got up and invited the real estate agent into the dining room.

"Let's do this," Beverly said.

Then Beverly Lamont signed the sales agreement.

"Make it happen as fast as you can," she added.

After the real estate agent had left, she turned to Matt and Rebecca.

"You'll need to do something with most of your stuff. We can't take it all to the new house."

"That figures," Matt shrugged.

Ted had always set the course for the family. Beverly had made it happen every day.

"Becca," she said, "put that picture of your father back up on the wall where it belongs. Then get your things together. You're going back to school today."

"Mom, I'm not ready."

"You'll never be ready. You can come home this weekend."

"And Matt, get dressed. You'll take Dad's car and give your sister a ride."

"But..."

"No ifs, ands or buts. When you get home, you're going to work."

After they got up from the table and went upstairs, Helen gave Beverly a cool look.

"Are you going to boss me around too?"

"Yes. Go home and have the house clean and dinner ready for Sean. Put some lipstick on. And be standing by the door when he gets home."

"Ha!" Helen folded her arms across her chest. "That'll be the day! We're equal partners."

Beverly stood up and started putting the piles of papers from her life with Ted Lamont into a banker's box.

"That's your loss, Helen."

AMERICAN VENICE

Two Saturdays later, Sean rented a U-Haul truck. When he backed it
into the driveway of the old house, he had to crane his neck and look
up to greet his kid sister. Rebecca Lamont was standing near the top
rung of an aluminum extension ladder with a hammer in her hand,
squaring off with a loose piece of trim at the ridge line of the roof.

"Hey! What are you doing up there?" he asked, even though her
task was obvious.

Fixing ten inches of loose trim to satisfy the people buying the
house was one of the things he had intended to do with Matt. Except
that Becca had put on her tool belt and beat the boys to it.

"It's about time," she smiled as she easily descended. "Now you
can help with the hard part. Getting this old ladder down."

Sean gave Becca a hug. The youngest sibling had been Ted's best
helper. Sometimes they all forgot that she was a girl.

The ladder was at least as old as Sean and spattered with paint.
Also slightly bent, which made it difficult to extend and retract.

"Should we put it in the truck?" Becca asked after they had it under control.

"I don't think it will fit. Anyway, Dad has a nice ladder at the new
house. Let's leave it for Mister Hoffman. He used to borrow it all the
time, anyway."

"Are all Dad's tools going to fit in the storage unit? Mom didn't want to take a lot of stuff to the new house."

"No way. But that's okay. I rented another unit, for us and Dad's tools. Here's a key. You can put anything you want in there."

"Way cool," Becca smiled as she took the key. Then she used the little saying which had been hers and Ted's, "Yes-sir-ee, bobcat-tail."

Becca started moving tools from the garage to the U-Haul while Sean went in through the back door to find Matt.

Walking through the nearly empty house was an ethereal experience. There was hardly any food in the kitchen. The appliances were all gone, save one coffeepot. The hutch had always been there. The dining table there. In the living room, the piano and the rug under the sofa and chairs had left shadows where the hardwood was not so worn.

Sean hardly noticed that there were no curtains on the downstairs windows. He couldn't remember when they had ever been closed, anyway.

He went upstairs and found his older brother talking on his cell phone in their bedroom, smoking a cigarette. His feet were on the windowsill, with a cup of coffee on a saucer in his lap.

"No smoking in the house, loser."

"What do you care? It's not our house anymore."

Most traces of Sean were gone from the room. He hadn't really lived there since the day he enlisted in the Marines.

It still bothered him that Matt was flicking the ashes of his cigarette into the saucer under his coffee cup.

"We could use a hand with Dad's tools."

"Okay. I'm coming. But I've been doing all sorts of stuff for Mom while you and Becca weren't around, you know."

On the way downstairs, Sean looked into his parents' bedroom. It was completely empty. After seeing no furniture or clothes in the closet nor pictures on the walls, going down the stairs seemed like an out-of-body experience.

Sean and Becca had only started emptying Ted's tools from the garage when Father Nick arrived. He drove a priestly midsize sedan and wore civvies. Dungarees and a polo shirt with the tail hanging out, and a small clerical collar underneath.

"Look who's here, Becca. I guess the diocese can keep the faith for one day without Sneaky Nick creeping around."

"Hi, Becca. Actually, this is my first day off since I was ordained. It's been the Church or the Mission, every day."

She smiled and put a circular saw and a router in a cardboard box into the U-Haul.

"It's great you can spend it with us, Nicky."

"Where's Helen, Sean?"

"She's got the car. She's going to join us for dinner at the new house. You're coming, aren't you?"

"I don't know. I borrowed the monsignor's car to get here. I should get back to…"

"Oh, come on Nicky," Becca offered. "You can ride with us."

"Okay," Father Nick smiled and helped Sean heft the table saw into the truck.

When Matt came downstairs and out the back door, he headed straight for his car.

"Since you've got this under control," he said, "I'm going to pick up Bernadette and go help Mom at the new house."

Sean muttered, almost under his breath, "Sure, you won't take the time for a quickie," as Matt drove away to his girlfriend's house in Ted's car.

They emptied the garage and took a few things from the basement, too.

Sean was surprised to see that the antique NYPD call box, which had always been mounted near where Ted and his friends played poker, had been crudely pulled off the wall. The piece of cop memorabilia from the days before two-way radios was sitting on the floor amid a small pile of drywall.

"Becca, did you yank this old police call box off the wall?"

"Wasn't me."

"It's not a big deal. We're taking the call box, of course. Except now, we'll have to patch the drywall."

"Must have been Matt." Becca shrugged.

Sean was happy to have Nick. Becca was as willing as always, but he was really helpful getting things up the basement stairs. Besides, when he caught Nick's eyes, it was nice to have a friend who knew how traumatic leaving the old house was, without saying it out loud.

When they climbed into the U-Haul truck for the trip to the storage facility, Becca sat between Sean and Nick on the vinyl bench seat.

"I don't know," she said as they drove away and lost sight of their home. "I feel so adrift, without that old house in my life."

"We'll figure it out later," Sean said. "Just stay close to me."

"Yes sir-ee, bobcat-tail."

Sean turned the U-Haul at the corner at the end of their block.

"That goes for you too, Nick."

The Montauk Highway forms one continuous main street for many of Long Island's south shore villages. It runs east and west, between Sunrise Highway and Great South Bay, from Amityville to the Hamptons. There are many places where saltwater comes right up to the Montauk Highway, and even more boatyards.

In the village of Lindenhurst, across from a laundromat and a little red barn where one can drive through and purchase milk and bread, there is a boatyard where two Venetian winged lions stand alongside the highway atop tall concrete columns, facing each other. The statues are unmistakably replicas of the one in Saint Mark's Square in Venice, Italy.

Framed by these inscrutable sentries, a dredged canal behind the boatyard extends all the way to Great South Bay. This grand canal connects to many others south of the Montauk Highway in the village of Lindenhurst. Eight decades years earlier, there were gondolas in the canals and a developer with a dream to turn the area into the American Venice. He called it Venetian Shores. The development was curtailed by the Great Depression, but the winged lions and the canals and the streets with Italian names remain. Riviera Drive. Doges Promenade. Neptune Avenue.

The houses came later, mostly after the Second World War. Some started as vacation homes, and most had been renovated and added to a least once. Nearly all showed an unpretentious front to the neighborhood, which was decidedly working class. A place where a tradesman or a professional, or a retired city cop, might own a home right on the water.

The kitchen was the centerpiece of Beverly's home on the West Lido Promenade. More than any other room in the house, it expressed her sense of understated elegance. Luxurious countertops and the best appliances. Indirect lighting. Rich wood cabinets and drawers which opened and closed silently and smoothly. Every item was reassuring to the touch.

Matt was cooking dinner in Beverly's kitchen. It would be a buffet for twelve. Roast beef, chicken casserole and baked stuffed shrimp. The sink was already full with dirty pots and pans.

Beverly knew she would be cleaning up a royal mess when her eldest was done with his culinary magic. She was setting the table and organizing the serving counter while Matt's girlfriend watched television and talked on her cell phone. They had been together for nine years and there was no mention of marriage. Bernadette also seemed content to live with her parents. Matt was someone to take vacations with.

Aunt Jean had come out on Saturday and stayed over. Beverly was happy to have her friend there, and she wondered how the house would feel after her children and friends went back to the city.

She and Jean were done setting the table when the U-Haul arrived. Sean backed it into the driveway, and Beverly was somewhat dismayed to see that they had brought Matt and Becca's beds from the old house.

"You can just leave those beds in the garage for now," she told them.

Maybe I wasn't clear enough, Beverly rued. *Those beds were supposed to go into the storage unit until Matt and Becca find places of their own. We already have beds in the guest bedrooms here.*

"Hi, Mom. You look great," Sean said as he flew through the house. "I'm going to take a look at Dad's boat. Come on, Nick."

Ted's boat was still tied up against the bulkhead in the canal behind the house. Sean and Nick went out to check the mooring lines and see how much water was in the bilge.

Which was something that Beverly had not done. She had not even been beyond the deck behind the house since Ted had left her. Going down the steps to the bulkhead at the water's edge was not something she would normally do, anyway.

Becca elbowed her way into the kitchen against Matt's protestations and began cleaning the mess in the sink.

"Okay, just stay out of my way," Matt said, opening the oven to check the roast.

"Really? Get a grip, Mattie. You're overcooking everything. Again."

Beverly saw a shiny black Land Rover pull into the driveway. Dexter Birmingham and Joyce had arrived.

"You look terrific." Dex handed her a bottle of Merlot at the front door. "How are you doing?"

"We're hanging in there," Beverly smiled.

Sy Levinson arrived with his daughter Miriam. His wife had died of cancer the year before.

Becca went straight to Miriam when the Levinsons arrived. They had formed a special bond at the funeral. She was a newly minted lawyer working as an assistant district attorney in Brooklyn, who had been able to speak to Becca from her own experience with losing a parent.

"A hundred people might tell you that time heals all," Miriam had told Becca. "Don't believe it. The hurt never goes away. You just bear it through the funeral and the day after. Then the week after. You just carry on. But don't expect the pain to ever diminish. You just find ways to deal with it. Life goes on."

Helen had driven out from Queens by herself and she was the last to arrive.

When they sat for dinner, Sean and Sy Levinson took the seats next to Beverly. There were good friends, good food, and laughter.

Even the cat—Smoky—abandoned his hiding spot and made a brief appearance under the table.

Afterward, Beverly saw Dex, Sean, Sy and Miriam circled in a corner of the living room.

"The case is at a dead end, for now," Sy told Beverly when she joined them.

"Someone will talk," Dex Birmingham said. "Someone always does. Then we'll know."

"I just hope this doesn't drag on for too long," Beverly said. "Sitting through a trial years from now would just be too much."

"We have to get justice for Ted," Miriam said.

"Justice for Ted would be if the killer resisted arrest," Beverly said. "I know it's awful, but that's what I'm hoping for. No trial."

She excused herself from her guests and stepped onto the deck. It was dark by then and, for a moment, she thought that a shadow at the water's edge might be Ted coming up from the boat.

Sean came out and stood at her side.

"I guess we'll have to pull Dad's boat out of the water soon. I'll take care of that."

"I suppose. Right now, I'm rather angry with your father, Sean."

Sean bit the corner of his lower lip. A gesture she hadn't seen since he was much younger.

"Ted could have retired years ago. There was no reason for him to still be on the streets, looking for trouble."

"Gee, Mom. I…"

"Save it, Sean. Just listen to me. There's something I have to tell you."

Beverly turned and took Sean's hands in hers.

"I held you when you were a newborn baby, and I knew you were special. I just knew what you would become."

Sean shook his head.

"You already told me this once, Mom. When I decided to go to the police academy."

"I'm telling you again, in our new reality. You can do so much more. Don't waste your life in the city. Get out, now."

"I don't know, Mom. It's not like that. It's hard to explain. As Dad used to say, being a cop in the city is a ringside seat on the greatest show on Earth."

"Don't tell me, Sean. I saw your father become a bitter old man. He could always turn it off around you and Becca. But there were years when he was miserable to be with. It was only recently … only since we fixed up his dream house on the water … that he came out of his funk."

"I remember, Mom. He wasn't as good at turning off his type-A cop persona as you might think. We knew he was pretty tense for a while."

"I don't want my baby to be that way."

"Becca is the baby of the family."

"No. You're wrong about that, Sean."

"Jeez, Mom. I'm twenty-five years old. And I'm married now."

"You're my baby, and you always will be."

She leaned close and kissed him.

"There," Beverly waved her hand. "Now that you know how I feel let's not mention it again. It's your life."

"Okay, Mom. We should go back inside."

"You go ahead. Give me a moment."

"Are you going to be okay out here, Mom?"

"I'm fine. I'll be right in."

"No. I mean, are you going to be okay in this house? Is this really where you want to be?"

"It's where your father wanted to be, Sean."

"You could probably sell this place if you wanted to."

"Not really. We put everything into this house. We never intended to sell. This was it, for us. We'll never get it all back."

Sean was quiet.

"Besides," Beverly said, "your father and I have unfinished business here. This is a good place to sort some things out, in my own mind."

"Uh … okay, Mom. I'll see you inside."

So this is home now, Beverly thought, looking at the black water in the canal after Sean went inside. *I suppose I can put up a fence along the bulkhead, now that Ted won't object.*

"You stay down there," she whispered to the water as she turned to go back into the house, "and I'll stay up here."

THE CALM

The last Friday in October began with Sean bringing morning coffee to Helen in bed, where she sat up and watched the news on TV while he dressed for work. He and Erik Ramos were working one last day shift before going on the first watch, from midnight to eight.

"Sean, did you see what this hurricane did to Jamaica?"

"Another one?" He leaned in to see the television screen. "I wonder how that resort we stayed at last year made out."

"Those poor people," Helen said. "And there's flooding in Haiti and the Dominican. It's awful. What if the storm comes here?"

"It's kind of late in the season for a hurricane, Helen. The water is too cold."

"But they said it could come right up the coast."

"It won't," Sean said as he kissed her forehead and went for the door. "Love you, kitten."

"Be careful, Sean."

He took the subway into Manhattan and walked over to the Old Slip. It was a calm morning under high, thin clouds that hardly obscured the sun. He and Erik Ramos stood for roll call and took to the streets in their RMP. They had responded to a signal 10-10, suspicious person, and a signal 10-50, noise complaint, before they were dispatched across town to One Police Plaza to see Command Five, Deputy Chief Sy Levinson.

Assistant District Attorney Miriam Levinson, Sy's daughter, was leaving his office when the patrol cops arrived. She pulled Sean aside for a word or two in the outer office.

"Sean," she spoke clearly and quietly. "There is a snag in the investigation that we have to take care of."

"Okay."

"Ted's off-duty piece. A Smith & Wesson .38 snub-nose."

"Why is that a snag?"

"The task force has to examine that gun, Sean. To rule it out as the murder weapon. You know that they have to consider every possibility. We need to run that .38 through ballistics. That's the only way the task force will stop wasting time on nonsense."

"Yeah. I know they might think that my dad was carrying a back-up piece on the job. But he wouldn't do that. He always told me that holding on to one piece in a scuffle is enough to worry about."

"Some cops carry throw-downs."

"His .38 was no throw-down. It was registered and legal for off-duty carry."

Miriam looked out the window for a moment.

"What is it, Miriam?" Sean asked. "What aren't you telling me?"

"I don't even know if I should tell you this." The young ADA sighed. "Promise me you won't fly off the handle."

"I'm cool. Shoot."

"Fratricide, Sean. They can't rule out any member of your family, except you."

"What?"

"You were on the job, in Manhattan. They can't firmly establish the whereabouts of anyone else at the time of the shooting."

"Miriam … I don't want to talk about this."

"It's a credible theory. They have to rule it out."

"Do you realize how nuts you sound? I mean … no way! Beverly and Rebecca were home in Queens that night, and my brother was at the restaurant."

"First of all, Sean … and please don't ask me how I know any of this … Matt was not working at the restaurant that night. Secondly, Becca was home from Hofstra, but she had gone out with a friend. She won't tell us who, or where. And that left Beverly home alone. So we're not absolutely certain where any family member was."

"Miriam, I don't even want to talk about this. It's crazy talk."

"Sean, listen to me. The task force is getting wrapped around the axle on this investigation. It's out of control. It's not only the detective bureau. There are State Police investigators and FBI agents and even ATF guys working on this. And they are considering every credible possibility."

"They're barking up the wrong tree."

"I know that as well as you, Sean. But it's a red flag that Ted's .38 is missing. We've got to find it. That's the only way they will move on to other leads."

"Yeah," Sean shrugged. "Right. Thanks, Miriam."

Sean regrouped with Erik Ramos in the outer office, and they both went into the deputy chief's office.

"Come in, Sean," Sy Levinson said, at the door to his office. "There's someone here I want you to meet."

The man in Levinson's corner office stood up when Sean entered. He was middle-aged. Haggard. Nervous. Dressed in casual civilian clothes. They had never met, but no introduction was necessary.

"Hi, Murph," Sean said.

So Miriam wasn't here just to visit her father, Sean realized. *She was re-interviewing Ted's partner from that night.*

Murph took Sean's hand when he offered it, mumbled something and looked at the floor.

"Officer Murph is applying for disability retirement," Deputy Chief Levinson said. "He was upstairs filing the papers, and I asked him to come down and meet you."

Poor guy, Sean thought. *He's a mess.*

"Sorry to hear you're having a tough time, Murph."

"Post-traumatic stress," Murph mumbled.

"Yeah," Sean said. "It's been a tough time for all of us."

"Officer Ramos," Sy Levinson said to Erik as he led him out of the office, "let me buy you a cup of coffee."

Sean and Murph sat down when the other men left them alone in the office.

"Murph, can you tell me what happened that night?"

"I don't know. I've already told everybody about it."

"I just want to hear it myself. Straight up."

"Honest, Sean. I wasn't gone that long. I just went in to say hello…"

"I don't care why you left my dad in the car, Murph. He let you go, so he must have been okay with it. Just tell me what happened."

"I don't know, Sean. I really don't. I didn't hear anything. Nobody did. I just came outside … like always … and found him there."

"That doesn't make any sense. They said it was a .38 revolver. Those make a pretty loud report."

"I don't know. Maybe, with all the windows in the car closed…"

"The car windows were closed? That doesn't sound right, either."

One of Dad's quirks, Sean thought. *He always had the window cracked a bit, at least. Even in the family car. Even in the winter. On plainclothes patrol in good weather, he would have had the windows in the unmarked minivan at least halfway down.*

"My dad always told me that a cop had to listen to the street. I can't imagine he'd be on the job with all the windows closed."

"Jeez, I don't know, Sean. I'm pretty sure they were open when I left the car. But I don't know. My memory is a mess. When I came outside and saw Ted … your dad … I … just …"

When Murph finally looked at Sean's eyes, emotion overcame him.

"What's done is done," Sean said, standing up and putting a hand on the man's shoulder. "I hope you can live with it."

He found Sy Levinson and Eric Ramos sitting in the outer office. Paper coffee cups in hand. Sean almost felt bad about interrupting their little chat.

"Feel any better, Officer Lamont?" Sy Levinson asked him.

"Not really. Except that I just found out that the windows in the unmarked car were closed tight."

"That sounded strange to me, too," Sy nodded.

"I don't know," Sean looked out the window. "How could someone shoot a .38 seventy-five feet from Atlantic Avenue, and nobody heard a thing? Nobody saw a thing? It doesn't make sense."

Erik Ramos offered a theory.

"A silencer?"

"No," the deputy chief flatly said. "Forensics was very clear that it was a short barrel .38 revolver. Suppressors don't work on that sort of piece. And the murder weapon was pressed directly into the skin."

When Sean looked at Sy Levinson, he saw that the deputy chief was studying him.

"It's been seven weeks," Sean said. "Can you remember any cop shooting that went that long without an arrest?"

"Personally?" Sy said. "No. Maybe too many cooks really do spoil the soup."

Sean cocked his head. *Huh?*

"That special task force they put together to solve this one is top heavy," Levinson rued. "Homicide. Major Crimes. Internal Affairs. FBI and State Police. Miriam says they're stumbling over each other trying to figure out who shot Ted. And why."

"So I hear."

Sean turned to Erik Ramos.

"We better get back on the job ourselves."

"I have a better idea," Deputy Chief Levinson said. "*Law and Order* is filming in Chinatown today. Why don't you drop by and see Dex Birmingham? As a retired detective—who everybody loves—he's in a better position than me to keep an eye on the investigation. The brass in Brooklyn South get a little huffy when I stick my nose into their business."

"Yeah. That would be good."

"Go ahead. I'll clear your car out of service with Old Slip."

"Thanks."

Sy Levinson was behind his desk by then, confronting a pile of crime reports and departmental memos. He looked up with an afterthought when Sean and Erik were halfway out of the door to his office.

"And Sean…"

"Yes, sir?"

"Keep an eye on this hurricane down in the Caribbean. Some of the projections have it smacking us in the nose in a few days. If that happens, your mother might want to be somewhere other than in her new house on the water."

"Yeah. What are they calling this one?"

Inspector Sy Levinson shuffled papers at his desk and did not look up when he spoke.

"Sandy."

———

"Oh, those darn trucks!" Beverly complained to a neighbor, when another big tow truck rumbled down the West Lido Promenade and nearly hit her cat.

"They don't care," the neighbor shrugged.

Beverly watered the flowers in front of the new house nearly every morning. It was a task she enjoyed, and she did it at a time when many of the neighbors were also outside, doing chores or taking a stroll. She always wore a long-sleeved shirt, gloves, and a wide-brimmed hat. Even though the sunlight was not strong at that hour.

"Why don't the people complain?"

"My husband thinks that Bruno is great," the neighbor offered, tilting her head towards the biggest house in the neighborhood. "Bruno throws a big party every Fourth of July, with fireworks. And kegs of beer."

Beverly coaxed the cat out of hiding from behind a rose bush and picked him up. She held him tightly and put him down inside the house. Then she followed the faint but unpleasant scent of a lit cigarette through the house to the back deck.

Matt was on the deck smoking a cigarette and drinking a cup of coffee. His cell phone was set precariously on the railing, and he was staring out into space.

The slider off the dining room was wide open.

"Please keep the doors closed, Matthew. Smoky was nearly hit by a truck."

"Uh … okay. But the cat can take care of himself, you know."

"No, he can't. If he doesn't get hit by one of those darn trucks, he'll fall into the canal and drown. So I'm asking you … again … please do not carelessly let him outside."

Matt sighed and exhaled smoke.

"Sure, Mom."

Beverly slid the door shut and went out the front way. She put the garden hose away and then walked down the street.

The big new house at the end of the street was actually a compound, bordered by a very tall privacy fence. The front yard was all gravel and was used for parking several tow trucks and cars. A young man was pressure washing the truck that had nearly hit Smoky.

"Excuse me, I'm Beverly Lamont. I live up the road."

"I know who you are."

You say you know me, Beverly thought. *But you don't know enough to introduce yourself in turn. Nice manners.*

"Please slow down. You could have hit my cat."

"Then keep your cat out of the road, lady."

The overly muscled young man shut off the power washer and went into the house.

Beverly stood there for a short while trying to decide what to do next. The trucks were all apparently new, with flashy paint jobs and abundant chrome. They each had big exhaust stacks alongside the cab and the name of a different auto body shop on the door. The family probably owned several businesses and lived together. Which accounted for the huge house, and the small fleet of gleaming sport fishing boats at their private dock.

When an older man came out, she guessed that it was Bruno himself.

"What do you need?"

"I came to ask that young man to slow down in front of my house."

"It only looks like we're going fast because the trucks are big. The speed limit is thirty."

"That's too fast for a big truck in a residential neighborhood."

"Nobody else seems to mind."

"My house shakes from the noise."

"These trucks are supposed to be loud, for safety."

"He almost hit my cat."

"Look, we all just get along here," the apparent king of the neighborhood said, climbing into a diesel pickup truck. "Everybody likes us."

With that said, the man who might be Bruno closed the truck's door and drove away.

Beverly walked home, forcing a smile and a wave for the neighbors. She found the old Italian man who walked the street and inspected the neighborhood every day standing in front of her house. He was thin, bent, and spry. And he stood with his hands behind his back and a smoldering cheroot in the corner of his mouth.

"A storm is coming. You better tie those trash barrels down."

"Oh. Well, we'll put them in the garage."

"That's no good. You need to tie everything down, with sturdy rope. I can show you how to tie the right knots."

"We'll be ready," Beverly said. "How about the water?"

"It will fill the roads and a basement if you have one. Just the low spots. No, it's the wind that does the real damage."

"You're sure that the water won't come as high as my first floor?"

"No, no. I've lived here sixty-five years. I know all about hurricanes. It's the wind that makes a mess. I can tell you're not ready. Your things will blow around and damage your neighbors' houses."

"We have a few days to get ready."

"You'll see. You don't know. One loose shingle and your whole roof will be gone. You'll see."

The old *Pisan* moved on to resume his inspection of the neighborhood. Beverly was not quite in her front door when the engine of the big flatbed tow truck started in the compound in a cloud of exhaust smoke. The truck approached her house and slowed, with the engine resisting. *Blatt! Blatt! Blatt! Blatt!*

In front of her house, the young man driving looked directly at her from the high cab. The flappers on top of the exhaust stacks were opening and closing with metallic clicks. Then he shifted and revved the engine to make the truck jump ahead with a burst of speed and rude explosion of noise.

———

Sean and Erik found half of Pell Street in Chinatown shut down to vehicular traffic for a few hours. They parked their patrol car and walked towards a brace of gray moving vans, which had taken over one side of the street behind yellow barriers.

"Hey, you guys can't come in here," a pencil-neck kid from the mayor's film office said. "No autograph hunters. Get out."

The kid had a clipboard and an important-looking ID card on a lanyard. He took a step back when Erik leaned into his face.

"How about I throw you and your little clipboard over those barriers?"

Sean tried not to laugh while he thought about how he might have to restrain his partner. Until he heard Dexter Birmingham's tenor call.

"Dennis! They're with me."

Dex was sitting at a folding table inside the line of moving vans, waving the two cops in. There were lights and cameras set up on the sidewalk, and power cables leading in the front door of a restaurant, where interior scenes must have been filming.

The kid from the mayor's office was irked. But he pretended to study his clipboard and stood aside.

"Chill, pal," Erik whispered. "You're on our street. Nobody tells us what to do here."

"Sean! Erik!" Dex called. "Come over here."

Dex was seated with a small group, who were talking and pointing to the sidewalk where the lights and reflector screens were set up. He made a quick round of introductions. The producers. The assistants. The director.

"Go over there and meet the talent," Dex said, waving them to the chairs where the actors sat. The two stars were typecast faces from half a dozen cops-and-robbers shows over the years. The scruffy pair who did the grunt work to back up the glamorous pair in suits. They were talking to another actor who looked vaguely familiar—he'd been the perp in a dozen TV shows—and a harried script assistant.

Sean expected little more than a nod from the stars. He'd seen them before. The rich and famous were often at arm's length when working security details in the city, but it had never occurred to him to bother the actors on location.

"Hey, guys," one of the stars said, deepening his voice into his stage persona as they approached. "What's up?"

"Just wanted to say hi," Sean said. "We're fans of the show too, you know."

"Well, hell," the other star said. "In that case let's get some evidence. You got your cell phones handy?"

The actors put down their scripts and stood with Sean and Eric while the script assistant snapped pictures with their cell phones.

"This is cool," Eric said. "I've been watching you guys for years. Even before I was a cop."

"Ha! I've done so many cop shows that I should get a pension from the NYPD," the husky actor said. "Then I'd be all set, like Dex Birmingham."

"I know," the thin actor offered. "Even my neighbors forget that I'm not a real cop. They ask me to fix their parking tickets."

Then the assistant director made an announcement.

"Two minutes!"

"Showtime." The tough-guy actor smiled, shaking Sean's hand. "Stick around. Let me know if I do this arrest right and proper."

"I think you've got the routine down pat."

An assistant producer was watching the posing, and she stepped in as soon as the actors went to their marks with the director.

"Erik, have you ever thought of acting?"

"No," he laughed.

"We're always looking for real officers to help us. We could use you in a scene."

"How about my partner?"

"Well…"

"Ha!" Dex laughed. "They have all the pretty little white boys they need signing up. You've got *eth-ni-city*, my man."

"Put together a portfolio," the producer said. "Face and body pictures. List your stats. Height is important because we can't use you with certain actors if you tower over them. I'd use a professional photographer."

"That sounds like a lot."

"It'll be worth it. Have you ever done any singing?"

"You want me to be a singing cop?"

"No, but we might have a minor speaking role, with that baritone voice of yours. Singing experience helps with delivering the lines."

"I was in the chorus in school. And the senior play. *West Side Story.*"

"You're perfect!" she said. "E-mail your package to me."

She handed Erik a card.

"That's my cell phone number, too."

"Thanks," Erik said. "I'll talk to my wife and let you know."

The real cops stood with Dex Birmingham while the actors and the director walked through the scene with the crew. Sean thought that it looked fairly complicated but when "action" was called, the stars made it look easy. They were talking to witnesses when they sighted the perp coming out of the restaurant. A chase past the steady cam operator ensued. He backed up a few steps and then panned to follow them to the alley. Another camera was already set up in the alley to capture the action when they knocked over trash cans and collared their man. A sound man with a boom microphone and a recorder pack on his hip caught the snappy dialogue.

"Cut."

The actors and the director huddled in front of a video monitor to watch the scene.

"No good," the director said. "Try to keep the pickle out of the next take, Pete."

"Sorry. First day on the job," the veteran sound man said, raising his hand.

They quickly shot the scene again. This time it was right, and the crew began to pack up while the actors hopped into a black SUV and headed to the next location.

While the crew disbanded, Erik talked to the real uniformed cop who had been in the scene. Sean huddled in the alley with Dex Birmingham.

"I just saw Murph in Sy Levinson's office. He's a mess."

"He ought to be."

"Yeah. He told me that the windows in the unmarked van were all shut tight. That doesn't sound right."

"I know. None of us know what to make of that. It might not be a big deal."

"What are those guys on the task force thinking?"

"Well, you know that the shooter was in the back seat, right?"

"I guess so."

"Half of them think Ted was taking a nap, and the shooter opened the back slider and jumped in before he could react."

"What about the other half?"

"The others think he had some civilian in the van. Someone who shouldn't have been there."

"You've got to be kidding me, Dex. Those assholes think that my dad was taking a bribe? Or drugs? What the hell!"

"Sean, they're treating Mary Love as a person of interest."

"Who the hell is Mary Love?"

"A well-known transvestite prostitute. She works that corner."

"What?"

"That's where they're at, my friend."

"What do you think, Dex?"

"They're idiots."

"Yeah. Miriam Levinson said something about them getting all wrapped up on Ted's .38 snubby."

"You better find that piece soon, Sean. You know that you should have reported it stolen right away."

Sean just shrugged. He didn't have an answer.

"Sean," Dex continued. "That task force is spinning their wheels. We have to do something."

"What did you have in mind?"

The crew had the equipment loaded by then, and the vans were ready to pull away.

"Jake Morrow is coming up next week. We need to talk. You and me. Jake and Sy. About Ted. And about that other thing."

"Why the mystery, Dex? Just tell me about that other thing."

"I can't. Not without Sy and Jake."

"Sy Levinson didn't say anything about getting together with Jake. Why is that?"

"Damn, Sean. He's high brass. A damn good street cop who worked his way up to the number five spot in the Service. The commander of Manhattan South. He has to be real careful what he says to one of his junior officers. Just go with me on this one."

"Okay, Dex. I'm ready for anything, at this point."

Dex Birmingham put his hand on Sean's shoulder.

"I know it's eating at you, man. People think you're handling it so well … we know better. Hang tough, man. Just hang tough. We're going to have to figure this one out ourselves. But we have to be very careful. We have to play it cool. Okay?"

"Right."

They walked out of the alley towards the police car, where Erik was waiting.

"What about this damn storm?" Sean asked as they walked. "Will Jake come up anyway?"

"Come on, man," Dex beamed. "You know what a hurricane does in the city. Just a load of wind and rain. The beat goes on. We'll give you a call, my friend."

"Right. See you, Dex."

Erik took shotgun in the RMP so that Sean could drive when they called dispatch and put themselves back in service.

"Hey, Hollywood," Sean said. "So are you going to start whistling show tunes now, or what?"

"Shut up, Sean."

"Really? *West Side Story*? I bet you were the leader of the Sharks. Weren't you?"

"No. I was Tony. The white kid."

"How did that work out?"

"Hey, there were so many Ricans and blacks in my school that we couldn't find a white boy for the part."

"This is great," Sean laughed as he drove towards the Bowery. "I'm going to have a ball with this."

"Thanks for having my back, partner."

"Tell you what," Sean offered. "It could stay our little secret … if you help me haul my dad's boat out of the water on Saturday morning."

"What? Drive out on Long Island to mess with a boat? We start the night watch at midnight on Sunday."

"That's my price," Sean smiled. "Take it or leave it."

"You're driving, right?"

"You'll have all day Sunday to take a nap before watch."

"You don't know Sundays with my wife. Catechism class, Mass, lunch, prayer circles … Sometimes I wish I was on the job every Sunday."

"That's too bad. I guess I'll have to reveal your secret past, *Tony*."

"Okay. What can I say?" Erik shrugged. "Breakfast and lunch better be included."

IN NOVISSIMA CENA

"**C**heck out these lions," Sean said as he turned the car off Montauk Highway and into Venetian Shores. It was the morning of the last Saturday in October. Erik Ramos was riding shotgun for the drive out from Queens to Beverly's new house in Lindenhurst. Father Nick was in the back seat with Helen.

"Nice," Erik offered. "They look like something from ancient Rome."

"Yeah. But they make good landmarks. I'd have a hard time finding the new house without them."

Beverly greeted them at the front door. Sean gave her a long bear hug. She had coffee and pastries ready for them all. Becca was happy to see them, too. She was at the new house every weekend since Beverly had given her Ted's car to take to school. Matt was watching television. The Weather Channel.

"I wouldn't go out on the boat today if I were you guys. There's a hurricane coming."

"That's why we're hauling it out today," Sean said.

"Don't get lost. If you're not back in time, you're all goners."

"The storm is far away, Matt."

"What if the boat breaks down?"

"The Coast Guard won't leave us out there, Matt."

"They say that hurricane winds can come suddenly."

Sean laid his hand on Matt's shoulder.

"You really need to get out more often, my brother."

Sean turned to his crew that was devouring the pastries and snacks which Beverly had laid out for their arrival.

"Let's get going a bit early, guys. I promised Erik a spin around the bay before we go to the boatyard."

"It better be a nice ride after you dragged me all the way out here."

Erik and Father Nick went to the boat with Sean and Becca. Helen stayed behind with Beverly and Matt. She would bring the car around to the boatyard to pick up the crew and bring them back to the house.

Ted's boat was tied to a small float along the bulkhead behind the house. It was nearly high tide, so they only had to negotiate two steps on the ladder to get down to the float, which was a bit tippy when they all stepped on it.

"You're going to drown me, aren't you?" Nick said.

"What?" Sean joked. "You can't walk on water yet?"

"That's reserved for a much higher pay grade in the Church, Sean."

"Hang on," Becca said, offering Nick a hand to climb up to the boat.

She was wearing tight shorts and even Sean had to admire her legs when she supported the young priest. They only looked petite until she summoned the muscles and tendons to show themselves.

"Okay," Father Nick said, once he was on the solid deck of Ted's boat. "This is much better."

When Sean opened the engine compartment and leaned in to open the seawater valves to cool the engine, his sweatshirt rode up in back, revealing the 9mm strapped to his waist.

"Are you two carrying your guns?" Becca asked.

"Of course we are. We're cops."

"Remember what Dad always used to say to his cop buddies when he took them fishing? No matter what, don't shoot a hole in the bottom of the boat."

"I'll keep collateral damage in mind," Erik smiled.

Sean went to the steering station and turned the key to start the engine. Erik instinctively went to the stern to watch for the overboard discharge of cooling water in the exhaust.

"I didn't know you knew about boats," Sean said when Erik gave him a thumbs-up.

"Sure. My people are from an island. There's saltwater in my blood."

"Erik, you were born in the Bronx."

"Yes. But my soul is from Puerto Rico."

"Maybe your great-grandfather's soul. You speak more Mandarin than Spanish."

"Occupational hazard," Erik smiled. "I've been a cop on the Lower East Side for too long. Chinatown and Little Italy."

Sean moved away from the wheel and waved his sister in.

"Becca, why don't you drive?" Sean suggested.

"Sure," she said, standing behind the wheel. "Untie those lines, boys."

Becca easily backed Ted's boat away from the float. She sat up on the seat back, the way her father used to, so that she could see over the windshield on the way out of the narrow canal.

Father Nick took the seat behind the windshield next to Becca. Sean and Erik sat next to each other on the stern boards, where they could see everything. It was a beautiful morning. The boat idled slowly out of the canal, lined with houses.

"I love watching her drive the boat," Sean said.

"I'm impressed," Erik nodded. "She really knows what she's doing."

"Yeah. My dad spent more time with her than any of us. He might have treated her like a boy ... he taught her how to play ball and nail a board and drive a boat ... but he loved having a little girl. Most of all."

"Then you need a daughter of your own. Someday."

"I'm ready now. I'd love to have kids. Helen is the one dragging her feet. But she's a good kid. She'll come around."

"You're only twenty-five. Wait until you're thirty."

"Yeah. I'd rather start while my mom is still around."

"What? She's a young woman, Sean. She looks great. You've got plenty of time."

"None of us knows how much time is in the world, Erik."

They reached the end of the canal. Becca pointed the boat into Great South Bay and gave the motor some gas. Spray began to kick up at the stern when they sped up, and Sean and Erik got up and moved up to where Nick and Becca were seated. Becca was still up on the seat back, so her legs were even with Nick's head.

"Stop ogling my sister's legs," Sean joked. "You're a priest now, for Christ's sake."

"Nicky has always been a leg man," Becca laughed. "He had his hand on my thigh when he made his pass at me, back in the day."

By then, the boat was up to speed and cutting through the water nicely. Prancing over small wavelets with spray flying aside off the bow.

"What?" Sean turned to Nick, laughing. "You made a try at my kid sister? When did this happen?"

"You were away in the Marines," Becca laughed.

"Becca, you were … what? Fourteen?"

"Sixteen. And Nicky was very sweet."

"You hit on my sister when she was a kid?" Sean said, with a grin that betrayed his mock anger. "What an ass."

Father Nick was mortified.

"It wasn't like that, Sean."

"Now, Nick," Becca laughed. "It was just like that. It's okay. I was flattered. You were just a little too old for me."

Sean watched Father Nick's face turn crimson. He bowed his head and raised both hands to his brow.

"And nervous," Becca laughed. "I was afraid that you might pee your pants."

"Good thing Dad never found out," Sean said. "He would have killed you, Nick."

"He was very sweet," Becca reached over and touched Nick's knee. "A true gentleman."

"That's okay," Erik said to Nick, over Sean's shoulder. "You're only human, Father. But I'm sure you were more dangerous than sweet."

"Isn't it time to head for the boatyard?" Father Nick suggested.

They made a wide turn around the bay before heading back towards shore, enjoying the ride. Huddled behind the windshield to avoid the spray when they motored into the wind and singing the chorus from *Gilligan's Island*, "A Three-Hour Cruise."

"You're cutting it close," the manager of the boatyard said when Becca nudged the boat into the slip to be hauled. "I'm going home as soon as I get you out of the water."

"Thanks for doing this on short notice," Sean offered.

"No problem. A lot of my regulars wait until the last minute. You guys need to get out of the boat before I pick it up."

They climbed out of the boat, and the manager revved the motor on the mobile boat lift. Wide straps under the keel raised Ted's boat out of the water and held it over the ground.

The boat hauler was waiting with a special trailer behind his heavy-duty pickup truck. Still dripping saltwater, the manager set the boat on the trailer, and hydraulic arms swung up to cradle it. When the lifting straps were removed, the boat was ready to travel.

"Where is your dad?" the boat hauler asked Sean as he checked Ted's boat to make sure it was sitting correctly on the trailer.

"Sorry to say, he has passed away."

"Aw, that's a shame," the man said. "Sorry to hear that. He was a great guy."

"He always enjoyed this stuff with the boat," Sean shrugged.

"Oh, I know. Always a big smile and a joke or two. He was a piece of work, your father was."

Helen arrived with the car. Becca, Erik, and Father Nick went to Beverly's house with her. Sean took shotgun in the boat hauler's truck. It was only a few miles to the house. Then the boat hauler expertly backed the trailer into the driveway at Beverly's house, with Becca directing him, and sidestepped the boat alongside the garage. There was just enough room between the garage and the fence. The grass had never really healed from having the boat stored there on previous winters, so they all got their knees dirty when they slipped big wooden blocks under the keel.

Sean and Becca set the screw jacks in place to support the sides of the boat. Then the boat hauler lowered the hydraulic arms and pulled the trailer clear.

Ted had always paid the boat hauler three hundred dollars in cash for his service, and Sean was prepared to do the same.

"Hey, how about just fifty bucks for my gas?" the man said.

"I can't do that. You came out on short notice, just for us."

"No problem. This one is for your dad. I'll make my money in the spring, when we put the boat back in."

"Thanks," Sean said, handing the boat hauler a fraction of the usual fee. "If Ted is watching, I bet he's relieved to have the boat high and dry, in case we get the hurricane."

"Yup," the man said, climbing back into his truck. "You better tie that thing down, real good."

Beverly had prepared a late lunch for the crew. Soup and sandwiches. She came outside to call them all into the house while the soup was still hot.

"You guys go ahead," Sean said. "I can finish here."

Father Nick and Erik went into the house to eat. But Becca stayed at the boat with Sean.

"Get serious," she said to Sean. "You can't do this without me. I used to help Dad block up the boat every year."

"You're probably right," Sean said, crawling under the boat to drive wedges so that the weight was evenly distributed on the keel. Becca sat next to him on the patch of sparse grass, handing him wedges and swinging the hammer herself when she had a better angle. The rain began with a smattering of hard drops.

"Your gun is showing again," Becca pressed a finger on the pistol in the holster on her brother's belt when his sweatshirt rode up.

"Don't touch my gun."

"I can touch your gun if I want to."

"No, you can't."

Sean was prone and reaching around the wood blocks under the keel of Ted's boat. Becca sat where there was more headroom. It began to rain hard all around them, but they were dry under the boat.

"You look so much like him, Sean."

"I miss him too, Becca."

"Mom wants you to get out of the city."

"I know," Sean said. He crawled out of the tightest spot under the keel and sat next to her in the dirt near the propeller and rudder. "What do you want me to do?"

"Whatever's right for you. I know that means staying on the job."

"You don't sound very convincing."

"Sean, I couldn't go on if something happened to you."

"Nothing is going to happen to me. Besides, you're going to find a great guy of your own and get married."

"Sean, where am I going to find a boy like you?"

"You will."

"Definitely not a cop!" Becca laughed through tears.

"Can't argue with that."

The hard rain ended as suddenly as it had begun.

"I miss Dad."

"So do I."

They hugged, sitting in the dirt under the stern of Ted's boat. She whispered in his ear.

"Yes sir-ee, bobcat-tail."

———

Beverly was tossing the salad when the rain began splattering on the roof. It made her uneasy that Becca and Sean were still outside at the boat. But the rain stopped suddenly and her children came in the house as she was setting the salad bowl on the table.

"Get out of those wet clothes. You'll both catch your death of cold."

When they peeled off their sweatshirts and joined the rest of the group at the table, Beverly wondered what had transpired between them. The raindrops on Becca's face didn't hide her teary eyes. And Sean was laughing something off. Feigning nonchalance.

Becca will tell me later, Beverly decided. *But Sean is still crawling off in the corner to be alone, the way he did when he lost a ball game or a fight as a young boy.*

"What's the latest with the weather, Matt?" Sean asked as he sat down between Helen and Father Nick.

"Sandy has made the turn towards the northwest, just like they said it would. Now it's headed straight for Atlantic City."

"Then we're all going to die, anyway," Sean shrugged, overdoing the graveyard humor. "This is the last supper."

"Sean," Erik remanded, "there's a priest at the table."

"It's okay, Erik," Father Nick nodded, with the same innocent smile he once used when he was caught stealing at the candy store. "Sean will allow God's grace into his life someday. We'll just have to wait for that moment."

"Don't hold your breath," Helen said, reaching for the salad.

"Sean is more spiritual than he lets on," Becca said. "He's just shy."

"Easy, now," Sean laughed. "Is this Pick-on-Sean Day or what?"

"You're an easy mark," Matt scoffed. "You might want to try taking things less seriously now and then."

"Here sits a true stoic," Father Nick offered, putting a hand on Sean's shoulder. "An island unto himself. A true disciple of Marcus Aurelius, if ever there was one."

"Really?" Matt said. "Maybe he's just afraid of reality."

"You don't know how wrong you are," Helen said. "Courage is my husband's biggest problem. A little fear would do him good."

"Let's talk about something else," Sean stated, with more than a hint of impatience.

His discomfort gave them all reason to pause.

Beverly not only knew that modesty was deeply rooted in Sean's complex psyche, but also the moment it became embedded there. Ted had taught him to run the bases with his head down like Joe DiMaggio after a home run. She could still hear the father's words to his son across the years: "Don't embarrass the opposing pitcher. Save the celebration for the dugout. Make it a team achievement."

It isn't necessarily a good trait, she decided. *Sean could do so much more if he were not so damn unassuming at times.*

"Erik," Beverly turned to their guest, "I hope you'll bring your wife and daughter out to visit me soon."

"You're on," Erik smiled. "We'd love to come out. I would have brought them today, but this was sort of a working trip. Just to get the boat out of the water. Even though I didn't do anything."

"You're welcome anytime."

"You should get his autograph, Mom," Sean said. "They want Erik to play a bit role on the *Law and Order* television series. You know, the uniform who briefs the detectives at the crime scene, or takes the perp away after the big arrest."

"That's wonderful," Beverly smiled.

"Hold on a minute," Erik said. "I'm not sure I'm going to do that. My wife and I are still talking about it."

"It's a no-brainer," Sean said. "The producers were all over Erik when we visited Dex Birmingham on the set in Chinatown. They wanted to sign him up on the spot."

"We'll see," Erik shrugged.

"I can see it," Becca offered. "You've got a great look, Erik. Quite the dashing figure."

"Jeez," Sean laughed. "Get those raging hormones under control, Becca."

"No," Helen said. "Your sister is so right, Sean. Erik brings it, big time."

"Oh, if you only knew!" Sean laughed.

"Hey, partner!" Eric laughed. "I'm enjoying this if you don't mind."

"Yeah. I hate to cut this meeting of the Eric Ramos Fan Club short, but we've got to get going. I need a nap before the night watch. It ought to be a real cluster, with a hurricane on the way."

"Me too," Father Nick said. "I'm going straight to the Mission. I'll be there all night, I suppose."

"Won't everyone just stay indoors until the storm passes?" Helen offered.

"You'd think so," Erik answered. "But the crazies will all come out. It will be a real freak show if the wind and rain get strong enough."

"Becca," Sean offered, "you're coming to our place, right?"

"I wasn't planning on it."

Beverly agreed with Sean.

"You need to go with them, Rebecca. You've got Ted's car now."

"I was going to stay here with you and Matt."

"Don't be ridiculous. You'll be snug as a bug with Helen."

"For sure," Helen said. "Sean will be off saving Gotham City. I don't want to be alone."

Beverly knew that Sean wasn't done.

"You should come to Queens too, Mom."

"I don't think so."

"We have plenty of room," Helen said. "You and Becca could share the spare bedroom, and Matt could take the couch."

"Screw that," Sean interrupted. "Matt can mooch off Bernadette's family for a change. While he's at it, he could see if they still have a job for him at the restaurant."

"Someone has to stay here with Mom," Matt insisted.

"Sean," Beverly said, "I can't leave this house. Your father and I worked for years to get it ready. We put everything into this place. I can't just walk away."

"This might be a bad storm, Mom. What if the water comes out of the canal?"

"If the water comes that high, I'll be right over to your apartment with Helen and Becca."

"It'll be too late. You won't be able to drive at the height of the storm."

"Hey, I got this," Matt insisted. "I've been following this thing on TV all the way. It's going to pass south of Long Island. We'll be okay."

"Don't be so sure," Becca piped up. "Dad used to say that hurricanes don't care what the experts say. Not even a little. They go wherever they want to go, and do whatever they want to do. Nobody knows."

"You'll see," Matt said. "I've got this all figured out."

"I believe that a prayer is in order," Father Nick said. "Will you join me in asking for God's grace?"

"That's a great idea," Erik said.

"Of course, Nick," Beverly said.

Father Nick and Erik crossed themselves before the group held hands around the table.

"Jeez," Sean laughed. "I'm not going to hold your hand, Sneaky Nick."

"Do it!" Helen whispered, holding Sean's left hand in her own.

Sean completed the circle by taking Father Nick's hand.

"Heavenly Father, we ask that you watch after this house and keep Beverly and Matt safe at all times. Be with Helen and Rebecca, and stand with Sean and Erik as they defend the city. We pray for peace for Ted's soul. In Jesus's name we ask, Amen."

Beverly was astonished to see that Matt made the sign of the cross after the prayer.

Sean noticed, too.

"What the hell was that, Matt?"

"I'm thinking of converting. Bernadette's parents want me to, before we get married."

"Matthew," Beverly exhaled. "Your father is rolling over in his grave right now."

WALL TOSS

On most Sunday mornings, they only got out of bed to make coffee and get the newspapers from the front door. The *Sunday Times* for Helen and the *New York Post* for Sean. Then they would prop themselves up with extra pillows and watch the news on TV.

On that last Sunday in October, the news was all about the storm.

"Sandy, Sandy, Sandy," Helen said. "Can't they talk about anything else?"

"I know."

"They do this every time. They make a big deal about some hurricane and then it turns out to sea at the last moment. Then they're like, sorry never mind."

"Yep."

Helen dropped the *Times* to her lap when the television made dire predictions. A diagram of Manhattan in profile. Streets under water. Blue water halfway up the first floors of buildings.

"This storm won't hit the city, will it?" Helen wanted to know. "I mean, it couldn't. Could it?"

"Hurricanes do whatever they want to do. Nobody knows."

"Well, what do you think?"

"I don't know." Sean shrugged as he put down the sports pages and rolled onto his side.

He pinned her to the mattress. Drank in the way she smelled and tasted. He knew that his feelings for her had started as a chemical reaction. That was fine. She was his drug. *This is the one.*

They had been married for almost one full year.

"Sean, will your mother be okay?"

Jeez, he thought. *Don't talk about my mother when I'm on top of you.*

"I don't know," Sean said. "They might lose power for a few days. Maybe some shingles on the roof."

"They say that a big storm surge could hit the city. At high tide and on a full moon."

"I'm not going to drown in Manhattan, kitten."

Not unless I fall into the river, he thought. *Or a sewer.*

"Sean, you've been a cop for two years, and you've never taken one sick day. Why not call out tonight?"

"Are you kidding? I can't leave my guys when the going gets a little tough. That would make me the worst kind of cop. The kind nobody trusts."

"Your guys? What about me, Sean?"

"Helen, it'll probably miss us. Let me go look."

He sat on the edge of their bed and pulled on pajama bottoms and a T-shirt.

Sean opened the slider and stepped onto their balcony. The wind was rustling brown and yellow leaves on the trees below. Transit buses and light traffic moving on Queens Boulevard. Pedestrians strolling on the wide sidewalks.

A lazy Sunday morning, Sean thought.

"I'm no weather man," he said. "But the wind is coming from the northeast. So it should push a hurricane away. Towards New Jersey."

"That's what they're saying."

"When is this thing supposed to get here?"

"The storm surge is supposed to hit tomorrow afternoon."

"Okay," he gripped the railing with both hands and stretched his frame. "I'll be off duty by then. The second watch can deal with it."

He saw Helen sit up on their bed and point at the TV.

"Sean, they're going to shut down the MTA. Today!"

"What?"

"That's what Governor Cuomo just said on the television. The subway and all buses will stop running at seven p.m. this evening."

"Okay. You'll need to drive me to work tonight. And make sure to fill the car with gas when you get home. Just in case."

———

Beverly arrived home from the King Kullen with a trunk full of groceries at around an hour before noon. After a hot summer, it was one of the first pleasantly cool days on the West Lido Promenade. Neighbors watering the flowers. Kids playing in the street. A chorus of lawnmowers harmonizing in the distance.

When Beverly deposited the first two bags of groceries on the kitchen counter, Matt was still in his pajamas. Sitting in front of the TV.

"Help me bring this stuff in, Matt."

"Just a minute. This is breaking news, Mom."

"Nonsense. They'll still be calling it breaking news next week. Just to keep you mesmerized."

"No. This is a big deal. A tall ship is sinking down by Cape Hatteras. The Coast Guard is sending a helicopter to rescue the crew."

"The Coast Guard doesn't need your help, Matthew. Come rescue the ice cream from the car before it melts."

He went out to the car with her and began carrying bags into the house.

"Jeez, Mom. Did you buy the whole store?"

"We might as well stock up, just in case. Don't forget the bottled water."

"Dad has plenty of water in the garage."

"You never know," she said and began putting things away.

The TV was still turned on. As soon as all of the groceries were in the door, Matt returned to the screen. A moth to the flame.

"I thought that you and Bernadette were going apartment hunting today?"

"Not with a hurricane coming."

"Really, Matthew. There's always a reason to put it off, isn't there?"

He was talking to her but looking deeply into the TV screen.

"I don't know if we can afford a place of our own."

"I told you that I'll cover the first and last month's rent. Just get a place you can afford. The two of you ought to be able to do that."

"Sure, Mom."

"Matt, how long is the restaurant going to hold a job for you?"

"They said I could come back whenever," he shrugged.

Beverly stepped out onto the deck. She left the door wide open. Maybe the fresh air was the elixir he needed to draw him away from the tube.

When she came back inside, she glanced at the TV briefly. The angry dark spot in the center of the satellite image of swirling white clouds looked like the eye of an octopus, or a spider, creeping up the east coast.

She went outside to take in some of her flowers so they wouldn't get destroyed by that thing coming towards them. Beverly was down on her knees unearthing an impatiens when a black Land Rover pulled up.

"Hi, Bev," Dex Birmingham said as he dismounted.

"This is a pleasant surprise," Beverly said, pulling off her gardening gloves.

Joyce Birmingham came straight to Beverly with a hug and a kiss on the cheek.

"We just ran out to the Hamptons to check on our cottage. We thought we'd stop by and see if you were ready for the storm."

"I'm glad you did." Beverly stood up. "How about a cup of coffee?"

"A beer would be better," Dex said, helping her to her feet.

"Sure," Beverly said, leading Dex and Joyce into the kitchen. "I think I have a cold one in the back of the fridge someplace."

Matt said hello to the visitors without getting up from the TV as Beverly handed the retired detective a bottle of beer. She took a Coke from the refrigerator for herself. Joyce took a glass of water.

"Let's go out on the deck," Beverly offered.

"I'll be right out," Joyce said, pulling out her cell phone and a small notebook. "I'll sit right here and make a few phone calls if you don't mind."

Dex followed Beverly outside. They sat on the deck, overlooking the canal.

"Nice," Dex smiled, with a nod to the Jersey Skiff in the backyard. "I see that you got Ted's boat out of the water in time."

"Sean and Rebecca came out with some friends yesterday."

The cat appeared on the deck and circled at a distance.

"How about you, Bev? Are you going to stay with the house for the storm?"

"I guess I have to," she shrugged.

"You're welcome at our place until it all passes," Dex offered. "Hurricanes don't cause much of a commotion on the Upper West Side."

Smoky jumped up onto Dex's lap and Beverly began to shoo him away. But Dex signaled that it was okay and began to stroke the feline behind the ears.

"At least the storm won't sneak up on you," Dex laughed and pointed through the window at Matt in front of the TV, still in his pajamas. "It looks like Matt is keeping a close eye on it."

"I wish he wouldn't watch TV while there is daylight outside."

"That's a good policy," Dex nodded.

For a moment, they looked at each other and nothing was said.

"Beverly, we need to talk about a thing that happened … with Ted … when we all worked together at the Old Slip … Sy and Ted and Jake and I."

"That's all ancient history. Isn't it, Dex?"

"Actually, this thing left us with a big problem. I was just wondering if you knew."

"What sort of thing are you talking about?"

"Things happened on the job," Dex shrugged. "It didn't always go according to Hoyle, you know."

"I know that Ted had to do some terrible things when you were on the Stakeout Squad if that's what you mean."

"Those things really are ancient history. We all just did what we had to do. This was something else altogether."

"It sounds like you could go to jail," Beverly intuited.

"We could all go to jail. Maybe for the rest of our lives. After all, we're not kids anymore."

"Isn't there a statute of limitations on most things? Except murder?"

"We didn't murder anyone, Bev."

"What did you guys do, Dex? Does this have anything to do with Ted's killer?"

"We don't know. That's the thing. We have to figure it out."

"Dex, I hate this guessing game. Just tell me, please."

"I can't, Bev. I've never even told Joyce. None of us were supposed to tell our wives. I just had to be sure that Ted never told you."

Beverly looked at Dex Birmingham.

"Why are you telling me now, Dex?"

"This is unfinished business. We're going to have to bring Sean into our group."

"Don't do that, Dex. Please. Just leave that boy alone."

"It has to be this way, Bev. After the hurricane, Jake Morrow will come up from North Carolina. Then the three of us will sit down with Sean. All you need to know is that as long as we stick together, everything will be okay, Beverly. Just trust me on that."

"Don't you dare drag that boy into your web. I won't allow it."

"Trust us, Beverly," Dex stood up to leave her. "Let's never talk about it again. And please, never ask Sean about this thing."

"I don't like this, Dex."

"Neither do I." He shrugged as Joyce came outside and joined them on the deck.

The threesome spoke of other things for a while. City politics and the storm.

"Take care, Bev," Dex said as he held the door to his Land Rover after the visit. "Trust me. Everything will be all right."

Joyce blew a kiss as the Land Rover backed out of the driveway. Beverly stayed outside and watched them drive up the West Lido Promenade.

A tow truck huffed past the house. The young driver scowled at her as he downshifted to make more noise, and then sped away.

———

Since before sunset on the last Sunday of October—a full twenty-four hours before Hurricane Sandy was forecast to brush past the Verrazano Narrows—Lower Manhattan was eerily quiet. South Street Seaport, the Fulton Fish Market and the Statue of Liberty were all closed. Subways and buses throughout the city had suspended operations. For the first time since 9/11, Wall Street and the entire financial district would not open for business on Monday morning.

Blame it on Sy Levinson.

In meetings with the mayor and the governor, the commander of Manhattan South, along with his counterpart in the Fire Department, had argued for securing Lower Manhattan well in advance of the storm.

So on Sunday night, Deputy Chief Sy Levinson drove his city SUV away from his office at One Police Plaza though nearly empty streets. A light breeze swirled through the tall massifs of the canyons of commerce. The placid black water in the East River reflected the lights of the Brooklyn Bridge like a mirror. But for a few taxis and pedestrians venturing out before the total curfew, the most expensive real estate in the world looked like an abandoned ghost town.

He intended to visit all nine of the precincts under his command that night. But Sy Levinson arrived at Old Slip in time for the change of watch. He parked his SUV under the large American flag over the doors. By force of habit, he reached out with his hand and touched one of the massive bronze lanterns framing the entry as he passed through.

In recent weeks, he had been inside the old first precinct often. There were memories everywhere.

The first floor of the House had not changed much since he had been a patrolman and a sergeant there. The imposing wooden desk facing the front door looked the same. Except that the handwritten blotter and typewriter had been replaced by a computer. The holding area and the drunk tank looked exactly as they did when he, Ted Lamont, Jake Morrow and Dex Birmingham used to collar perps on the street and drag them in through the front doors. Exactly as it had on the night of *that* other thing, long ago.

The first watch was milling about in the muster room. Talking and laughing and finding their spots. They gradually formed into two standing ranks, facing the desk.

After a few words with Captain Sweeney, Deputy Chief Sy Levinson spoke to the oncoming watch. They deserved to get the bad news straight from him.

"You'll all be working double and triple shifts until after the storm passes. I need all hands on deck. So break out the cots upstairs and tell your families that you'll see them in a few days."

He looked directly at Sean Lamont as he spoke. The young cop standing in the ranks looked exactly like Ted had looked when they were all *rookies*. But he did not acknowledge him. Not even a casual nod.

The last thing that kid needed was a reputation for being buddy-buddy with the brass.

When he left the Old Slip, Sy Levinson drove uptown. Unlike the financial district, there were plenty of people on the streets and in the establishments of Little Italy and Chinatown. It appeared to be a normal Sunday night. As if New Yorkers were saying, "forget about it," to the storm.

He was driving slowly on the Bowery when he saw a group of kids on the edge of Chinatown. Skinny teenagers, wrapped in Abercrombie and Old Navy. Preppie rich kids, standing close and passing something and stumbling over each other like they couldn't decide which way to go. Or who should go first.

They didn't belong there.

A street cop in a white shirt with stars on the collar and with master's degrees in criminology and government affairs was still a street cop. So Deputy Chief Sy Levinson turned and drove around the block. When he came at the five kids again, he abruptly stopped his SUV and stepped onto the sidewalk.

"Get up against the wall," he pointed, with his portable radio in hand.

"Who, us?"

"Get your noses against the wall," he told the boys, grabbing the lead two by the arms and pushing them. His tone was matter-of-fact. New Yorkers walked past without paying much attention.

"We're not doing anything," the tallest boy said.

"Shut up and get against the wall."

"We're not doing anything!" one of the other kids pleaded.

"Get your nose against the wall and shut up, son."

"You can't touch me! My father is a lawyer."

"Your father will thank me tomorrow morning," Sy Levinson said, all in his routine voice. He was big and imposing enough to dispense with the growling. He was doing these boys a favor.

He had the five boys against the wall before he reached in the leader's pockets and came up with large industrial markers. Magnums of permanent ink with wide felt-tips.

"That's an illegal search!" the lawyer's son said.

"Ask Daddy about stop-and-frisk when he picks you up at the First Precinct," Sy Levinson sighed.

The deputy chief had been holding his radio in his hand throughout, and he used it to call for backup as soon as he found the markers.

"Where do you live?" Sy asked the boys while he waited for a patrol car to roll up.

"Riverside."

"Do your parents know you're over here late on a Sunday night?"

"No school tomorrow, because of the storm."

Some tough Chinese youths came out of a nearby alley and walked by in groups of twos and threes.

"Keep moving," Sy Levinson told the Asian gang members. "This doesn't concern you."

"Good evening, Officer," the gang members facetiously muttered as they passed. Looking long and hard at the preppie kids against the wall.

Sy Levinson let the kids from Riverside turn their heads enough to watch the tough youths walk away.

"Are you really dumb enough to come to Chinatown with markers? Those guys would break you apart for disrespecting their home. Now get your noses back against the wall."

When the first police unit rolled up, he wasn't surprised to see Sean Lamont and Erik Ramos step out. They quickly moved towards the kids.

"What have you got, Deputy Chief?" Erik Ramos asked.

Sy Levinson handed the magnum markers to Sean Lamont.

"These young gentlemen were loitering in the wrong neighborhood," Sy said.

"Are you guys crazy?" Sean asked one of the kids as he searched him against the wall. "You'll get cut to pieces for tagging in Chinatown."

Another RMP rolled up and the uniforms searched and cuffed the youths. When the wagon arrived, they put them all into the box and drove to Old Slip. The deputy chief followed in his SUV.

When his cell phone rang as he drove, Sy Levinson wasn't surprised to see that Dex Birmingham was calling.

"Hey, Sy! How you doing?"

"My city is about to get hit by a hurricane. How do you think I'm doing?"

"Are you on the job? On a Sunday night?"

"Chinatown. I just tossed some rich kids from Riverside. Just in time, too. Or they would have got hurt."

"Ha! Don't you know you're too old and fat for a wall toss?"

"Some things never go out of style. And guess who my backup was?"

"Sean Lamont?"

"You got it. Sean looked just like his old man when he got out of the RMP. It was eerie. For a moment, I really thought I was seeing a ghost."

For a few seconds, nothing was said.

"So," Dex offered, "I went out and saw her today."

"Okay. How did that go?"

"She doesn't know a thing."

"That's good."

"I also talked to Jake. He'll come up after the storm. We've got to do something. Work it out."

"Yes. And we have to bring the kid into this."

"That's risky."

"It is. But he's a good kid. We can bring him all the way in. Then decide."

"Okay. You're right, of course. We really don't have any choice."

"Later, Dex."

What a mess, Sy Levinson thought. *Prison was a very real possibility if this thing turned out badly. For all three of them.*

But what did it matter? He had lost Hoda, either way. She had fought the cancer like a lion, all the way to the end. Without her, prison was just another place to live.

When he arrived at Old Slip, he knew that after he processed these kids, it would too late to go to his home in Brooklyn. Now that Miriam had moved out to a place of her own, the big house seemed painfully empty.

He would sleep at One Police Plaza. Without Hoda, his own bed was no better than the sofa in his office.

As Sy Levinson went between the big green lanterns flanking the entrance to the First Precinct, he wondered if he could ever be with another woman.

It didn't seem possible. But, after the storm—and the other thing—he needed to find out.

RED SKY MORNING

Dawn came to Lower Manhattan on the last Monday in October as a magenta glow over the warehouses and piers across the East River in Brooklyn. Joggers and dog walkers enjoyed a mild morning on the Battery Park Promenade. Traffic was light on FDR Drive, and delivery trucks were being diverted away from the Financial District. Hurricane Sandy was then over three hundred miles south-southeast of the city—it had already taken the turn towards the Jersey Shore —and most New Yorkers felt assured that it would blow by with little effect on their lives.

Sean Lamont and Erik Ramos were in the last hours of the first watch when they parked their patrol car in front of the old Governor's Island Ferry Terminal at the foot of Whitehall Street. The night had been uneventful.

Standing on the sidewalk at the southern tip of Manhattan in the ethereal calm of that morning before the storm, Sean could sense the enormity of the city resonating off the bedrock below. The background hum of ventilators purging the air in the subway tunnels underfoot. Tide rips churning around the pilings of the ferry slip. The first light glinting off the windows of skyscrapers high above. Cars on the FDR Drive and the diesel engines of tugboats singing against the tide as they chugged upriver for shelter.

They checked the benches and corners on the promenade. Then they climbed the stairs at the fluted iron columns and decorative trim of the abandoned ferry terminal. The once-grand facade was sporting a fresh coat of green paint.

They found a young man sleeping in the door alcove.

"Hey, are you okay?"

A clean young face turned up and greeted the officers.

"Uh…"

"Wake up, buddy. Time to rise and shine."

"I'm okay."

"Sure you are," Erik said. "Sit up for me. Okay?"

When Sean helped him sit up, he felt fine wool fabric in the shoulders of the young man's suit.

"There you go."

"What are you doing here?" Erik asked.

"Uh … just taking a break. I came down to sit on one of the benches and think about things."

"What time was that?"

"I don't know … One? Two?"

"Okay. What time is it now?"

"Uh," the man searched his wrist for a watch, which wasn't there. "I don't know."

"Got some ID?"

"They shut the damn subways down," the man said, shaking off a hangover and hunting through his pockets. "Who would do that? How was I supposed to get home?"

"The shutdown was announced well in advance."

He found his wallet. The cash and his American Express card were gone, but he pulled out and presented his Connecticut driver's license. The address was in Greenwich.

"Sorry. I have a job. I just had a tough night."

"Where do you work?"

"Morgan Guaranty Trust."

Morgan? Sean thought. *This lucky guy is on his way to being a multi-millionaire. If he doesn't get derailed by booze first. Or knifed by a mugger.*

"Ready to get up?" Sean asked him.

"Sure."

He helped him stand. The man rubbed the back of his neck. Sean quickly frisked him for weapons.

"Why were you down here on a Sunday night?"

"We took some clients out to dinner. I guess I let the limousine leave without me. I thought I could take the train home."

Erik handed his license back.

"Robert, it's a good thing you have identification. Otherwise, we'd have to arrest you. You're free to go. But we really don't want to see you down here anymore."

"You won't."

"Where are you going to go now?" Sean asked.

"Home."

"Is there someone you can call?"

"My wife. Except ... I guess I lost my cell phone."

"Well, you can't wait for her here. You should meet some people who can help you."

"I'm okay," Robert said, searching his wrists again for a watch which wasn't there.

"What kind of watch did you have?"

"Patek Philippe."

"Are you kidding? Do you want to report your cell phone and wristwatch stolen?"

"Uh ... no. I don't think so. I just want to go home."

"Sure you do," Sean said. "Let us give you a ride."

"Am I under arrest?"

"No. We'll give you a ride to a safe place. I just have to handcuff you before I put you in the car. For everybody's safety."

"Okay."

Sean snapped his cuffs on the man and got into the back seat of their RMP with him. Erik drove up Broad Street and through the Financial District, which was eerily deserted. They drove up Park Row and passed by Columbus Park and turned onto the Bowery. Sean handed his cell phone to the man and told him to have his wife pick him up at the Bowery Mission.

The car rolled up on Father Nick Shellaine at the sidewalk in front of the Mission. The priest was taking the last few steps on his walk over from the rectory at St. Mary's.

"Sean! Good morning. And Erik, good morning to you!"

"When did you get to be so chipper, Nick? You were never a morning person."

"By God's grace, it's a beautiful day, Sean."

"Sure it is. Here, we brought another soul for you to save."

Sean got Robert out of the back seat and took the handcuffs off.

"You look okay to me," Nick said.

"I've had better days," Robert muttered.

"Call it an intervention," Sean offered. "Robert needs a place to wait for his wife to come and pick him up."

"Why don't you come in and have breakfast at the Mission?"

"I'm not a derelict," Robert said. "I have a good job."

"Come in and have breakfast anyway. You could even make a donation."

"Okay."

"Sean, why don't you and Erik join us?"

Sean looked at Erik, who nodded approval.

"Sure."

They went through the big front doors of the Mission with Father Nick. Breakfast was being doled out by volunteers at a long table upstairs. Most of the down-on-their-luck diners avoided making eye contact with the police officers, but they were happy to see Nick.

Sean could see the discomfort in Robert's features when they sat at a table with some men and women who also might have slept in the streets the night before. As soon as he finished eating, he excused himself.

"Am I free to go, Officers?"

"Sure," Erik replied.

"Thanks. In that case, I'll go downstairs and wait for my wife."

"You bet," Sean said. "Take care."

When Erik got up to walk around the dining hall and meet some of the patrons, Sean and Father Nick were left alone at the table.

"Sean, how is Helen?"

"She cries enough for both of us."

"You should take some time for grieving yourself."

"Maybe. I'll feel better after they find the shooter."

"Revenge, Sean?"

"No. Justice. And answers. The worst part is not knowing who it was."

"There is grace in forgiveness, Sean."

"Fine. Who am I supposed to forgive?"

"Yourself, Sean. Allow yourself to grieve. It isn't healthy to carry a burden like that. Let it out."

"Like I said, after they find the shooter."

Looking out the window near their table, Sean saw a shiny gray BMW sedan pull up in front of the Mission. Robert got into the car, and it quickly drove away.

"Listen," he said to Nick, "I think something is wrong. Some things about Ted's murder just don't sit right. His oldest friends—guys I've known all my life—are acting strange. I don't know who I can trust, Nick. Other than my family. What's left of it."

"I'm always here for you, Sean. Tell me all about it."

"Yeah," Sean laughed. "Like I would ever cry on your shoulder, Sneaky Nick."

———

The basement of Old Slip had flooded in the Great Storm of 1938 and again in Hurricane Carol in 1956, and the surge from Hurricane Sandy was predicted to rise even higher than either of those epic events. So when Officers Lamont and Ramos repaired to South Street after leaving the Bowery Mission early Monday morning, they found the precinct buzzing with last-minute preparations.

Sean and Erik went down in the basement and helped to carry old desk blotters—hundreds of handwritten logbooks—upstairs. Captain Sweeney had them deposit the bound volumes wherever they could find space on the second floor.

The community-relations officer had a small desk in a windowless gallery on the second floor, which used to be a pistol firing range. The narrow space had been divided into a series of interconnected offices. Rows of filing cabinets lined the walls. When Sean and Erik pushed her chairs aside to stack the logbooks on the floor in her tiny space, she muttered in resignation.

"I don't get any respect around here."

"Time to take one for the team," Sean chuckled. "Give us a hand, why don't you?"

Officer Rhoda Abernathy took half of the books out of his arms and stacked them between overflowing filing cabinets and her desk. She had beads and dreadlocks in her hair. Her pile was neater than the ones Sean and Eric made.

"At least leave me room to get to my desk. Okay?"

"Why?" Eric chided her. "After this storm, there isn't going to be any community around here to relate to."

"Eric, don't you know that the NYPD has to generate its own weight in paperwork every day, storm or no storm?"

They succeeded in filling Rhoda's niche in the ancient pistol range halfway to the ceiling with logbooks dating back to 1954. Then Captain Sweeney came to the door.

"Nice work, Ramos and Lamont. Now go up to the third floor and take a nap. You're both going out on foot post with me this afternoon."

"I helped too, you know," Rhoda said.

"Good. You can go out on foot post too, Abernathy. Do you have departmental rain gear?"

"Of course I have rain gear. I'm a cop."

"Really? When was the last time you used it?"

"Who says I ever used it? It doesn't rain on the second floor of Old Slip that often."

———

It might have been a holiday Monday on West Lido Promenade. People stayed home, walking and drinking a few beers and talking to neighbors. Fathers and sons played stickball and tossed footballs in the street. Not many windows were boarded up. Storms gone by were remembered fondly, like long lost friends. *Carol, Bob, Hortense, and Irene.*

Beverly's car had a full tank of gas. She and Matt had packed bags in case they had to leave the house. Other recommended precautions, like filling the bathtub with water, seemed too ridiculous to follow.

The torrential rain came in midafternoon, driving nearly everyone indoors.

Sean called her cell phone not long after the real rain began. Beverly assured him that she and Matt were snug and secure in the house. She was more worried about him in the city.

"Relax, Mom. We've got everything under control here."

"Well, be careful anyway."

"I will. Love you."

Beverly sat in the kitchen after talking to Sean and watched the water rise in the canal. It came up slowly, until it reached the level of the highest tide. About a foot from the top of the bulkhead, but still contained.

The afternoon had become gloomy and dark. Beverly settled into Ted's chair with Smoky on her lap.

"If the water comes up much more," Beverly finally said to Matt, "we're going to get out of here."

Matt was sitting in front of the TV.

"It's going to miss us," he said. "They're waiting for Sandy to come ashore in New Jersey. Those guys are really in for it. But they're not saying anything about us."

A flash of lightning cut through the rain.

Beverly looked out the window and saw that the big drops were falling sideways.

A moment after the lightning, there was a deep bomb-like explosion, as if a mortar shell had landed nearby. Sparks flew from somewhere near the Montauk Highway, and the lights went out all through the neighborhood.

Smoky leaped off her lap and disappeared behind the couch.

"What was that?" Beverly recoiled.

"The lightning hit a transformer." Matt jumped up from the blank TV screen. "We're screwed now."

Beverly had never heard rain pound on the roof so hard. When she looked out the front windows, all the leaves had come off the trees. The suddenly-bare branches looked like gnarled fingers raised in agony. The foliage had fallen onto a few inches of water in the street, which was being beaten into a mousse by the wind and rain.

"Look at this, Mom," Matthew called.

He was standing in front of Ted's brass clock and barometer in the living room. The ship's weather instrument had been mostly decorative, until then.

"That can't be right," Matt doubted. "The air pressure can't be falling that fast!"

When Beverly looked out the back windows, she was horrified to see the gray saltwater spilling up over the top timbers of the bulkhead. The grass near the deck was already underwater.

"We might have to get out of here," she said, in a surprisingly calm voice.

"Jeez," Matt uttered when he came to the window. "I guess so, Mom."

The two of them were transfixed by the sight of the rapidly rising water. It came up to the back of the house in sheets of windblown wavelets.

"It's rising so fast!"

Beverly went across the kitchen to the door to the garage. She reached for the button to raise the outside door. Hit it several times before she remembered that there was no power.

Two inches of water covered the garage floor.

"Matt, do you know how to open the door with no power?"

"Sure."

Matt pushed by his mother and bounded down the two steps to the garage floor. He sloshed over to the door and pulled the release rope for the automatic opener. When he raised the door slightly by hand, a wave of water rushed in.

Within moments, six inches of dark water filled the garage.

"Matthew! Get up here!"

"Uh, it might be too late to leave in the car, Mom."

The water was up to the fenders of the car. Beverly and Matthew were stunned when the spare refrigerator in the garage started to bobble and float. When it toppled and fell onto her car, Beverly closed the door and they retreated back to the kitchen.

"I can't believe how fast the water is rising," Matt said in a hollow tone. Disbelief turning to shock.

The wind was roaring against the windows. Water lapped at the planks of the back deck. Ted's brass clock was chiming eight bells— four p.m.—when Beverly dialed 911 on her cell phone.

There was no service. But she tried calling Sean anyway.

Nothing.

At that moment, Ted's boat floated off the blocks in the backyard and crashed into the house. The wind pushed the prow of the sturdy boat against the cedar shingles outside the kitchen. The angry little waves sweeping across the backyard drove the side of the boat against the deck repeatedly, and the railing soon gave way.

"Come on," Beverly tugged Matthew, who was mortified by the sight of the boat smashing against the house, to the stairs leading to the bedrooms on the second level.

———

The wind was rising and just starting to whip the water in New York Harbor into whitecaps when Captain Sweeney took his platoon of officers to the streets of Manhattan. Sean and Erik were detailed to a foot post near the intersection of South Street and Whitehall Street, across FDR Drive from the abandoned ferry terminal where they had encountered the sleeping young financier a few hours earlier.

Lower Manhattan was under a mandatory evacuation order by then, and their orders were simple: there would be no looting or loss of life on their watch.

Their post was at One New York Plaza, the southernmost sky-scraper in Manhattan, where financial giants such as Morgan Stanley and Goldman Sachs were housed on fifty floors of offices. A subterranean parking garage and a retail concourse containing upscale stores were located below street level.

The mezzanine was at least ten feet above street level. Two cops had been posted at each entrance. Sean and Erik were on the southwest side, overlooking Whitehall Street. From there, they could see the harbor, the walkway around the Battery, and the glass facade of the subway station at the new Staten Island Ferry Terminal. There was an entrance to the subway beneath where they stood, which had been secured with yellow police line tape, as well as a wide stairway leading down to the shopping mall. The ramp to the parking garage was also under their post, and a trickle of cars was leaving. The afterguard of the financial houses was evacuating the building.

The heavy wind began that afternoon.

When the wind turned the rain into a horizontal deluge, they retreated into the lobby. The glass entry doors were rattling in the breeze when Captain Sweeney and Officer Rhoda Abernathy arrived with hot coffee and sandwiches.

"Building security has cleared the upper floors," Sweeney told them. "You guys have front row seats on this thing."

"Hey," Rhoda said, looking at a TV which had been left on in the display window of an electronics store. "A crane is out of control uptown. It's swinging all over the place, nineteen stories up."

The rest of them joined her in front of the TV.

"That thing is coming down," Sean said.

"It might take the building with it," said Sweeney.

"Don't even say that," Erik laughed.

After Sweeney and Rhoda had left to continue their round of the concourse, Sean noticed that Erik Ramos was unusually quiet and preoccupied. He was watching the rainwater fill the streets outside halfway to the tops of the curbs and watching the crane on TV at the same time.

"What gives, Erik?"

"Dammit, this part sucks."

"Quit your complaining," Sean laughed. "We're sitting pretty here. High and dry."

"No, man. I have a recurring nightmare that the whole damn city falls down. I wake up in a cold sweat some nights, with visions of Manhattan skyscrapers tumbling down like dominos."

"What are you babbling about, Erik?"

"I was a student at Hunter College on 9/11. It seemed like the city had been rocked down to the bedrock underneath. Like it was all unstable. When the twin towers fell, I thought they might take the whole damn city down, too."

"The city is not going to fall down, Erik."

"Probably not. But I wish I'd never seen what I saw that day."

When they looked outside, the streets were filled with rainwater. It was coming down fast, with no place to go, and it lapped at the tops of the curbs and ran to lower ground in rivulets.

The patrol unit which had been sitting outside the building was forced to retreat. The officers yelped their siren twice before they pulled up Whitehall Street.

"There goes our ride out of here," Sean laughed. "We're really screwed now."

Half a dozen high-end sedans came speeding up the ramp from the parking garage. They charged up Whitehall Street throwing wakes like speedboats and sprays of water from their wheels.

"Good luck," Sean laughed as the cars sped away. "Those guys are really cutting it close."

"Those guys are nuts," Erik shrugged.

"Yeah. Maybe the building is really empty now."

By four p.m. all electrical power had gone out. It was dark as nightfall and seawater were spilling over the bulkhead at the Battery. It came at them from all directions, rushing across Pearl Street and Water Street and up Whitehall Street and Broad Street.

"Look at this, Sean. It's coming up fast."

"Yeah. Makes you wonder where it's going to stop, right?"

They could see the water swirling around the green iron railings of the subway entrance and spilling down the steps to the platforms below.

"Holy shit," Captain Sweeney said, when he and Rhoda Abernathy joined them to watch the parking garage and the lower-level shopping mall filling with cascades of seawater.

"The whole subway system couldn't fill up with water," Sean said. "Or, could it?"

"It looks like it's filling up to me," Sweeney muttered. "You guys better turn off one of your radios, to save the batteries. We're going to be here for a while."

"Captain, I think I'll stay here and keep an eye on these two characters," Rhoda said.

"Whatever," Sweeney shrugged. "Just don't go outside for anything. You could get sucked into the subway pretty easily."

Sean tried to call Helen and Beverly again after Captain Sweeney left. But the cellular networks were all jammed with calls and failing due to power outages by then. He and Erik were looking out at the water rising over the plaza when they heard a voice behind them.

"Excuse me, Officers."

They turned to see a gray-haired man in an expensive suit and perfectly clear gold-rimmed glasses.

"My Lexus is underwater," the man said, apologetically. "How do I get out of here?"

"You don't," Sean said. "We're all stuck here."

Erik recognized the man.

"Hey, aren't you Lou Meltzer? Chairman of New Amsterdam Investments?"

"I am."

"You manage our pension fund."

"Well, yes. My people do, anyway."

Erik turned to Sean.

"Sweeney is going to love this!"

Rhoda Abernathy was ignoring their conversation with the financial magnate. She was looking out the glass doors to the street.

"Hey. We got a situation out here."

Sean and Erik spun around and joined her at the doors. They could hardly believe their eyes. There was a figure coming up out of the subway entrance, holding the railings. Straining to climb against the cascade of seawater.

Sean spoke into his radio as he and Rhoda shot out the door into the rain and wind.

"10-24 at the Hole on Whitehall. Civilian in distress."

Erik was right behind them.

"Stay right there, Lou!" Erik said as he ran out.

They sprinted off the mezzanine and down to street level. There was six inches of water on the sidewalk and as they neared the subway steps, they could feel it tugging at their ankles. Pulling them towards the Hole.

The man was almost free when he stumbled and fell backward. Down the steps. Rhoda Abernathy started down after him.

"Rhoda!" Sean called. "Be careful! Let me in there first."

"Hold me!" she yelled, reaching for the man.

Sean had Rhoda and Erik was holding them both with one arm on the railing. The wind blowing across the subway entrance made a deafening hollow sound. Water cascading around their ankles. Sean could see the subway platform in the darkness below, awash in a foot of splashing water.

The man reached for Rhoda's hand, and they all began to inch back up the stairs.

They didn't see Captain Sweeney come charging down off the mezzanine with half a dozen cops and two paramedics. Not until the reinforcements encircled them and pulled them clear of the stairway.

"Is anybody else down there?" Sweeney asked.

Rhoda and Sean had the scrawny man by his arms.

"Well?" Rhoda asked. "Is anyone else down there?"

"No."

"I'll be damned," Sean said to Erik. "Look who it is."

"No kidding. His rathole must be down there."

Jimmy the Finder looked around. Held up by Sean and Rhoda. Disoriented. Windblown rain pelting his face.

"Hey, Jimmy," Sean said. "Jimmy the Finder. Remember us?"

"Who, me?"

"You know this guy?" Lieutenant Sweeney asked.

"Yeah," Sean said. "Jimmy the Finder is an old friend of ours."

"Right," Sweeney muttered. "Let's get him inside and have the paramedics check him over. Then he's your problem."

They all trooped back to the mezzanine and into the lobby of One New York Plaza. The cops closed the doors to the wind and rain and shook the water off their jackets.

Lou Meltzer was waiting inside the doors

"Okay. Now, who are you?" Sweeney asked.

"Lou Meltzer."

"Of course you are," Sweeney muttered, recognizing the face from the financial shows on TV. "You might as well go back to your office, Lou. Nobody is leaving here for a few hours."

"My office is on the top floor."

"Okay. We've set up a command post in the building security office on this level. You can wait there."

"Can I stay with these officers?"

"Suit yourself."

"We'll keep an eye on Jimmy, too," Sean said.

Lieutenant Sweeney left Sean, Erik and Rhoda with the two civilians. They gave cups of coffee and blankets to Lou Meltzer and Jimmy the Finder. Then their own sandwiches and a candy bar.

Jimmy didn't recognize Sean and Erik. He talked to Lou Meltzer for a long time before he crawled into a blanket and slept in a fetal position.

Lou had settled onto the polished marble floor by then. He sat with his back against the wall not far from Jimmy. His thoughts seemed far off, and Sean guessed that he was pondering how the storm was going to disrupt his financial empire.

The cops stood at the glass doors, watching the water rise.

"It's not too late to become a social worker," Erik said to Sean, when he caught him looking at the sleeping form of Jimmy the Finder.

"I'm a cop. I'm supposed to help people."

"You can't change that guy, Sean. He's always going to live down in the subway, or in a cardboard box in some abandoned building. That's who he is."

"No. But we can make sure he doesn't drown tonight. I guess that's enough."

By around nine p.m., there was two feet of water covering White-hall Street.

The sound came slowly. Gurgling, choking. A murmur in the wind.

It grew louder. When the mezzanine vibrated slightly under their feet, Sean ventured outside to take a look.

"Captain," he said into his radio. "You need to see this."

Sweeney arrived as Erik and Rhoda also went outside. Even Lou Meltzer joined them. The rain had paused, and the wind had diminished, but it was still howling.

Cars were floating out of the parking garage under the building. They rose to the surface on the ramp under the mezzanine in a capillary motion, bumping and jostling. Floating in the entrance to the garage. Running aground on the ramp.

"Lou," Erik asked, "what color is your Lexis?"

"White."

"Is that it?"

"Yup. It was a good car, too."

At that moment the building shook, ever so slightly. A bubble of trapped air burped out of the subterranean garage as a giant air pocket surrendered to the flood.

"God damn it," Erik said. "I hate sitting here watching my city get trashed."

THE SEARCH

The floodwaters began to recede from Lower Manhattan after midnight. By six a.m. on Tuesday morning, the sidewalks had reappeared. Police cars resumed patrolling the streets. A platoon of replacements arrived at One New York Plaza.

Sean and Erik were standing outside on the mezzanine above the flooded parking garage when a black Hummer sped up, and two armed security men hopped out.

"We're looking for Lou Meltzer."

"He's in here," Sean pointed over his shoulder to the lobby.

Sean escorted the security team into the lobby. Rhoda Abernathy was watching over Lou Meltzer and Jimmy the Finder. The two civilians were sleeping on blankets on the polished marble floor.

"Jimmy," Lou said when the security team helped him to his feet. "Why don't you come with me?"

"No. I can't leave," Jimmy rued. "This is where I find things."

"Jimmy is right," Rhoda said. "We'll take care of him."

"But … I could take him to Greenwich. Get him a place to live. And a job."

"It's a nice thought," Sean offered. "It really is. But let us take care of Jimmy."

"Where will you take him?"

"The Bowery Mission. Their doors are always open. He'll be able to go there whenever he needs a meal. Or medical care."

"Officer Lamont is right," Rhoda said. "You can't change some people. The streets are their lifestyle."

"I have a friend at the Mission, who will look after Jimmy," Sean said. "It will always be a safe place for him to go."

Lou Meltzer looked at Jimmy. Then at the officers.

"There are a lot of Jimmies in the city, aren't there?"

"You bet," Sean said.

"I wish I had noticed them before this."

"They prefer to stay out of sight."

"I'm going to look into this. I might have to get involved. What is your friend's name at the Mission?"

"Good for you, Lou. Father Nick Shellaine. He's there nearly every day."

Lou Meltzer departed in the black Hummer just as Sy Levinson arrived in his SUV, splashing through deep puddles. The deputy chief leaned out the window towards Sean and Erik. He recognized Jimmy the Finder.

"Where did you find this one?"

"He came out of the Hole when it flooded," Sean said. "And landed in our laps."

"Lucky for him. You can turn him loose. We don't have time for social work today."

"Chief, we should take him to the Bowery Mission."

"Like they would have room for one more?"

"I can get Father Nick to keep an eye on him," Sean offered.

"Okay," the deputy chief acquiesced. "Get in."

They drove uptown. Jimmy between Sean and Erik in the back seat.

"How did your mother make out?" Sy Levinson asked, over his shoulder.

"I don't know," Sean shrugged. "Not yet."

"You haven't talked to her?"

"No. Her landline and cell phone aren't working. Apparently."

"Listen, the reports say that the area south of the Montauk Highway on Long Island got hit pretty hard. She's probably not even at the house. Most likely she got evacuated to a shelter."

"We'll see."

"Sean, you look terrible. Get some sleep."

"I'll let Helen drive ... take a nap in the car."

Father Nick met them in front of the Mission. A Con Ed generator on wheels was humming at the curb. The lights were on inside the double doors.

"How was your night?" Sean asked.

"We survived, by God's grace. You?"

"No problem. Got room for one more?"

"No. Sorry."

"Yes, you do. This is Jimmy. Jimmy, this is Father Nick."

"I've got to go," Jimmy said to Nick. "I have to get back to my place."

"Where is that?" Nick asked.

Jimmy the Finder shrugged.

"A hole in the Hole," Erik said. "It's underwater right now."

"How about some food first?" Nick asked.

"I don't know," Jimmy looked aside.

"Just have some breakfast. Then you can go back to your place."

"Okay."

"Thanks, Nick," Sean said when he got back into the deputy chief's SUV.

"Oh, by the way, how is your mother, Sean? Didn't the south shore get a lot of damages?"

"I hear it's a mess," Sean said out the window. "I'll let you know."

Deputy Chief Sy Levinson gave Sean and Erik a ride back to Old Slip. This time Sean sat in the front seat.

"You're going out to find Beverly as soon as you get off watch, aren't you?"

"You bet."

"I'd say that you should get a few hours sleep first. But you won't."

"There will be plenty of time to sleep later."

They arrived at Old Slip, and Sean and Erik got out of the SUV. The deputy chief had some final words for Officer Lamont.

"Sean, we have to do something about that other thing. But it may be a few days before Jake Morrow can get up here. So hang tight."

"I know, Chief."

When Sean and Erik went up the steps and between the green lanterns at the entrance to the precinct, Erik had a question.

"What is this other thing that Sy Levinson is talking about, Sean?"

"You don't want to know, Erik."

"It's about your father, isn't it?"

Sean shrugged. The Old Slip was a mess inside. The water had apparently risen as high as the floor in the muster room. The basement was still flooded.

"Do you need me to help with your mother?" Erik asked as they turned in their radios.

"Thanks. But you'd better get to your own family, Erik. I'm sure they're worried about you."

"Anything you need, just let me know, Sean."

A large contingent of exhausted cops was standing in the muster room, waiting for transport out of Manhattan. The holding cell was empty. The door was open. Sean and Erik took seats behind the bars.

Sean leaned back against the pock-marked brick wall. He exhaled before he spoke.

"Erik, I can't tell you too much. But the guys who were in my dad's Stakeout Squad are up to something. I don't know much about it. But I'm starting to think they did a bad thing, a long time ago. And that it has everything to do with Ted getting shot."

———

The National Guard Armory on Mott Street in Brooklyn had been designated as an evacuation point for the cops from Manhattan South. Sean found Helen there, waiting in the car.

He tossed his gear in the back seat and climbed in next to her.

"Sean, you look awful."

"I just need a shower. Then we're going to my mother's house."

"There's no electricity at our apartment. No hot water."

"What does it matter, at this point?"

Sean called Rebecca's cell phone as soon as his own phone was connected to the charger in the car.

"I'm fine," Becca laughed. "They told us to stay in the dorms. We have no power, so we're having an English Pub Party. Warm beer."

"Have you talked to Mom?"

"No. I'm worried, Sean. Can you pick me up?"

"Stay put, Becca. I'll let you know as soon as I find Mom and Matt."

The Forest Hills section of Queens had been spared the brunt of the storm. But the elevator was not working in their building, so they climbed the three flights of stairs. The super had the furnace running by then, so at least they had heat when Sean took his cold shower.

He dressed in jeans and an NYPD sweatshirt. He strapped his 9mm on his hip and slipped Ted's blackjack into his back pocket.

"You drive," he said, when they went back downstairs.

Helen slipped behind the wheel, and Sean again plugged his cell phone into the charging port. He tossed his shield onto the dashboard of their car and tried to find a position which might allow him to sleep in the passenger seat.

His eyelids were heavy. They closed easily, and time became elastic.

When he woke up, Helen was shaking him hard. They were at a roadblock somewhere, with Suffolk County cops standing on both sides of the car. There were Red Cross vans and TV remote broadcast trucks on both sides. Sean only knew where they were when he saw the winged lion statues at the road into Venetian Shores.

"You can't go in there," the county cop was saying. "Residents only."

Sean rolled his window all the way down. Forty winks in the car had only made his head hurt more. His mouth was dry, his eyes burned, and his body ached.

"My mother and brother are in there."

"Are you sure? They might be in a shelter."

"Look, I don't know where they are," Sean said, feeling weary and irate. "I was up to my ass in floodwater on the job all night. So I'd appreciate some professional courtesy."

The Suffolk County cop looked at the NYPD shield on the dashboard and then at Sean.

"I hear you, but we can't let cars in. You'll just get stuck in the standing water, and that makes big problems for us."

"Then we'll walk," Sean shrugged.

"What street is the house on?"

"West Lido Promenade."

"Jeez! That area got hit pretty bad. Are you sure she isn't at a shelter?"

"We've got to check."

"Okay, park your car right here. We'll keep an eye on it. The National Guard will give you a ride in."

Helen parked their car as the county cops waved a National Guard Humvee over.

"Just come right back, okay?" the cop said. "We can't leave your car here too long."

"The keys are in it," Sean said as he took his shield from the dashboard and helped Helen into the military vehicle.

A courteous, young National Guard corporal drove the Humvee through flooded residential streets. TV news crews were also cruising the streets in the back of a pickup truck. A trio of kids in a red canoe were mugging for the cameras and some guy was splashing around and pretending to scuba dive in the street, even though the puddle wasn't deep enough to get the air tank on his back underwater.

Sean took a deep breath when the corporal stopped the Humvee in front of Beverly's house. The spruce tree in the front yard had fallen into the picture window in the living room. The garage door was open, revealing a toppled refrigerator and soggy debris, which spilled out into the driveway.

"Thanks for the lift," Sean said to the guardsman.

"I'll be cruising the neighborhood, sir. Just flag me down if you need anything else."

"You bet."

Beverly fell into his arms at the front door.

"They wanted to evacuate us, Sean. But I knew you'd find us if we stayed here."

"Okay. Let's get out of here. Have you got some things ready to go?"

"Yes. Except … I can't leave Smoky."

"Where is he?"

"We can't find him," Matt chimed in.

"Okay. Forget about the damn cat. He'll be fine. When you come back in a day or two, he'll be ready to come out of hiding."

"I'm leaving some food out for him," Beverly said, going to the kitchen.

Sean surveyed the living room and kitchen with his brother.

"How high did the water get, Matt?"

"The waves were over the deck. There were only a few inches on the floor here, but it made a mess."

"Uh-oh," Helen said, at the back of the house. "This doesn't look good, Sean."

Sean's heart sank when he joined her at the sliding door off the kitchen. Ted's boat was laying on its side alongside the deck, with the point of the bow stuck into the garage wall.

"Okay. We'll worry about that later. Right now, we have to get Matt and Mom out of here."

Sean turned to his brother.

"Matt, do you think you could stay at Bernadette's house for a few days?"

"Maybe. But I'll crash with you tonight. I need sleep."

"Lucky me."

They went outside after they had gathered some necessities. Sean and Helen carried suitcases of clothes. Matt had a backpack. Beverly clutched a box of papers and photographs. Memories of Ted.

Bruno came by in a flatbed tow truck. He stopped in front of the house with the big diesel motor idling. He leaned out of the cab.

"How are you making out, Beverly?"

"Good. We're leaving now."

"That's a good idea. Hop in."

"Thanks, Bruno. But the National Guard will give us a ride."

"No way," he said, climbing down and opening the passenger door for her. "We've got a first-class ride, right here."

Beverly climbed in up front, with a hand from Bruno. The truck had a crew cab with a back seat for Sean, Helen, and Matt.

"We'll try to keep an eye on the place," Bruno said as he drove through standing water. "Nobody in this neighborhood is going to touch any of your stuff. The cops will keep everybody else out for a few days. Until we can get boarded up."

"Thanks, Bruno," Beverly said, "Mostly, I'm worried about my cat."

"The dark one? I'll keep an eye out for him, Beverly. He'll turn up."

———

The car was mostly quiet on the drive to Queens. Helen was nominated to drive since she had slept through the brunt of the storm while Beverly and Matt dozed and watched the scenery from the back seat. Sean slept most of the way and only woke up when they pulled into the parking area at their apartment building.

That was when he saw the unmarked unit parked across the street.

Sean turned around and spoke to his older brother as Helen parked the car.

"Matt, you're not going to bring anything into my apartment that you shouldn't, are you?"

"What do you mean?"

"I mean that I don't want anything illegal in my home. So if you have something in your bag, don't bring it in. Toss it on the ground now."

"Don't worry about it."

Beverly looked at both of them.

"Sean, what's going on?"

"Probably nothing, Mom."

"Yeah," Matt mumbled. "Nothing."

The elevator was working once again, so they rode up together. Beverly clutched the box filled with her memories of Ted. Sean and Helen carried her bags into the spare bedroom, while Matt dropped a bulky backpack with his things near the couch in the living room.

Sean went to his own bedroom and took off his sweatshirt. He placed his Glock on the shelf in their bedroom closet.

With electricity and hot water restored, Helen started cleaning a backlog of dirty dishes, which had been accumulating in the sink, while Sean opened the refrigerator.

"That stuff is probably all spoiled," Helen said. "I'll empty it later."

"Okay. What else have we got to eat?"

Beverly opened a cabinet. "Here's some peanut butter. I'll make you a sandwich."

"I'll get that," Helen said, turning away from the sink.

"Go ahead and finish the dishes, Helen. I can get it."

"No. I'll get Sean's sandwich."

"Okay," Beverly backed away. "Whatever."

Tired as he was, Sean would have been happy to make his own sandwich. But he sat down at the table and waited for someone to bring him food.

"Do I have a clean uniform?" he asked Helen, when she set a peanut butter and jelly sandwich in front of him.

"You can't be serious. You worked for two days straight. You can't work tonight."

"I wasn't planning on going in tonight. But I've got to be ready in case they call me."

"They've got to give you some time off. Tomorrow night, too."

"I've got to muster for the first watch tomorrow night."

"I'll do a wash," Beverly offered.

"No," Helen said. "I've got it."

That was when there was an ardent knock at the front door.

"Who could that be?" Helen said, moving to answer the knocking.

"Let me get it," Sean insisted.

He stood up and walked to the door.

"Everybody just take it easy," Sean said to the room after he looked through the peephole. "This shouldn't take too long."

He opened the door to Frick and Frack. Detectives Dick Francis and Frank Capella, Internal Affairs. Along with the two plainclothes officers who had been parked across the street, and four uniformed officers.

"Well, isn't this nice," Sean said.

"Search warrant," Frack said, handing the paper to Sean and coming into the apartment.

"Come on in," Sean said after the officers were inside. "What's the object?"

"A .38 revolver."

"I told you, we haven't found my father's .38 snubby."

"We're looking for any .38," Frick offered. "Maybe Ted's. Maybe another one."

"This is outrageous," Beverly said, reaching for the telephone. "I'm calling Deputy Chief Sy Levinson."

"Go ahead," Frack shrugged. "Deputy Chief Levinson signed off on this warrant four days ago."

"My piece is on the top shelf in the bedroom closet," Sean said. Then he sat back down and calmly picked up the half of his sandwich, which already had a bite out of it.

"Just relax, Mom. They'll go away when they don't find anything."

"Hey!" Helen objected when the detectives went into her bedroom and began rifling through drawers. "Really?"

"They've seen it all before," Sean shrugged. "Relax."

"Sean," one of the uniforms said. "We're just on the job. You know."

"No hard feelings."

"This is one hell of a way to treat survivors of the shield," Beverly said to Frick as he entered the spare bedroom. Her suitcases were still packed when he opened them.

"Sorry, Beverly. Just following orders."

"That box is off limits," she said as Frack looked through the cardboard box, which she had carried out of her house.

"Sorry," Detective Frank Capella said as he started to look through the box, over Beverly's objection.

Sean was looking directly at Bad Cop Frack through the door to the spare bedroom. When the detective saw that the box contained the documents and pictures of Beverly's life with Ted Lamont, his features became ashen. He backed off with a pained look. *Sorry.*

"Jeez, Beverly … I …"

"My house is on the West Lido Promenade in Lindenhurst," Beverly glumly offered. "You won't need a key to search there, too. Just push the tree out of the way and climb in the living room window."

"Sorry, Beverly. This investigation is making us all crazy. We have to look under every rock, again and again. We thought that since you were all together here, we could get this over with one stroke."

"It's okay," Sean said. "Do your thing."

"Right," Good Cop Frick said as he moved towards Matt, who was sitting on the couch in the living room. "How about this backpack, Matthew?"

"Suit yourself," Matt shrugged.

The detective emptied Matt's backpack. He found nothing.

"Get up," Frick said to Matt.

"What?"

"You heard me. Stand up."

"Why?"

"Get up, Matt," Sean said.

When Matt was standing, the detective pulled the cushions off the couch. He came up with a baggie of green leafy substance.

"That's not mine," Matt said as if by habit.

"Sure," Frick said as he tossed the baggie on the table in front of Sean. "We'll let your brother dispose of that."

"Thanks, Detective," Sean nodded.

"Are we done here?" Frick asked Frack.

"Yup. Sorry for the intrusion, Beverly. Just doing our jobs. You understand, don't you?"

"It is what it is, Detectives," she said.

The uniforms turned to Sean on the way out, "Are we okay, Sean?"

"You bet. No problem. I'll do the same for you sometime."

As soon as the door was closed, everyone in the apartment breathed a collective sigh of relief. Matt made a move to take the bag of marijuana from the table.

"Forget that," Sean said. "I told you never to bring that crap into my house."

"Jeez, little brother. You're not really going to take my stuff. Are you?"

"You bet I am."

Sean took the baggie to the bathroom. He had to flush three times to get every last bud down the drain.

"Good night, everybody," he said, just before he collapsed on the bed.

Matt sat on the couch and sulked while Helen and Beverly cleaned up in the kitchen.

"I've never felt more violated," Helen said, rinsing the plate from Sean's sandwich. "Our house got robbed once, when I was a kid. This was worse than that."

"It's over, Helen. Let it go."

"They didn't have to go through my personal things … some very personal things. That was awful."

"It is what it is, Helen. We're all exhausted. Go to bed. I'll finish up here."

"You have to be more exhausted than me, Beverly. It must have been awful in that house last night."

"Whatever," the older woman shrugged. "The important thing is, you should be with Sean now. Lying next to him when he reaches for you. I've got the dishes."

WALLS TALKING

Sean Lamont slept straight through to Wednesday morning. The apartment was quiet and the sounds of a few cars and buses on Queens Boulevard greeted him when he stepped outside onto their balcony. The day was cool and calm. Life appeared to be returning to normal.

Whatever normal is, Sean thought.

He went to the kitchen and started cooking breakfast. Scrambled eggs, bacon and toast. A large pot of coffee. It felt good to have his family under his roof. But the warm feeling didn't last for long.

Sean turned away from the stove when he smelled tobacco. Matt was sitting up on the couch. With a lit cigarette.

"Are you crazy? Put that thing out."

"I always have a smoke when I get up."

No kidding, Sean thought. *How could I forget my older brother sitting on the edge of his bed in our room, with a hangover and a cigarette? Trying to hide the scent of the smoldering nicotine, lest Dad comes into the room and smacks his head.*

"Not in my house," Sean insisted.

"I'll go out on the balcony."

"The hell you will. Helen is sleeping."

"Jeez, don't get all bent out of shape, Officer Lamont."

Matt snubbed it out with his fingers. A practiced move to save the rest. Some ashes didn't make it to the saucer he was using as an ashtray. They landed on his knee and he brushed them off.

Sean went back to the stove. Poured some batter for pancakes. Small circles, the way Helen liked them.

Matt didn't get up from the couch. He began sipping the cold coffee left in his cup from the night before. After he slurped the last drops, he held the cup and saucer up towards Sean.

"How about a warm-up here?"

"Get up and get it yourself, Matt."

Helen was up by then. She appeared at their bedroom door in a short robe.

"What's that smell? Is the place on fire?"

"Nope. Just Matt. He lit up a cigarette."

"Really, Matt. If you must smoke, go out on the balcony."

"Sean told me not to."

"Whatever," she said, and went into the bathroom and closed the door.

Then Beverly was up.

"I'm going to tell Rebecca to go to classes today," their mother said as she sat at the dining table. "She can help us this weekend."

"I'm not so sure about that, Mom," Sean said as he put a cup of coffee in front of Beverly. "Becca is really handy with tools. We could use her help."

"Hofstra University isn't free, you know. She can't afford to cut classes."

He put down two plates of food and sat with her.

"The family comes first," Sean said. "She's smart enough to make up one or two days."

"Maybe Becca should come," Matt yawned from the couch. "My back is acting up. I probably won't be able to lift much stuff."

Sean cocked his head and leaned sideways in his chair.

"Matt, why don't you and Bernadette go find an apartment today?"

Helen came out of the bathroom and sat across from Beverly with a cup of coffee, snuggling her robe tight for warmth.

"Nothing is going to be available," Helen said. "Not with all the people who lost their houses in the storm."

"See?" Matt agreed.

"You lost your house in the storm," Sean said, looking at his brother. "You can't sleep on my couch for the rest of your life."

"Sean is right," Beverly nodded. "You and Bernadette had better start looking, at least. My house isn't going to be livable for quite a while."

"With my back acting up, maybe I'll just hang out here today."

"I don't think so," Sean smiled.

"Your couch sucks, by the way."

"Call Bernadette," Beverly said. "Have her come pick you up."

"You never should have sold our house in Queens."

"It's not our house anymore, Matthew. There's a nice Pakistani family living there now."

"Let's get moving," Sean said. "Take your showers, or whatever. And dress warm. It's cold out there today, and there won't be any heat in the house."

"And Matt," Sean added. "No smoking in our place while we're gone."

"Okay, Dad."

———

Sean drove out onto Long Island wearing a New York Yankees sweatshirt over jeans. Helen sat next to him in their car, with Beverly in the backseat, also dressed for work. He took Queens Boulevard to the Van Wyck, and then got onto the Southern State Parkway.

There was slow traffic on the Montauk Highway as if the damage on the South Shore had become a tourist attraction. They turned into Venetian Shores at the winged lion statues, where the Suffolk County Police were keeping the rubbernecks out of the harder hit neighborhoods.

Sean didn't need to flash his badge. The same officer was standing alongside his cruiser, and he waved them through.

"You ought to be able to drive in there today," the officer said. "Just go around the deeper puddles."

"You bet," Sean said.

"Good luck."

The rattle of chainsaws and the rumble of pumps and generators grew louder as they neared the heavily damaged areas. Residents and aid workers shuffled around as if in a daze. Front yards were filling up with water-damaged furniture and appliances.

"Puddles?" Sean said as he turned around a street that was still underwater and blocked off with sawhorses. "These are more like ponds."

The curbs were lined with debris. Some of the trash had been blown around. Branches and shingles and mangled patio furniture. But the bigger piles had been dragged out of flooded homes. Carpets and mattresses and leather recliners.

Ted's Ford was in the driveway. Rebecca had arrived before them. But there was another car ahead of the Ford. An older Cadillac, with a North Carolina license plate.

"Is that Jake Morrow's car?" Beverly asked.

"Looks like it," Sean said as he pulled into the driveway behind both cars.

They found Becca and Jake behind the house, standing alongside Ted's boat. Which looked like a beached whale, high and dry. Laying half on its side and still stuck into the back of the garage.

"Look who was here to greet me when I arrived," Becca said.

"Beverly!" Jake limped towards Beverly with open arms. "You poor thing. Don't worry, we'll make this right."

"Jake," she hugged him. "This is a surprise."

"I came up yesterday to check on my daughter in Bellmore."

"How did she make out?"

"Oh, she's fine. Her house is miles from the water. No real damage at all. Nothing like this."

"Let's go in and take a look," Sean said. "Be careful on these stairs. The deck really took a beating."

"Did I forget to lock the back door?" Beverly asked as they went in.

"Does it matter?" Helen offered. "There's a tree where the picture window used to be, and a boat is stuck in the side of the garage."

They walked through the kitchen and living room and found the floors still wet.

"Let's not go upstairs," Beverly said. "The bedrooms are relatively unscathed. I don't want to track this mess up there."

"You can't say that for the garage," Sean said, going down the steps to the concrete floor. "This place is a mess."

Water spilled out of her car when Sean opened the passenger side door.

"This is a total loss, Mom."

"We should see if it starts, anyway."

"Yeah. We'll push it out into the driveway later. After we get this refrigerator out of the way."

Rebecca looked into the utility room at the back of the garage.

"I'm afraid that your furnace and hot water heater are also trashed, Mom."

The sturdy prow of Ted's boat had come through the outside wall and into the small utility room.

"I hope the homeowner's insurance will cover that," Beverly rued.

"If you don't mind a dumb question," Jake asked, "do you have flood insurance?"

"I'm actually not sure about that," she frowned. "Ted took care of all that. I hope."

"You may not have power for a few days anyway," Sean said. "We'll figure something out."

When they went back up the steps into the kitchen, the cat nonchalantly sauntered up and rubbed against Beverly's shin.

"Smoky! Where have you been?"

When she tried to pick up the feline, he jumped away and hid under the kitchen table.

"I guess Smoky is a little spooked by all this," Becca offered.

"He must be hungry, too," Beverly said as she opened a can of cat food and put it on a dish. Smoky approached her offering warily.

"Okay," Sean rubbed his hands together. "Now that we're all accounted for, let's start cleaning up this mess. We're going to have to empty everything out of the refrigerators and the freezer. It's all going to spoil before power is restored."

"I'm on it," Helen volunteered.

"The trash cans are in the garage," Beverly said. "I'll help you with the food."

"Good," Sean continued. "We're going to have to do something with this tree. Then we can toss the living room carpet out through where the window used to be. We'll board it up after that."

"I'll get Dad's bow saw," Becca said. "There are two sheets of exterior plywood above the rafters in the garage, too."

"I'll say this for the old man," Sean smiled. "He was always ready for trouble."

"He *loved* trouble," Becca laughed.

Jake watched and offered bits of encouragement while Sean and Rebecca attacked the downed tree limb with a deep-toothed bow saw. They quickly parsed it into manageable sections and tossed the limbs to the curb for removal.

Sean knocked the remaining shards of glass out of the picture window with a hammer. Then he and Rebecca and Jake Morrow began pulling up the carpet. They rolled the sections up and tossed them out the window opening into the front yard.

The mat under the carpet was more problematic. It was already disintegrating into soggy clumps. Carrying all of it to the curb proved to be the bigger job. Beverly and Helen had finished emptying the refrigerator by then, and they helped to carry the mess outside.

"You shouldn't be doing that," a neighbor kibitzed as he walked by.

"Oh?" Sean questioned as he dropped a soggy heap of matting near the sidewalk.

"No. You should just leave everything, or the insurance won't pay. They have to get a contractor to do all the work."

"Yeah. We can't wait for that."

"Then you're on your own for damages," the man scoffed as he walked on. "You'll see."

"Could he be right?" Rebecca asked as she deposited her own armful of soggy mat.

"Who cares?" Sean shrugged. "You'll hear a lot of rumors and bad information after a deal like this."

Jake hobbled out with some wet carpet matting and shook his head.

"Some people love to talk through their asses," he said.

They were about to turn back to the house when a big flatbed wrecker huffed to a halt in front of them.

Bruno leaned out the window of the cab.

"Is Beverly in there?"

"She's cleaning up."

"Good. How are you guys making out?"

"The roof is intact," Sean waved back at the house. "And we might get the place sealed up today. After we figure out how to take care of the boat."

"Okay," Bruno shifted the truck into gear and reached for his cell phone. He was already pulling away when he said, "Maybe we can do something about that."

The wrecker powered through puddles towards the Montauk Highway.

"Let's get the picture window boarded up."

They took one sheet of CDX exterior plywood down from the garage. With the tree removed, Sean and Becca boarded up the window.

Beverly was carrying some more of the soggy carpet matting to the curb when another tow truck stopped in front of her house. The driver was the young man who had almost run over her cat.

"My father told me to come help you move your boat, Miss Beverly."

"Great," she said. "Let's take a look."

The others joined them on the side of the house.

"I brought the truck with the extending boom." Bruno's son surveyed the scene. "I could back in through here."

"Fine," Sean said. "Let's do it."

"It's a heavy truck," the driver said. "It's going to make a mess of this wet soil."

"No problem. The boat is the bigger problem."

The young man backed the truck alongside Beverly's house and extended the boom over Ted's boat. He got yellow straps out of the truck's box, and Sean and Becca put them under the boat's keel. Then he revved the engine and pulled the boat into the backyard.

Sean and Becca put big wood blocks under the boat, with advice from Jake. When they removed the straps, the Jersey Skiff was sitting upright again.

"Damn it," Sean said. "Look at those broken planks on the turn of the bilge."

"Probably a few frames underneath, too," Becca said.

"What does that mean?" Beverly asked.

"That might be a mortal wound," Becca rued. "That's a lot of damage to repair."

"We'll worry about the boat later," Beverly decided. Then she turned to the young tow-truck driver. "What do we owe you?"

"Nothing," he shrugged as he put the yellow straps back in the truck's box. "My dad wouldn't charge for helping a neighbor."

Beverly reached for his hand.

"What's your name?"

The young man wiped his hand with a rag before he took Beverly's.

"I'm Tony."

He flashed a disarming smile.

"Thank you, Tony."

They were all in the front yard watching the tow truck pull away when a black Land Rover stopped at the curb.

"Well, look who it is," Jake Morrow said.

Dex Birmingham and Sy Levinson got out of the Land Rover. They were carrying sandwiches, coffee, and donuts.

"Isn't this a nice surprise," Beverly said.

When they took the food offering inside, Sean and Helen and Becca suddenly realized how hungry they were. They stayed in the kitchen while Beverly and Jake walked through the damaged areas with Sy and Dex.

"How can we help?" Sy Levinson wanted to know after their look around.

"We've got it under control," Sean said. "We've got another sheet of plywood for the hole in the garage where the boat smashed through. Helen and Becca can help with that."

"Actually, I have to go deal with the insurance company and FEMA," Beverly apologized. "They're set up in tents on Montauk Highway. I should get some claims started today."

"Well, we hate to steal one of your helpers," Dex smiled. "But we're going to drag Jake away. We need to have lunch together and talk over a few things. Don't we, Jake?"

"Sure. Sounds like a plan."

With that decided, they all went out to the front of the house and said their good-byes. Beverly took Sean and Helen's car and the three old cops departed in Dex's Land Rover and Jake's old Cadillac.

"That wasn't very useful," Helen said as the cars drove away. "Stealing our help."

"Jake wasn't much help," Becca shrugged.

"Yeah," Sean stood in front of his mother's damaged house and watched the older generation leave with a jaundiced eye. He put his arm around Helen and turned to his kid sister.

"Becca, you've been around the NYPD all your life. So let me ask you something."

"Shoot."

"What is the commander of Manhattan South doing way out here in Suffolk County while his district is a disaster zone?"

———

Beverly found a place to park in a strip mall on Montauk Highway, amid businesses which were already boarded shut, and walked to the tent which FEMA had set up. She stood in line for about twenty minutes. Then she was handed a form to fill out.

When she finally sat down across from an agent, the woman began asking questions.

"Do you have flood insurance?"

"Yes. At least, I believe so."

"What is your policy number and effective date?"

"I'm not sure. Don't you have that on the computer?"

"No. You need to provide that information, to protect against false claims."

"Well, my husband took care of all that."

"Then he should come in and make the claim."

"He died six weeks ago," Beverly shrugged. "I'm still sorting through paperwork."

"Oh, I'm so sorry. Is this your primary residence?"

"Yes."

"Hmm," the agent gazed at her computer screen. "It is listed as a secondary home."

"We sold our house in Queens three weeks ago. This is home, now."

"Unfortunately, that's not what our records show."

"In that case, you should update your records."

"It's not that easy, Beverly. You'll have to fill out a form Twelve Dash Nine. In triplicate. With copies of the transfer of deed for your former residence. And proof that the house here is your primary residence."

"Is that all?"

"Yes. I can't issue a check to you right away. Since you may have flood insurance, we'll have to wait for them to pay for damages."

"So," Beverly shifted in her chair. "Let me get this straight. If I didn't have flood insurance, FEMA would provide assistance now. But since I bought flood insurance, I'll have to wait?"

"Correct."

"That's ridiculous. Why would anyone have flood insurance?"

"That's the way it works, Beverly. Go find the documents, and we'll get your claim started."

"Okay. I'll be back."

"Don't worry, Beverly. The system works. We'll take care of everything."

———◆———

Even with the big door opened, it was dank in the garage. And cold. Sean could see Helen and Rebecca's breaths turn to vapor as they stood in there facing the drywall, which enclosed the utility room.

"The wet drywall all has to go," Sean said.

"Yes," Rebecca agreed, holding a twenty-two-ounce framing hammer. "But it just seems wrong to tear down something Dad put up."

"It will just spread mold all over the house if we don't tear it out. You know how bad Mom's allergies are. The sooner we get it out of here, the better."

"Okay. I guess it has to go."

Rebecca took a mighty underhand swing with the hammer and pulverized a chunk of the Sheetrock.

"Let's get it done," she said as she hooked the hammer behind the drywall and pulled down another big chunk of Sheetrock.

Rebecca continued to swing the hammer while Sean and Helen carried the stuff to the curb. They soon fell into an agreeable rhythm, which would make short work of the task. The drywall came down, exposing the two by four studs underneath.

Their rhythm was broken when Rebecca froze and lowered the hammer to her side. She looked at her feet. Dumbfounded. Something most unexpected had fallen out of the wall when she pulled the Sheetrock away.

"Hey! What's *this*?"

Helen bent over and reached into the pile of damp debris at Becca's feet. She came up with a small green bundle.

"It's ... money," Helen stammered.

Sean dropped his handful of broken Sheetrock.

"What...?"

He came and stood with the women as they passed the bundle of cash from hand to hand. As if they had to touch it to believe that it was real.

"These are one-hundred-dollar bills," Helen stated the obvious.

The bills were bound by a brown-paper band bearing the seal of the Federal Reserve Bank. And labeled—in large red numerals— $10,000.

"Dad...?" Becca wondered aloud.

"Dad definitely Sheetrocked this wall," Sean said. "I'm sure of that."

"Wait," Becca said.

She reached up behind the remaining drywall and more bundles of cash fell to the floor at their feet.

Thunk ... thunk ... thunk. Thunk.

Four more bundles of C-notes fell onto the pile of broken Sheet-rock.

"Don't pick it up," Sean said, reaching his arms to hold the women back momentarily. "Let's think about this for a moment."

"What does it mean?" Rebecca wondered.

"It means we're rich," Helen laughed.

"No," Sean said. "Hang on a minute."

He went to the front of the garage. Looked around and up and down the West Lido Promenade. Then he pulled the garage door down and closed it all the way.

Without lights, the garage was dimly lit by the light coming in through the small windows. It took a few seconds for their eyes to adjust.

"There's more," Becca said, reaching behind the drywall.

"Just wait," Sean said. "Let me think about this a minute."

He bit his lower lip. His stomach was doing flip-flops. He couldn't wrap his mind around the cash. He'd seen big piles of cash before. In bank vaults and in the evidence room at Old Slip. Those were just paper. Meaningless.

This money was different. Mysterious. Powerful. Ominous.

It was hard to think about anything else when that amount of cash was lying at his feet. But Sean reached into the pile of cash and came up with a small green notebook. It contained cryptic entries in his father's handwriting. Numbers and a date on each line, followed by a tally of cash.

"Helen, let's start taking this into the house."

"And then what?"

"Just pile it on the kitchen table for now."

"Okay."

Rebecca continued to pull wads of cash out of the wall. Sean and Helen took it up the steps into the kitchen in handfuls.

They soon had a pile of bills the size of a breadbox stacked on the kitchen table.

"I think that's all there is," Rebecca said when she came inside. "I figured out that you could get to it by unscrewing the fuse box in the utility room. Dad … or somebody … installed the wires in a way that allowed the fuse box to swing out of the way."

"Let's count it," Helen said.

They all counted and restacked the bills.

"Eighty-four bundles of Benjamins," Sean muttered.

"That's eight thousand and four hundred C-notes," Helen said. "Eight hundred and forty thousand dollars."

"And this notebook," Sean muttered. "Whatever it means."

When someone knocked at the front door, Sean raised a hand to signal the women to sit tight.

He instinctively drew his Glock and held it hidden at his side when he cracked the door with his left hand. Ready to block with his shoulder.

The man standing outside had a clipboard and an ID card on a lanyard around his neck.

"Hi, I'm Jay Newton from the insurance company. May I come in?"

"No, the homeowner isn't here. You'll have to come back later."

"But … the sooner I survey the damage, the sooner we can get a claim started."

"Yeah. But the homeowner isn't here. Come back later."

"Well … in the meantime, I'll just look around the outside."

Not while there's a pile of cash just inside the glass slider to the deck, Sean thought.

"I don't think so, buddy. Come back later."

When Sean closed the door, he turned to see Helen and Becca stuffing the bundles of cash into the oven. They closed the oven door and sat at the kitchen table when he approached.

Helen asked the question.

"Sean, what is this all about?"

"Give me a minute to think."

Even though there was nothing to think about. The truth was stuffed into his mother's oven.

"Sean," Becca offered, "you can put your gun back in the holster now."

———

When Beverly arrived home, she found them sitting quietly around the dining table. The last of the coffee, which Dex and Sy had brought, was in front of them.

Sean spoke.

"Sit down, Mom."

Their expressions were as cold as the damp interior of her once-vibrant house. Beverly sensed a serious mood before she sat down.

Had another bad thing happened? For some reason, her first fleeting thought was of Sy Levinson. Who knew why?

"Mom, we found something hidden in the wall in the garage."

"Oh?" she relaxed. "Did your father hide a rifle there? He always threatened to do that, you know. Build an untraceable gun and ammunition into the wall, just in case the country descended into chaos."

"No, Mom. Not a gun," Sean said. "Show her, Becca."

Rebecca stood up and went to the oven. Opened the door and stood aside.

In the dim light across the room and inside the oven, Beverly could only discern a shape on a cooking rack.

"What is that?"

"It's money, Mom."

Becca took four bundles of one-hundred-dollar bills and put them on the table in front of her. "Forty thousand dollars." Then she went back to the oven and got more. The bundles of cash kept coming until all the money was stacked on the kitchen table.

Becca sat with them when she was finished.

"You found this?" Beverly asked. "In the house?"

"In the garage," Sean said. "We were all there, but Becca actually found it."

Beverly bit her lower lip.

"Touch it, Mom. It's real."

"Maybe later," Beverly kept her hands down. "Have you counted it?"

"Eight hundred and forty thousand dollars," Helen said.

"You look surprised," Sean said.

"I had no idea."

"He never said a word? Never hinted?"

"Ted was nothing if not direct. He never hinted, Sean. But he always did keep his silence about some things."

"Yup," Sean nodded.

Beverly turned to Becca.

"Show me where you found this."

Becca took her to the garage.

"It was here. Apparently, he could get to it through an unused circuit breaker panel."

Becca lifted a false two-by-four brace between the bare studs to demonstrate how the hiding spot was reached when the Sheetrock was in place. Then they went back into the house.

"Are you okay, Mom?"

"Why wouldn't he tell me about this?"

"Maybe this wasn't his," Becca offered. "Maybe he was holding it for somebody."

Beverly looked into the distance.

"The Pad?"

"No," Sean knew. "Dad wasn't on the Pad. He wouldn't take a

bribe. Anyway, this didn't come in piecemeal, like payoffs. This was one amount."

"Maybe it fell off an armored car," Helen guessed.

"Not our Dad," Becca said.

"Who cares where it came from?" Helen said. "You know what they say, possession is nine-tenths of the law."

"No," Sean said. "We can't touch any of this until we know more."

He held up the notebook that had been in the wall with the money.

"This notebook will explain it, I'm sure. We just have to figure it out."

"We know everything we need to know about this money," Becca said. "It's here. What else matters? Look around at this house. It's a godsend for Mom."

Helen had an idea.

"Maybe a disaster like this was exactly what Dad was saving for?"

"No. We can't touch this money until we figure out where it came from."

"How can we ever know that?" Helen wondered.

"I don't know … yet," Sean answered. "In the meantime, don't anybody say a word. It has to remain among just us. Don't whisper any of this to your friends."

"Except Matt," Becca said. "He has to know."

"Matt is the last one who should know."

"We can't exclude our brother just because he wasn't here when we found it. This is his money too."

"It's not our money, Becca. So we can't tell Matt. He can't even hang onto his tips from waiting tables."

"Sean is right," Beverly glumly said. "I love him, but Matt has no sense for money. Or secrets. When he knows, the world will know."

"So … what do we do with this?" Helen asked.

"Put it in the trunk of your car for now," Becca offered.

"A safe deposit box would be better," Helen said.

"No," Sean said. "We can't remove it from the property."

"Why not?"

"We could be receiving stolen property."

"That's too awful to think about," Becca moaned.

"Let's at least make it hard to find," Sean decided. "Come upstairs with me, Becca."

There was an access to the attic in the closet of the master bedroom. They moved some of Beverly's clothes. Then Sean lifted his sister—she still felt as light as she did when they used to play together—and she pulled herself up.

"Pull up a roll of insulation at the far end up there," he told her. "Lay the bills flat between the rafters. Then cover them with the insulation."

"This stuff makes me itch. I hate touching it."

"So does everybody else."

Sean, Beverly, and Helen carried the bundles of bills upstairs and handed them to Becca.

"We can never speak about this," Sean uttered. "To anyone."

"Of course," Beverly nodded. "Sean knows best."

———————

It was just the two of them in the car on the way home. Sean drove with his jaw set. The way he held it when he was in no mood to talk.

"Sean, please talk to me."

"Give me a minute."

Until he merged onto the Long Island Expressway, those were the only words spoken.

Helen couldn't stand the silence any longer.

"Sean, we've got to talk."

"I'm thinking."

"Think out loud."

He kept his eyes ahead. Did not look at her.

"I hate it when you shut me out like this, Sean."

He was driving in the middle lane, not particularly fast, when she noticed tears running down his cheeks.

"Sean, you're crying."

He held his silence and the set of his jaw. Until the tears became so thick that he had to wipe his eyes with his hand. Then he pulled the car over and stopped in the sandy grass beyond the breakdown lane so he could wipe his eyes with both hands.

She reached for his shoulder, but he didn't seem to feel her touch.

Sean laid his forearms and brow on the steering wheel. Soon he was sobbing. Heaving. Choking. Muttering unintelligibly.

She had waited so long for Sean's sorrow to surface that she was unprepared for the emotion when it came. She couldn't make out the words. They were not particularly meant for her.

Helen held Sean by his shoulders. Then he was saying the words out loud. Beating his head on the steering wheel.

"Dad was a bad cop."

"Sean, it's okay."

"My dad was a bad cop."

Helen was afraid her words were having the wrong effect. He seemed out of control. She was only vaguely aware of the white highway patrol car when it pulled up behind their car. A dozen blue and red strobe lights flashing frantically. A loudspeaker shouted some commands. She couldn't make any sense of those words, either.

After what seemed like several minutes, the officer approached the passenger side of the car. Helen reached in Sean's pocket and found the leather carrier with his shield and ID.

"Hands on the dashboard!" the officer commanded.

Helen ignored him and held Sean's silver badge in the window.

"My husband is a member of the service. His father was a plain-clothes officer shot in the line of duty in Brooklyn last month."

The highway patrol seemed confused.

"You still have to follow my commands. Hands on the dash-board."

"We're having a situation here. Can't you see?"

The officer spoke past her.

"Sir, are there any weapons in the car?"

"He carries his piece in a holster," Helen answered for her husband. "On the right side."

"Any other weapons in the car?"

"Of course not," she said.

"Sir, are you okay?"

Sean raised his head from the steering wheel and nodded. When Helen saw his face, she was shocked. His features looked washed-out. Blanched. Exhausted.

The officer spoke to Helen.

"Do you have a driver's license?"

"Yes."

"Let's see it. With the registration and proof of insurance."

Helen handed the officer the documents.

"This is your address? In Queens?"

"Yes."

"Stay in the car."

The highway patrol officer went back to his cruiser. He sat in it for several long minutes before coming back to Helen's window.

"Can you drive, Helen?"

"Yes."

"Are you sure you don't need a rescue?"

"We'll be okay as soon as we get home."

"Okay. Come around to the driver's side. Then follow me."

Helen went around the car and pushed Sean to the passenger seat. The county highway patrol officer pulled slowly into traffic and Helen followed. In a few seconds, they accelerated into the high-speed lane. Cars ahead merged to the right.

"What are you doing?" Sean asked her. Regaining his bearings.

"Getting you home."

"Okay."

Then Sean sat quietly. His head fell on her shoulder. They went ninety miles an hour, all the way to the city. At the Queens County line, the county highway patrol officer pulled right and waved Helen past.

When their escort left them, she slowed down, but only a little. With Sean's shield on the dashboard, she didn't really care if they were stopped in the city.

He leaned on her in the elevator up to the third floor. Matt was on the couch in their apartment. The older brother was watching afternoon TV in his underwear.

She spoke as soon as the door was open.

"Take a walk, Matt."

"You're kicking me out?"

"Give us a few hours."

Sean went into the bathroom on his own. He turned on the water and splashed his face in the sink.

"What happened to him?" Matt asked.

"What do you think happened? Give us a little space."

"He's my brother, you know."

"He can be your brother later, Matt. Right now, he's my husband. Go."

"Where should I go?"

"I don't care. Go down to the corner and have a few beers."

"I don't have any money."

She tossed him a twenty.

"Give us a few hours, Matt."

Sean came out of the bathroom after Matt left the apartment. They sat down at the kitchen table. She poured him a cup of coffee.

"Feeling better?"

"Yeah. I'm okay."

"You scared the crap out of me, Sean. Don't hold things in like that ever again. It isn't healthy."

He shrugged and took a sip of black coffee.

"Sean, are you ready to talk to me now?"

"What does it matter, now?"

"Now, what?"

"Now that everything has changed, kitten."

"How have things changed? The money?"

"Yeah. Dad was a bad cop. That's what's changed."

"Sean, the detectives have questioned all of us. They've searched our home. They went through my underwear drawer and saw our sex toys, for Christ's sake. Then this money in the wall. What is going on?"

"It was all a lie, that's what's going on. A big, fat lie."

Helen sipped her own coffee and looked at the table in front of them. She waited for Sean to speak.

"I knew it, kitten," he eventually whispered. "I knew it the night Dad was shot. And at the funeral. Something was very wrong. Sy Levinson and Dex Birmingham and Jake Morrow, the old Stakeout Squad, they were all wrong."

"What is a stakeout squad, anyway?"

"There aren't any squads like that anymore. We can't do the job that way now. The media would crucify us."

"Sean, I don't understand."

"They used to bait bad guys, Helen. Our guys would set up an ambush in a convenience store or package shop. A place that was likely to get robbed. Anyone who came in with a gun ... well, they forfeited their right to life. Plain and simple."

"The cops would fire warning shots, wouldn't they? Shoot the robbers in the leg or something."

A look of disgust crossed his features. Then a flash of anger. But it quickly passed. He almost chuckled.

"Jake Morrow was famous for saying, 'Halt, Police!' to the perps. After they were lying on the floor, dead or dying."

"That's awful, Sean. I don't like it when you talk like that. Not about people who I know."

"You asked, kitten. The only rule for the Stakeout Squad was, 'We all go home at the end of our watch.'"

"I don't like that, Sean."

"It had to be that way. In the bad old days, crime was out of control. The murder rate was insane. The city was broke, and the police service was demoralized. That was when the NYPD became the toughest gang in the city."

"Are you talking about the seventies?"

"For sure. The end of the bad old days. The days when guys like Sy Levinson and Jake Morrow and Dex Birmingham did what they had to do, to get the city under control."

"And Ted Lamont."

"Yeah. The uptown yuppies called it *social unrest*. Until they got mugged in front of their apartments. Then it was *crime*. Then they didn't care what the cops did as long as they could walk the streets without fear."

"I knew that Ted was a tough cop," Helen said slowly. Carefully. "But I always thought those stories of the bad old days were just stories. He was always so calm. So gentle. I always felt safe around your father, Sean. Like nothing bad could ever happen around him."

"Yeah. Well ... I don't know."

Helen got up. Poured Sean another cup of coffee and sat down.

"Sean, let's get out of the city."

"Maybe."

"I don't want you to be that way. I can't stand it."

"I guess there's nothing for me in the city, now. I suppose we could move away. I could find another job."

"That would be wonderful, Sean. If you must be a cop, do it someplace safe."

"Yeah. Thing is, there is no safe place to be a cop, kitten. Bad things can happen anywhere. Patrolling highways and back roads ... without backup ... is the most dangerous police work there is. In the city, I can get on my little portable radio and have a whole platoon of backup there in ninety seconds.

"That doesn't make me feel any better, Sean."

"Listen, do you really want to know what the NYPD is all about? Do you want to know why I love being a cop in the city? Why it is so hard to quit?"

She nodded yes.

"Here it is, Helen. We can be your best friend or your worst nightmare. Just don't mess with us. We're the toughest gang in the city because we all trust each other. That's what being a cop in New York is all about."

FLOATER

Sean got up after Helen left their bed on Thursday morning, feeling fine. He couldn't remember taking his clothes off and getting under the covers. Or when he had slept so soundly, for so long. When he stepped out on the balcony, the morning was cold and damp, under low, gray clouds.

Helen was in the kitchen, dressed for work. Sweater, skirt, and boots.

"Good morning, sleeping beauty," Helen said as he kissed her cheek.

He liked the way her legs looked under the skirt, in tights.

Beverly was sipping a cup of coffee at the kitchen table. Sean bent over and kissed her forehead.

"More like a bear coming out of hibernation," Beverly said.

Matt was sitting up on the couch, head bowed and half awake. Holding an unlit cigarette.

"So," Sean said as he sat next to his mother. "What's the plan for today?"

"I'm going to the house. We have to settle with FEMA and the insurance company, so we can start having some work done."

"Do you want me to come along?"

"No. You'd better stay here and rest. You're working the first watch tonight, aren't you?"

"Yeah. But first, I have to go down to Old Slip to clean out my locker. They're closing the First Precinct."

"Oh? For how long?"

"Maybe forever, Mom. It took a lot of damage from the storm."

"That's a shame. You'd better go take care of business there. Matt will help me." She turned to her eldest, "If he ever gets up and gets dressed."

Matt lifted his head.

"In a minute, Mom."

"Why don't you pick up Becca?" Sean asked her. "You'll be going right past Hofstra."

"Rebecca has missed too many classes already. I'll take Matt."

"Matt, why don't you hold down the fort here?" Sean offered. "I'll help Mom today."

"What?" Matt was almost awake by then. "Why don't you want me to go with Mom?"

"I thought that your back was acting up."

"It's better."

Sure it is, Sean thought. *When the work is done.*

Matt got up off the couch and went into the bathroom.

"Sean," Beverly spoke. "Are you going to see Sy Levinson today?"

"Probably not."

"He'd be the one to talk to. About what we found. Don't you think?"

"Shush, Mom," Sean whispered. "Don't even mention that. Matt can't know."

"I know how to keep a secret, Sean. What are you going to do?"

"I have a few ideas. Talking to Sy Levinson isn't one of them."

"Dex Birmingham?"

"No. Not yet. Or Jake, either."

Helen put a plate of eggs and toast in front of Sean.

"I don't know about Jake Morrow," Helen said. "He sort of gives me the creeps. The way he keeps showing up at the new house."

"He was one of Ted's oldest friends," Sean shrugged. "The Medal of Valor, and the Combat Cross. That means a lot, you know."

"I know. But if Matt finds out, he'll go straight to Jake. Then the whole world will know. Those two are like peas in a pod."

"Yeah," Sean muttered. "They are."

Beverly poured another drop of half-and-half and watched the cloud blend with the coffee in her cup.

———

Sean drove. He gave Helen a ride to work at PS 133 on 86th Avenue. Then he went into Manhattan, where the streets were clogged with utility workers and cleanup crews.

There was a giant diesel generator humming in front of Old Slip. Cables were strung into one of the windows. He went up the steps with his bag.

Captain Sweeney was taking down the picture of Ted Lamont.

"Didn't expect to see you this early, Sean."

"I just needed to clean out my locker. Are you going to put those pictures up in our new precinct? Wherever it is."

"I don't know, Sean. Everything is happening a little too fast. We don't know how they are going to reorganize the precincts. But this house is done for."

The muster room was full of activity. Temporary lights were strung along the ceiling and workmen were removing furniture. Sean went to the locker room and put his uniforms and personal items into his bag. Then he went past the holding area and the interrogation rooms, and up the stairs.

On the second floor, workmen were removing the heavy filing cabinets from the gallery of the old pistol firing range. The doors were all open, so he could see all the interconnected offices in the narrow space. Rhoda Abernathy was cleaning out her desk.

"How are you doing, Rhoda?"

"Hey, Sean. Congratulations."

"What for?"

"Didn't they tell you? We're getting a commendation. You and me, and Erik. For pulling your friend out of the Hole."

"Yeah. I didn't do anything. But I'm happy for you, Rhoda. That will help you get your gold shield."

"Right. The Community Relations desk isn't exactly the fast-track to detective."

He touched the old desk blotters. They were still stacked halfway to the ceiling in her area.

"What are they doing with these?"

"Heck if I know," Rhoda shrugged. "They'll probably take them to some warehouse and forget about them."

"That's too bad." He opened a random book and leafed through it. "There's a lot of history here."

"I know. I looked through a few of them. But it was all routine stuff."

"Yeah. But there must be a few gems in here. You don't mind if I hang around for a few minutes and look through these, do you?"

"Knock yourself out."

Sean leafed through some of the old logbooks. The entries were in cursive writing. Many were made by *Sergeant* Sweeney. Some of the names were familiar, like an entry from 1975:

1915 hours. G. Smith, 42 y/o white male, simple domestic assault and disturbing the peace. Arrest by T. Lamont, foot post #7. Remanded to custody.

Sean put that book aside. He kept sifting through the stacks of books until he found what he was looking for.

This is it, Sean thought when he opened the book from October 1977. *This is the month of the first entry in the notebook that we found in the wall with the money.*

When he turned the pages of handwritten entries, he knew that he wouldn't find much useful information standing next to Rhoda's desk. He'd have to make a much closer inspection.

Rhoda saw Sean slip the desk blotter from that long-ago month of October into his bag.

"Just a souvenir, Rhoda. I'll put it back after I'm done looking at it."

"I didn't see a thing, Sean."

Sean walked out of Old Slip with the blotter in his bag. Trying not to feel guilty he was stealing city property.

He put his bag into the trunk of the car, got onto FDR Drive and headed towards the Queensboro Bridge. Drizzling rain falling from an overcast sky.

———◆———

Beverly let Matt drive out to Lindenhurst. The drizzle turned to the first sleet and freezing rain of the season when they were on Sunrise Highway. Traffic slowed to a stop around the inevitable fender benders. Beverly turned up the heater and defroster in Ted's Ford, while Matt kept his eyes on the road.

The county police were still keeping sightseers out of Venetian Shores. But the TV broadcast trucks—much to everyone's relief— had moved on to another story.

They checked on the house first. It was even colder inside than out. She opened the closet in her bedroom and looked at the access hatch to the attic. It appeared to be undisturbed. But a chill still ran up her spine when she thought about what was hidden up there, and what it meant about her life with Ted.

"Better bring a warm coat," she said to Matt when she went back downstairs. "And a hat. We might be standing outside in line today."

The mood was very different in the FEMA tent on day four after the storm. Somber. Some temporary heaters had been set up under the big top. They weren't doing much against the chill.

Reality is sinking in, Beverly thought as she and Matt stood in line. *All these people realize that rebuilding isn't going to be that easy. And certainly not that fast.*

After a forty-minute wait, she was sitting across the folding table from the same woman she had spoken with the day before.

"Name and address?" the woman asked in a weary voice.

"Beverly Lamont. West Lido Promenade."

"Is Lamont your given name?"

"No. Of course not. First name Beverly. Last name Lamont."

"Okay. Lamont, Beverly."

The woman scowled at her computer screen and thumbed through stacks of papers.

"I don't have a listing for Lamont, Beverly."

"How about Ted?"

"Could it be Lamont, Ted and Beverly?"

"It could be. Except that Ted is deceased."

"Not according to our records."

"Well, please update your records."

"That has to come through the regional office," the agent shrugged. "But anyway, the Gold Team has taken over your file."

Beverly looked around the tent.

"Where is this Gold Team?"

"They're set up in the Senior Center."

"Great," Beverly said as she got up. "Thank you."

They drove over to the Senior Center and had to park half a mile away. After walking in the cold rain, they stood in another line. The tail end of the line was outside the door for the first ten minutes of their wait.

After an hour and a half, Beverly sat across from two FEMA agents. A trainee and a trainer, of sorts. It was apparent from the start that the two agents would be confusing each other.

"Okay, let's start a case file for that property."

"I already spoke with an agent," Beverly pointed out.

"Well, I can't do anything until you fill out this form to initiate a file. Press hard, you are making five copies."

"I already filled one of these out."

"I have no record of that."

"Okay," Beverly said, quickly penning the information on the form. "Here you go."

"This has to be signed by both property owners."

"How many times am I going to have to say that my husband is recently deceased?"

"Oh," the senior agent seemed pleased to have the problem solved. "Now I see what's going on here. Your claim wasn't signed by both property owners so we couldn't enter the data into the master list. Why didn't you say so?"

They called over a supervisor. A mid-level, mid-age bureaucrat in a wool vest.

"So you do have flood insurance?" he said. "Then you have to deal with them first."

"The flood insurance people are not answering their phones," Beverly offered. "And their website has crashed."

"Then we'll keep your application open. But we have to deal with the people who did not have flood insurance first. Come back next week."

"Really?" Beverly was flummoxed. "We paid for flood insurance and kept the policy current. So I have to wait for aid from FEMA? In the meantime, my house is a shambles."

"That's the way we do it," the woman nodded. "Next."

It was past lunchtime when Beverly and Matt left the FEMA lines. They had to drive north of Sunrise Highway to buy sandwiches at a trailer, which had been set up in a strip mall. There was no place to sit, so they took the sandwiches out to Ted's Ford.

Beverly couldn't remember when she had eaten a meal in the car before.

It's a new world, she thought as she drove home.

"Look, Mom," Matt said when they got back to the house. "Isn't that Jake's car?"

Sure enough, Jake Morrow's red Cadillac was in her driveway. He was nowhere in sight.

"Lucky me," Beverly mumbled.

They went into the house through the front door. Jake was in the garage. He came into the kitchen to greet them.

"Bev! How the hell are you?"

"How does it look like I'm doing, Jake."

"I brought you a coffee."

"Thanks."

Matt went upstairs to his room to gather some more clothing to take to Sean and Helen's apartment.

Jake tapped on the walls in Helen's kitchen, as if he was an engineer performing a building inspection.

"Golly, there's a lot of damage, Bev."

"At least the house is still standing."

"It's a shame you have to start over, though."

"I'm not starting over. Just picking myself up again."

His bad leg gave him a bit of trouble when he sat across the kitchen table from her.

"You know, Beverly. We're both too old to go through something like this alone."

"I have my family."

"But they can't keep you warm at night."

"Where are you going with this, Jake?"

"Oh, I was just thinking of the old days. You know, we had some good times, didn't we?"

"That was a long time ago, Jake."

Matt came downstairs. He went outside to put some clothes in Ted's Ford.

"At our ages, neither one of us should be sleeping alone," Jake said while Matt was outside. "That's all I'm saying, Beverly."

When Matt came back in the house, he helped his mother with the cleaning and straightening up. It wasn't easy without electricity or hot water.

Jake Morrow stayed at the kitchen table, watching and talking to both of them.

"That damn bullet nicked the bone," he muttered. "Gives me hell when it gets cold. That's why I can't live up here anymore."

Beverly wanted a cup of coffee. But the coffee that Jake had brought had cooled by then. Tepid, at best. In the cold and powerless house, there was no way to heat it up.

———

Sean brewed a pot of coffee and sat at the kitchen table in his apartment. The desk blotter from October 1977 at Old Slip was open on the table in front of him. He read from the beginning, paying particular attention to any mention of the Stakeout Squad.

An entry for October 2 caught his eye:

2134 hrs. Sgt. Levinson, Stakeout Squad. Shots fired. Reports 2 perpe-trators deceased at the scene. One perpetrator in custody, transported to Bellevue hospital.

He read on. The last inch of coffee in his cup had turned cold be-fore he finished it. He poured another. The cat was annoying him for attention.

Another entry, dated October 17:

2237 hrs. Sgt. Levinson, Stakeout Squad, Reports body of white male and multiple bales of suspicious substance recovered from the East River at Roebling Pier.

He read the blotter from cover to cover. Then he lay down on the sofa in the living room with the book open on his chest. Went back and reread several entries. Dozed off for a few minutes.

He put the book on the top shelf of the bedroom closet when it was time to pick up Helen at PS 133. Kids were streaming out of the school while he waited for her at the curb. They came out of the brick building and walked along the black iron fence and watched intently and giggled when she got into the car and kissed him.

"Good-bye, Miss Lamont."

Sean drove home.

"So, what did you do today?" Helen wanted to know.

"Not much. Read a book."

"Oh? Something I might like?"

"No," he shrugged. "It was all cop stuff. Pretty dry."

Helen smiled at him.

"Do you remember what you told me last night?"

"Yeah. We're out of the city. As soon as this mess is over. Where do you want to go?"

"My sister is in Cherry Hill."

"Okay," Sean smiled. "As far away from Cherry Hill as possible."

"Very funny."

Frick and Frack were sitting across the street from their apart-ment building when they arrived home. This time, even Helen sighted the unmarked unit.

"Damn it," she said, "are they going to hassle us again?"

"I don't think so. They're probably keeping an eye on Matt."

"Why Matt?"

"Because he has an arrest record," Sean shrugged. "For possessing pot. And for breaking and entering."

"I didn't know that."

"We don't talk about it very much."

"Anyway, I don't like those two men very much."

"They're just doing their jobs."

"Especially the one you call Frack."

"Frank is Bad Cop. It's just a role he plays. Just on the job."

"How about you, Sean?" Helen asked when they were in the elevator. "Do you play a role on the job?"

"I assume my cop demeanor."

"So it is an act?"

"Sort of. Actually … Ted used to call it the greatest show on Earth."

"You love it, don't you?"

Sean put the key in the deadbolt and opened the door to their apartment.

"Not as much as I used to."

———

Sean and Erik mustered in front of Captain Sweeney at the Fifth Precinct at midnight, clad in NYPD turtlenecks and patrol jackets. Then Erik drove their RMP to the Lower East Side. Their streets. Three days after the storm, most of the businesses remained closed.

When they cruised past Old Slip, the ancient precinct house was dark. Deserted. The workmen's generator, which had been out front, had been removed. The basement windows boarded up. The green lanterns at the front door extinguished, for the first time in memory.

Utilities were being restored, one block at a time. Some bars on Beekman Street had reopened their doors. They parked their patrol unit at the corner and waited.

They rolled up when a group of people spilled out onto the sidewalk. The crowd loosely circled two men grappling on the concrete. As Sean dismounted from the car, he saw a third man in a green jacket, still holding a bottle of beer, kick the unwilling combatant on the bottom of the fight. A solid foot to the head. Then the kicker faded to the back of the spectators.

Sean and Erik pulled the winner of the fight off the loser. He was slightly bigger and a lot stronger. They had him against the trunk of their car when other units began to arrive. Erik got his handcuffs on him.

With the aggressor subdued, Sean turned back to the crowd. They were leering. Drunk. Enjoying the show. Most of the men and women were around his age. The other units were getting the loser up. His face was bloody.

Sean saw the green jacket at the edge of the crowd. He dove into the group, nightstick in hand, and charged the kicker. He was a huge man. Slightly older than most of the bar patrons. Heavy boned. And he knew that the cops would be coming for him.

Sean was almost on him when the kicker sidestepped behind a young woman. The man towered above her. Sean pushed her out of the way with his nightstick. With two hands on the stick, he jabbed the kicker in the solar plexus with an upward swing.

The strike should have sent the kicker to the emergency room. Instead, he took an ursine swipe at Sean's head. He had a moment to block. The bottle of beer in the kicker's paw glanced off Sean's shoulder.

Then the giant had Sean by his collar. He tossed him against the wall like a rag doll. He was hauling back to deliver a knockout punch with the bottle of beer when Erik grabbed his arm from behind.

Even with Erik holding him, the big man managed to swing at Sean. But he hit the brick wall instead. Then four more cops piled on him. They grappled the kicker to the ground. He was still holding his beer bottle. He only let go of it when a cop stepped on his hand and pried it away. Then they rolled him onto his stomach.

Sean was still against the wall, recovering his senses, when he saw Erik pull the giant's left arm out of the pileup. He held it out.

"Cuff him, Sean!"

Sean dove in with his handcuffs and snapped them on the man's fat wrist. They barely fit. Then he held on tight with both hands— *There's half the battle!*—while the other cops pried out the kicker's right arm from under.

When Sean had his handcuffs on both of the kicker's wrists, some of the cops stayed on top of him. Two others picked up the officers' hats and Sean's nightstick before souvenir hunters grabbed them off the sidewalk. Then the cops dragged the man to his feet. Sean and Erik slammed his face down on the trunk of their patrol car, none too gently, to search his pockets.

That was when the cell phones came out for pictures.

"Move on," the other cops were saying to the crowd. They knew that the cell phone pictures wouldn't show the big man kicking the loser of the fight when he was down. Or Police Officer Sean Lamont nearly losing his head. The only pictures to be posted would be of two cops slamming a suspect on the trunk of an RMP.

———

A few hours later, the loser was still in the emergency room. The winner was waiting to be released from night court and the kicker, who had a half dozen prior arrests for assault, was on his way to Rikers Island.

Sean and Erik were back driving dark streets in their patrol car.

"I can't believe I dropped my stick," Sean bemoaned, rubbing his sore shoulder. "It's embarrassing."

"No big deal," Erik shrugged. "We got it back."

"Yeah. I guess."

"At least it wasn't your radio," Erik laughed. "I lost mine in a foot chase once, and some punk ran off with it. We had to listen to him taunting us with insults on our frequency until the battery finally ran down. Called us every name in the book. I caught hell from the guys for that."

They were on Dover Street, literally under the Brooklyn Bridge, when Sean had an idea.

"Erik, let's go down to the Roebling Pier."

"The tugboat place? What on Earth for?"

"I just want to check something out."

The water under the bridge was umbra and glassy. Strings of lights above the bridge reflecting in silver streaks. Nearby streetlamps and traffic signals showing as tangerine and red smears on the surface.

Erik stayed in the car when Sean walked a short distance onto the pier. A man was standing on the aft deck of a tugboat. He had a wire rope in a vise with the strands un-laid. A steel spike in one hand. A cigarette in the other.

"Uh-oh. What did I do now?"

"No problems," Sean stood above him on the pier. "Just wondering if anyone was working here back in 1977."

"I was."

"Do you remember when a body was pulled out of the river here?"

"We see lots of floaters," the man waved to the water under the pier. "The current brings them here. Then they get hung up in the pilings."

"This one came in with a few bales of drugs."

"Sure. I remember that. I was just a kid. Working as a deckhand. I guess it would have been the summer of '77."

"You were here when they found it?"

"Sure was. I saw it first. Looked under there at sunrise, and there it was. Doing the dead man's float. We thought it was a bridge jumper."

"Why a jumper?"

"It was on the surface. Sometimes the jumpers stay on top if they never inhale water. Most drownings roll over and sink to the bottom pretty quick. They come up three or four days later, when the gasses swell 'em up. By then the crabs and eels have done their thing. It ain't pretty."

"Yeah. Was anyone else here?"

"Captain Bob," the tug man shrugged. "But he has been dead for … good Lord! Ten years, at least."

"Okay. What did you see?"

"I saw the floater. And a bunch of bales wrapped in black plastic garbage bags. You know, all bundled in duct tape. Sealed tight."

"Then what?"

"There were some cops sitting in the parking lot over there. We just waved them over."

"What were cops doing over there?"

"We used to see them over there all the time. Early in the morning. They used to just park over there and talk for a while. Drinking a few beers at the end of their shift, I guess."

"What kind of cops?"

"The kind you don't mess with," the tug man laughed. "Hard cases, in plainclothes. Badges on chains around their necks and guns showing. I remember that the cop riding shotgun really did have a shotgun on the floor of this unmarked car."

"What else?"

"Not much. We called them over and helped them pull the dead guy out of the water. Then they got on their radios and called the Marine Unit. In the meantime, we all started grabbing the bales. They stacked them on the pier. Then they put them in a police van, and the meat wagon took the floater away."

"You picked up the bales?"

"Sure. I grabbed them with a boat hook and handed them up to the cops. No problem."

"How many bales?"

"Jeez, I can't remember that. Six? Eight? Heck if I know. But the Marine Unit found a lot more of them later. They were all over the piers around here. Maybe twenty or thirty? Square groupers. That's what we call bales of drugs. They were all over the place."

"Anything else? Anything unusual about the cops?"

"One thing. One of them was driving a taxi."

"Oh?"

"Yeah. There was a black cop driving this taxi cab. The other cops were in unmarked sedans. But the black guy was alone in a hack. A regular checker cab. I remember that. It seemed a little strange."

"Okay. Thanks, pal."

Sean turned to leave the pier. But the tug man had a question.

"Hey, Officer. What's so interesting about some floater from thirty years ago? I mean … working on the water … here in the city … we see stuff like that all the time. No big deal."

"Yeah," Sean shrugged. "It doesn't matter. Forget about it."

BROOKLYN BRIDGE

Sean Lamont stepped out of the Fifth Precinct in Chinatown at the end of his watch. The morning was cool and bright. A pale blue sky. He started walking towards the subway at Canal Street for the train ride to Queens. He didn't get far before an old, red Cadillac stopped on Elizabeth Street.

"When did you get back into town, Jake?"

"Last night. Hey, Sean, how about joining us for breakfast. Me and Dex and Sy."

"Where are those guys?"

"They're down at Percy's, waiting for us. Hop in."

Sean tossed his bag onto the back seat.

Percy's was north of the bridges, on a street of warehouses and wholesale businesses. A narrow barroom in an ancient brick building, facing a plumbing supply place. Dex Birmingham and Sy Levinson were there. A booth in the back.

The barkeep came back to the booth in a dirty apron. Sean ordered an omelet. He got scrambled. Dex Birmingham spoke first.

"Sean, the investigation is hung up on Ted's .38 snubby. Does Matt have it?"

"I don't know. I don't think so. But, why is the task force so hot on my brother?"

"He wasn't at work at the restaurant. As he said he was."

"You think my brother…?"

"No. But he shouldn't have lied. Now there's a big hole in his story."

"There's just no way," Sean muttered.

"Sean, relax," Jake Morrow laid a fleshy hand on his shoulder. "We know where Matt was. He just needs to tell the Task Force guys the truth. Then he'll be in the clear."

"What's the truth?"

"I checked into that myself," Jake said. "I know some people. He was at a dog fight. He didn't want to rat on his buddies who run the damn thing."

"Matt?"

"It's a true story," Jake said. "The fights were held in the auto body shop across the street from the restaurant where Matt occasionally worked. LePage's."

"My brother was watching dogs kill each other? You've got to be kidding."

"He was more involved than that," Dex said. "We've learned that Matt has been kidnapping dogs for the ring."

No. Sean's stomach sank. *He couldn't steal innocent pets for the slaughter. A horrible death in the ring. Not my brother.*

"Bullshit," Sean pushed his eggs away. "I don't believe that."

Sure, Matt is lazy, Sean thought. *And annoying. A philosopher king who smoked and drank too much. Who couldn't hold a job and pontificated about Kant and Nietzsche. But nothing could be further from the way we were raised than this.*

Sy Levinson's words brought Sean back to reality.

"Sean, you called 10-7 at the Roebling Pier a few hours ago."

"I can't get away with anything, can I?"

"I scroll through the communications logs on my computer every morning," the commander of Manhattan South shrugged.

Dex Birmingham took over with another question.

"Why don't you tell us why you are interested in the tugboat pier?"

"Who said I was interested? Maybe I just wanted a break, down at the River."

"Don't be that way with us, Sean. We're on your side."

"Okay. I read about it. In a long-forgotten desk blotter from Old Slip."

"How in the world?" Dex wondered.

"I found a notebook," Sean told them. "In my dad's handwriting. The first entry was October, 1977."

The three older cops looked around the booth at each other. *How did we miss that?*

"Sean," Jake Morrow asked. "Is the package in a safe place?"

"Yeah. I have the money."

"Where is it, Sean?"

"I'm not ready to say. Not yet."

"Just be cool," Dex said. "We're all friends here."

"I don't give a rat's ass about your money. I need to know who killed my father."

"It's not our money," Dex said.

"Damn, Dex. I'm a rookie. But I'm not stupid."

"So what do you think?" Jake asked. "You think we sold drugs that we found in the river?"

"What should I think?"

"The drugs aren't the story," Sy Levinson said. He spoke slowly. Softly. "The floater isn't the story. The real story is something that happened on the Brooklyn Bridge, three months before we went down to the Roebling Pier that night."

———

Police Officer Theodore Albert Lamont was twenty-five years old, single, and a Navy veteran with two years of service on the NYPD when he walked into the First Precinct at Old Slip on August 8, 1977. Back then, his dark chestnut hair covered most of his ears. The mustache over his lip was a new experiment for his first plainclothes assignment.

That warm summer night, the city was still reeling from the widespread lawlessness, which had occurred during the blackout on the thirteenth and fourteenth of July, in which 4,500 looters had been arrested. Over 500 police officers had been injured. Many New Yorkers were still too terrified to venture out of their homes after dark.

Their fear was well-founded. A serial killer calling himself *Son of Sam* was continuing his year-long spree of random attacks. Killing and maiming mostly young couples, with a .44 Bulldog revolver.

To add to the misery, the city was broke. Long-standing budget deficits and short-term debt had brought the nation's largest municipality to the brink of default. Graffiti proliferated. Garbage remained uncollected. Burned-out buildings fractured the cityscape. Even the Yankees were inflicting discord upon New Yorkers, with redneck manager Billy Martin and superstar Reggie Jackson nearly coming to blows.

So, when Lieutenant Bill Sweeney said, "Welcome to the Stakeout Squad, Lamont," Ted had no idea why he was there.

For his first two years in the service, Ted had been walking a beat on the Lower East Side. It was a tough neighborhood. Nighttime break-ins and petty theft were common. Without a radio, he had to use a curbside call box to communicate with Old Slip, and hope that the next foot post would hear his whistle if he needed immediate help. He had used his nightstick more than a few times, and his five-shot Smith & Wesson .38 revolver had been out of the holster, but never fired.

Walking a beat, Ted Lamont had learned to think on his feet. But other than that, he had no idea why he had been assigned to the Stakeout Squad.

"Listen kid," Jake Morrow had said when they first met. Before they were friends. "This is your first time out. So, if anything happens, just take care of yourself. Let us take care of the perps. Got it?"

They entered the liquor store from an unmarked unit, through the back alley. High noon on a hot August day. Prime time for armed robberies. Jake carried a 12-gauge Remington Model 70-pump shotgun. Nine .30 caliber lead pellets of buckshot in the crimped head of each cartridge.

Cases of beer had been stacked three deep and chest high at the back of the store. Cans of Rheingold and Ballentine Ale. Jake and Ted sat on the floor behind that barricade. Bill Sweeney and Sy Levinson cruised the street in the unmarked unit.

They waited slightly over two hours before Sweeney uttered, "Showtime," on the radio.

"Here we go," Jake Morrow whispered as he clicked off the shotgun's safety. "Stay cool, rookie. And for God's sake, don't shoot me in the back."

They heard the perps barge into the store. "Money! Give it now, or you die, Mother!"

The cash register drawer opened with a wooden rattle and a *ding*.

That was when Jake stood up. Without a word, he leveled the shotgun and fired while Ted was still getting up.

One perp was reeling when Ted found his feet. A chrome-plated pistol in his hand still pointed at the clerk, who was diving for the floor. The perp went down without firing a shot. Jake ratcheted a second round into the chamber of the 12-gauge. He held the trigger down, so the muzzle barked as soon as the pump action went forward.

But the second perp was quick. He spun around and fired a .45 Automatic. Jake's second shot missed. He didn't swing the shotgun fast enough. The glass door shattered, sending shards onto the sidewalk. The perp backed out the door, screaming and shooting wildly.

Jake came around the stacks of beer. Ratcheted a third round into the shotgun and stood in front of the cash register, over the dying man. The smoking muzzle of the shotgun in his face. Kicked the .32 caliber Iver Johnson Saturday Night Special out of his hand, and sternly said "Halt, Police."

Ted had jumped over the cases of beer by then. Streams of foamy liquid were issuing from their barricade, marking the impacts of the wild rounds from the second shooter's .45 Automatic.

"No, Rookie! Don't!"

Jake Morrow's warning came too late. Ted Lamont was out the door in a flash. The second shooter was almost into the getaway car when he turned and waved the .45 Automatic at Ted. Screaming. Firing wildly.

Ted was close enough to see the intense anger and fear in the perp's face—tears and snot and spit—when he aimed the front sight blade of his .38 at the center of his chest and began pulling the trigger. The perp reeled but was held up by the car. Ted fired all five shots. Climbing the ladder, the front sight was up around the man's neck by the last. He could see the bullets impacting flesh above the collar of a dirty T-shirt.

The shooter rolled onto the ground alongside the car. Eyes wide open. Still holding the .45 Automatic. The slide held back by a magazine, which was empty by then. Ted was standing over him with his .38—also empty—when he saw the driver of the getaway car fumbling with something in his lap.

I'm dead, Ted thought when he realized he was looking down the twin barrels of a sawed-off shotgun in the hands of the driver.

And he would have been if Lieutenant Bill Sweeney and Sy Levinson had not screeched up in the unmarked unit at that moment. Sy stepped halfway out of the Plymouth and blasted the driver with 12-gauge buckshot. Point blank. Twice.

Ted saw the buckshot land. But he never heard the reports from Sy's shotgun. By then, the sounds of shooting had become one dull roar. Hollow. Near but far off. Rolling thunder, out of time with the lightning strikes of hot lead pellets.

The driver's body bounced off the backrest of the would-be getaway car and slumped over the wheel. The blare of the horn added to the otherworldly sounds. Most of the driver's brains were in the back seat when the car crept ahead and over the curb as his foot slipped off the brake. It stopped when the bumper hit a cluster of garbage cans. Trash scattered on the sidewalk.

Ted tried to move, but only achieved two circles where he stood. He felt a bizarre trembling coming up his arm and into his body as if the hand which held his empty .38 was stuck in an electric light socket. A blur of havoc and destruction as he turned. Beer and blood on the floor inside. The perp with his bullets in his chest, sprawled in the gutter. And the noise. The noise like rolling thunder, trailing away to the high-pitched squealing of the dead men, which lingered over the sidewalk after their last breaths like the song of banshees.

Ted Lamont puked on his own shoes. Then dry-heaved. When he came up for air, he could barely hear Jake Morrow yelling at him, like a voice underwater.

"Jesus Christ, rookie! What the hell was that? Don't go running out the door like that! The outside guys will shoot your dumb rookie ass by mistake."

———

Sean Lamont sat in the booth in the back of Percy's and faced the three older cops. Their faces were matter-of-fact. Sy Levinson had started their story, but Jake Morrow had finished the account of his father's first day on the Stakeout Squad.

A long moment of silence hung over the table before Sean spoke.

"I never knew it was like that," Sean finally said.

"Like what?" Jake asked.

"That ... hard core."

"Hey," Jake shrugged. "When you walk in someplace with a gun and demand money, you forfeit your right to life."

"But ... no warning ... that's ruthless."

"There was only one rule then," Sy Levinson shrugged. "The same rule as always: We all go home at the end of our watch."

Hard to imagine Dad that way, Sean thought.

"Lieutenant Sweeney?"

"Bill Sweeney," Jake said. "Your lieutenant is Tom Sweeney. His nephew."

"Yeah. So why are you telling me this? Tell the truth, I wish you hadn't. I wish I'd never heard all that."

"You have to understand what it was like in the bad old days, Sean."

"Right. Got it. But you said something about the Brooklyn Bridge?"

Jake Morrow and Dex Birmingham looked at Sy Levinson. The deputy chief sighed before he spoke.

"The shootout wasn't the only thing that happened that day, Sean."

———

Midnight, after the shootout at the liquor store, Percy's was full of cops. The third watch was stopping in for a few beers before heading home. Spirits were high.

The Stakeout Squad had finished their paperwork hours earlier. They had turned the scene of the shooting over to the detectives. The firemen had washed the blood away with hoses. The broken glass had been boarded up. The getaway car had been towed. The perps had all been transported to the city morgue. A two paragraph article for the morning edition of the *Daily News* was being prepared on a Linotype machine. It would appear on the third page.

Jake Morrow, Sy Levinson, and Tom Sweeney sat in the booth in the back. They had Ted Lamont cornered. The third watch was sending beers back to them. The empties were being pushed aside.

"You need to get a steady girl," Jake was saying to Ted. Spilling his beer by then. "You can't go home to an empty apartment after a number like that. It ain't healthy."

"I'll be all right," Ted muttered. "I'm over it."

"Sure you are," Bill Sweeney laughed. "That's why you were puking on your shoes a few hours ago."

"It was just … all the blood. I didn't expect that much. Is it always like that?"

"The human body contains nine quarts," Jake mumbled. "When we do our thing, most of it ends up on the floor."

Sy Levinson decided that the rookie had had enough.

"How are you getting home?"

"The subway," Ted said.

Jake Morrow slapped his back. Hard.

"Not tonight, Teddy. You're riding with me tonight."

They found their cars and headed towards the Brooklyn Bridge.

They were all near the top of the span—between the soaring granite towers, enclosed by the cage of suspension wires—when they saw the flashing lights of a patrol car ahead. Two cops from the first watch had stopped a car on the bridge. They were trying to make an arrest, but the cops were outnumbered. Four men were getting out of the suspect car to fight with the two uniforms.

Lieutenant Bill Sweeney stopped first, in his Chevy. Then Sy Levinson in his Chrysler. Jake Morrow and Ted Lamont went past in Jake's Cadillac and had to back up to join in.

The fight didn't last long. Jake Morrow pistol-whipped one of the thugs, and he went down with a gash on his head. Sy Levinson tossed one man to the pavement and pinned him so that the battered uniform from the first watch could get his cuffs on him. Bill Sweeney helped the other uniform get the upper hand, while Ted chased a perp who began to run in the lanes of travel. He tackled the man and dragged him back to the melee near the police car, which was over by then.

Backup was coming up the bridge by then. Six patrol units and the paddy wagon from Old Slip.

"We were never here," Jake laughed, climbing into his Caddy. "Come on, Teddy. Let's get lost before the cavalry arrives."

The off-duty Stakeout Squad was almost into their cars when the drunk driver came on at about eighty miles per hour. He might have been running from the lights of the backup units coming up the bridge. Maybe he was looking behind. Passing slower cars on the right. He never braked before he hit the trunk of the patrol car.

The uniforms saw the drunk coming. They were out of the way when he slammed into their unit, which folded nearly in half and slammed into the suspect car. The perps were all clear, too. Up against the suspension wires and the guard rail. Their car was pushed into Bill Sweeney's Chevy.

The lieutenant had stepped between the front of his car and Sy's Chrysler. Trying to get out of traffic. He turned and saw the other cars slamming into each other, like a sick game of buck-buck. But there was no time to react.

When his own family Chevy slammed into Sy Levinson's trunk, Bill Sweeney was crushed nearly in half at the thighs.

———

"Holy crap," Sean uttered to the older cops, huddled in the back booth at Percy's. "Tom Sweeney's uncle was killed in a traffic accident? After surviving a gun battle?"

"Not right away," Sy Levinson said. "He hung on in the hospital for a month. But there was no way. He was a mess."

"It was a terrible way to go," Jake shook his head. "I wanted to shoot him every time I saw him in the hospital. Tubes and stuff oozing everywhere. I should have put him out of his misery."

Something doesn't add up, Sean thought. He sat back in the booth and folded his arms.

"So, you guys were all working out of Old Slip, right?"

"Yup," Jake nodded.

"Well, I don't recall ever seeing a picture of Lieutenant Bill Sweeney hanging on the wall with all the other guys killed in the line of duty. What gives?"

"That's the rub," Sy shrugged. "The city denied that it was a line of duty injury."

"What? How could they do that?"

"The city was broke," Jake uttered, with obvious disgust. "The idiots at City Hall had run New York into the gutter with bad debt. They were robbing our pension fund and doing every shady deal they could get away with."

"You're kidding."

"No. I'm not. They refused to pay Bill Sweeney's benefits. Said he was off duty and drunk. Injured due to misconduct."

"Son of a bitch," Sean whispered.

"You ain't kidding," Jake said.

"It was a raw deal for sure," Sy nodded. "Bill Sweeney had four children, you know. All they got was his life insurance policy. The city didn't even want to pay his pension to his widow."

"How could they deny that?"

"In those days, City Hall used to pay us a few days late, all the time. It was one of their tricks, after they ran the city into the ground. So it was a long legal battle for the union, but they eventually got Bill's pension reinstated. No line of duty honors was part of the settlement. To save face for City Hall."

Sean looked across the booth at Dexter Birmingham.

"Dex, you've been awfully quiet."

"I wasn't on the squad when Bill Sweeney was in charge," he gently smiled. "Never met the man. I came along after Sergeant Sy Levinson took over."

"Yup," Jake laughed. "I didn't want to work with a black. Thought one of us might shoot him, by accident. But Sy insisted. Turns out, this guy," he put a hand on Dex Birmingham's shoulder, "is one of the best friends I ever had."

———

Halloween, 1977. They were on a rolling stakeout that night. Two unmarked cars and a Checker cab.

"This sucks," Dexter Birmingham laughed when Sy Levinson assigned him to drive the taxi. "You put the black guy downrange."

Dex was a thin young man then. With a full head of curly hair and an angelic smile. A charming southern voice.

"No, the new guy," Sy Levinson corrected.

"Listen," Ted offered. "I'll drive the hack if you don't want to."

"That's okay," Dex Birmingham's smile was irrepressible. "I'm cool."

They picked up the Checker at the taxi company garage, with a promise to repair any bullet holes before they would return it. They had an open microphone in the taxi cab, so the two unmarked units could hear every word spoken by Dex or his passengers. Then they went to the waterfront, where several cabbies had been robbed.

Dex Birmingham cruised for fares. He actually transported some genuine customers. Dex kept the tips, but their agreement with the cab company required him to turn in the receipts for the meter.

Just before ten p.m., their target customer hailed Dex's taxi on Beekman Street. An addict, desperate for his next fix. They hadn't gone far before he squeezed his skinny forearm around the barrier between him and the driver and threatened Dex with a steak knife.

The squad always attempted to strike as the money was passed. The perps were always transfixed on the cash at that moment.

This perp was exactly what they expected for a petty robber. When he finished robbing Dex, he tried to get him to drive the cab to pick up his next fix. Even after the two unmarked units pulled up and pointed their guns in his face, he was trying to find a way to keep the money.

"Out of the car," Ted Lamont said as he dragged the addict from the Checker.

"I didn't do nothing."

"Sure," Ted had him up against the car by then. Jake Morrow and Sy Levinson were putting their guns back in their holsters. Sy pulled the steak knife from the back seat, where the perp had stashed it.

"Where did you get this?" Ted asked as he pulled the wad of cash from the perp's pocket.

"That's mine!"

"How did you get it?"

"I didn't do nothing wrong."

"You didn't pull this steak knife on your driver?"

"Hell no. I never saw that knife before."

"He says you did."

"He's lying. I didn't do nothing."

"Really? You haven't been formally introduced to your driver, have you? Meet Police Officer Dexter Birmingham, NYPD."

"You're a cop? You don't look like a cop."

"But I am," Dex said as he snapped his cuffs on the addict. "And you're under arrest."

"Okay. Okay," the perp was sweating and mumbling. "You can keep the money. Just let me go."

"What?" Dex said as he stuffed the addict into an unmarked unit. "Do you hear yourself talking? You need help, man."

They took the addict to Old Slip. He suffered through the first stages of withdrawal in the holding cell in the muster room before he was transported to the Tombs.

The Stakeout Squad went back to the streets, but their watch was nearly over. They decided to park near the Roebling Pier to debrief the night's events.

"It's going to rain soon," Ted said when they circled the unmarked units and the Checker cab.

Jake Morrow popped open a can of Schlitz and handed it to Dex.

"You're a shitty hack, man."

"What?"

"You drive too slow. And you go the shortest route. You'd never make any money driving a cab in New York."

"Yeah," Ted said. "Better stick with police work, Dex."

Sy Levinson had a question.

"Why did you come to New York to be a cop, anyway? Weren't there police jobs back home?"

"Right. As if a skinny black man could ever get promoted to detective in my part of Mississippi. Besides, I'm too fashionable for that. I want to be a real big-city homicide detective someday."

"So, now that you've had a steak knife at your throat, how do you like the NYPD?"

"It's okay. By the way, that perp's arm would have been broken if you hadn't rolled up when you did."

Ted was the first to see the man waving from the tugboat at the pier.

"What does this guy want?"

They all heard the man after that.

"Hey, you guys need to see this."

"Better bring some flashlights," Jake said as the cops walked down to the pier.

"What have you got?" Sy Levinson wanted to know when they were looking down at the tugboat.

"That guy looks dead to me," the man pointed.

Ted dropped to the deck of the boat and shined his flashlight under the pier. The body was floating face down. Arms and legs hanging. Only the shoulders and the nape of the neck were barely above water. The spine was so relaxed it appeared to be hunchbacked. Classic dead man's float.

"Yeah," Jake said, joining Ted on the deck. "He's a goner."

"What's this other stuff?" Ted said. By then, they were all shining their flashlights under the pier. There were black bundles all around the pilings.

"Bingo," Jake said. "Drug bust."

"Great," Dex said. "Why does this stuff always happen at the end of a watch?"

The young tug deckhand was holding a boat hook. A bronze hook at the end of a long wooden pole.

"You want me to pull him over?"

"I guess we have to do something," Sy shrugged.

"Thing is," the deckhand said. "Sometimes these dead guys roll over and sink, soon as you touch them."

"Nothing wrong with that," Jake muttered. "The divers from the Marine Unit will find him later."

"Go ahead and give it a try," Sy said to the tug man.

The crewman reached under the pier and gently laid the boat hook on the floater's back. He pulled the dead man slowly alongside the tugboat. When he was a little closer, he deftly slipped the bronze hook into the man's belt.

"Nice move," Ted said.

"Got lucky there," the deckhand smiled. He could hold the floater up after that, no matter what.

"Now what?" Jake said.

"We need some gloves," Dex suggested.

"No," Ted said, resorting to his Navy training. "You must have a Stokes litter on this boat. Don't you?"

A new voice from above answered Ted's query.

"At the back of the deck house," an older man said, leaning out a wheelhouse window.

"Sorry, Cap," the deckhand said. "I was trying not to wake you up."

"Right. You're stomping around the damn boat like a bull in a china shop. What else is under there?"

"Square groupers," the crewman chuckled. "Lots of 'em."

"Great," the captain grumbled. "This place is going to be crawling with cops, soon enough. I'll put on a pot of coffee. No sleep tonight."

Ted and Jake retrieved the litter—a steel tube and chicken wire affair—and lowered it to the water with ropes. They scooped it under the floater.

"See if you can turn him on his back," Ted told the deckhand.

"You've done this before," the young man laughed.

"I was in the Navy," Ted shrugged.

Soon the Stokes litter was on the tug's deck. The dead man's skin was white and wrinkled as if he'd been soaking in a bathtub way too long. His arms and legs were pulled in. Almost a fetal position. He wore casual clothing, with no shoes.

"Bridge jumper?" Dex wondered, looking up at the span of the Brooklyn Bridge over their heads.

"You'll make detective someday, for sure," Jake chortled. "What do you think happened here? This guy didn't toss a truckload of bales into the river before he jumped."

"Right. I get it. Looks like a murder. Drug related."

"Welcome to New York," Sy patted Dex on the back.

They used the boat hook and a sharp fishing gaff to pull the bales of drugs closer. They were hard. Wrapped in black plastic garbage bags and duct tape.

"How do they pack this stuff so tight?" Dex asked.

"They run it through trash compactors," Jake said.

"I always thought the bales were bigger. And wrapped in burlap. Like coffee bags."

"These are sized for the forward hatch on a sailboat," the deckhand offered as he pulled another bale aboard. "Or a go-fast boat."

The four cops stopped what they were doing and looked at the young deckhand.

"What?"

"You seem to know a lot about this business," Sy said.

"I see things."

"You know you could call us when you see things."

"And end up under the pier like this guy? No thanks."

Sy had called the incident in, so other units were arriving by then. They all helped pile the bales on the pier. The paddy wagon was called to transport the contraband to the impound vault in Morningside Heights. When the Marine Unit arrived, they shined their spotlight under the piers. There were other bales under the next pier, so most of the cops went there.

The Stakeout Squad was left on the tugboat with the body. They had to wait over an hour for the medical examiner's wagon to arrive. Then their watch was over and they were getting back in their cars to return to Old Slip.

"Hey," the deckhand called, walking up the pier towards them with something under his arm. "You guys forgot something."

"Son of a gun," Jake said, taking the bale. "Where was this?"

"It must have got pushed under the gunwale when we were bringing them all aboard. It was pretty hard to see in the dark."

"Okay. Thanks."

The cops were left standing at the two unmarked units and the borrowed taxi. The piers were completely deserted by then.

"What do we do with this?" Ted took the bale from Jake. He hefted it in his hands, testing the weight.

"We drive it up to Morningside, with the rest of the stuff," Sy shrugged.

"All the way up there?" Jake groused. "Then back to Old Slip to turn in our units? It'll be noon by the time we get home."

"Why don't we just cut it open," Dex offered. "We could open it up and toss the stuff back into the river. That would get rid of it."

"I like that idea," Jake seconded.

Ted was still testing the heft of the bale in his hands.

"Yeah. This one feels different than the rest."

He handed the plastic-wrapped bundle to Sy Levinson, who agreed.

"It does feel a little different."

Jake had his pocket knife out by then.

"Let's take a look."

"Well…" Sy hesitated. Then he said, "Go ahead, Jake. Just one corner, though."

Jake set the bale on the hood of one of the unmarked units and slipped the blade of his knife under the duct tape and plastic covering the bundle. He sawed some of the wrapping away, under the beam of Ted's flashlight.

"What the…?"

"It's *money*," Dex half-whispered.

"No shit," Jake said, facetiously. "Brilliant deduction. You really are going to get a gold shield, someday."

They could see one corner of the bills. Enough for Ted to say, "Those are C-Notes, guys. Hundred-dollar bills."

"Hey, how much do you think that is?"

"I have no idea," Sy responded. "But it's a lot."

"So what do we do with it?" Jake asked.

"We take it to Old Slip for the detectives."

"Then what happens to it?"

"Then it sits in the evidence room. Until the case gets solved. Or forgotten. Then the money goes into the city's coffers."

"Great. The city can't even pay us on time. And they'll probably spend this to put gold plumbing in the mayor's toilet at City Hall."

"I know," Sy shrugged. "It's a shame. There's enough in there to pay Bill Sweeney's pension and benefits to his family. But they'll never use it for that."

For a few moments, nothing was said. The cops looked at the bale on the hood of the unmarked unit. With the corner cut open to expose the hundred-dollar bills.

"Sy," Ted said. "Are you thinking what I'm thinking?"

"I don't know. What are you thinking?"

"Same as all of us," Jake muttered. "We should give this money to Bill's family."

"That's insane," Sy said. "It would never work. They could never explain where the money came from when they start to spend it."

D.S. COOPER

"Not if we gave it to them in small amounts," Ted suggested. "Over time."

"You guys are nuts," Sy said. "We don't even know how much money is here. And it's probably counterfeit, anyway. Why would good money be mixed in with a load of dope?"

"We can figure that out later," Jake said. "Let's take it and count it. And see if it's not funny money. Then we can decide if we can give it to Bill's family. I like Ted's idea. Small amounts, over time."

Sy Levinson put his hand on the bale of cash.

"There's one big problem here, gentlemen. This is a lot of temptation. Are we talking about helping Bill Sweeney's family? Or helping ourselves to the money?"

"I'm in," Ted said. "If it all goes to the family. Every penny."

"How about you, Jake?"

"Okay. Sure."

"Dex, you didn't even know Bill Sweeney. But he was a good guy, and the city is screwing his family royally. All you have to do is look the other way."

"Hey," Dex's eyes opened wide. "I'm in this squad, too. I'm in, all the way."

"It's risky, rookie," Ted said as the cold rain began to fall again. "We could all spend the rest of our lives in Sing Sing if we blow this."

"I'll take my chances with you guys, if you don't mind."

———◆———

The old barkeep at Percy's wiped his hands on his dirty apron and unlocked the front door promptly at ten a.m. The cops in the back booth knew that other customers would be trickling in soon. It was time to end their conclave.

"Okay," Sean said, wondering if he should believe their story. "How did the package end up in my mother's garage?"

"Ted was nominated to take it," Jake said. "Sy was married, so he couldn't hold it. Too much to lose. Ted's uncle ran a small grocery store in Queens. He hid it there, in the crawl space."

"We used to play poker in the back room of that store," Sy picked up. "Just the four of us. It seemed like a good cover story. Except that when we got around to counting the cash, it was way more than we thought."

"How much more?"

"One million," Jake said, matter-of-factly.

"We started sending it to Bill Sweeney's widow. Your dad made the first payout. Just mailed a bundle of cash—ten grand—in an unmarked envelope. No return address. No explanation."

"They didn't ask where it came from?"

"Bill's widow mentioned it to me once," Sy shrugged. "I just smiled and said, 'Mum's the word.' We never talked about it again."

"But, didn't the city reinstate his pension?"

"They did," Jake said. "And at around the same time, we realized we had way too much cash in the attic of that grocery store. But then, two members of the service got shot in the Bronx. And we figured, what the heck. Their families needed some help, too. So Ted mailed them each ten grand."

"Sean," Sy Levinson said. "We've been mailing a ten grand to the families of every member of the service killed in action for the past twenty years."

"Those numbers in my dad's tally book," Sean mused. "I just realized … those are the shield numbers of dead cops. And the date a payout was made."

"Right on," Dex smiled. "9/11 put a big dent in the East River Trust … that's what we call it, among ourselves … but it could still keep going for a long time."

"Which is the point, Sean," Sy Levinson said. "We have to decide what to do with the East River Trust."

"It might be time to call the whole thing off," Jake muttered. "It's getting too risky."

A customer came in and sat down at the bar. The cops lowered their voices.

"What do you mean, Jake?"

"Sean," Dex answered for Jake. "We think the Trust had something to do with Ted's murder. Somebody must have figured out where the money was coming from every time a cop died. Somebody wanted the money."

"Who else knew?"

"Not a damn soul," Jake stated. "Just us. As far as we know."

"Listen, Sean. The package was in your basement for years. In the wall. When we got together down there, we did more than play cards. We were deciding on the next payout."

"Yeah. Now that you mention it, I knew that you only played poker whenever a cop got killed. I thought it was some sort of ritual or something."

"Sean, this is tough," Dex said. "But we've got to ask. Do you think there is any way Matt found the Trust?"

"That's crazy talk," Sean shook his head. "I don't want to hear it."

For a long moment, nothing was said. Two more customers trickled into Percy's.

"Maybe we should call it a day," Sy Levinson said. "We can get together later to decide if we want to keep the Trust going."

"Or…" Sean hesitated. "What?"

"We could just divide up what's left," Jake said. "Walk away from it, once and for all."

"Or, you could just keep it, Sean," Dex said. "Not that it makes up for your loss. But that would be okay with me."

"You've hit me with a lot already," Sean said. "I need some time to think about this."

"Sure thing," Sy Levinson said. "Just be careful, Sean."

The cops got up and went to their cars. Jake Morrow said that he had to get on the road, back to North Carolina. Dex Birmingham offered to give Sean a ride to the N-Train for the trip back to his apartment in Queens.

When they stepped outside, Frick and Frack were sitting across the street in an unmarked unit. Dex smiled and waved to them.

They didn't wave back.

SUSPECTS

It was almost noon by the time Sean walked home from the 71st Avenue subway station. The apartment was empty. Helen was at work, and Beverly and Matt were out in Lindenhurst.

He flopped onto their bed with his clothes on. Smoky joined him and snuggled uncomfortably close. Purring. His head on Sean's shoulder and his whiskers in his face. He thought about shooing the cat away, but he couldn't sleep, anyway. So he let him stay.

He heard Helen come in after work. She opened the bedroom door to check on him. The curtains were drawn.

"Hey. Come here."

He rolled over and pulled her down on the bedspread. Held her close.

"Are you okay?"

"Fine, kitten. Now that you're here."

"Do you want supper?"

"Lie here with me for a while."

He smelled her hair. Muzzled the nape of her neck. He wanted to tell her everything. But he couldn't get the breath over his tongue to make the words come.

He dozed off.

Sean woke up again when Beverly and Matt came in, hours later. Helen went out to the kitchen. He stayed in bed. The TV in the living room was on the other side of the wall. Matt was watching the news. Volume too high.

He didn't want to talk to his brother. Not yet.

Sean got up at eight p.m. and took a shower. When he came out, he announced that he was going to leave for work a little early.

"I'm going to see Nick at the Bowery Mission."

"I'll give you a ride," Helen started to get up.

"No," he kissed her forehead. "I'll take the train."

Beverly looked up from her book. The cat had found her lap.

"Is everything okay, Sean?"

"Fine, Mom."

He walked to the station wearing a New York Yankees sweatshirt over his uniform trousers. His 9mm Glock was on his hip, but he carried his car jacket and duty gun belt, handcuffs and nightstick in his watch bag.

The train was not crowded. It rattled and swayed and screeched through the tunnels into Manhattan, with Sean lost in thought. When he caught sight of his own reflection in the dark windows, his eyes and brow were dark shadows. He barely recognized himself. As if he had been expecting to see the carefree kid he had been, just a short time earlier.

Father Nick Shellaine was upstairs at the Mission. At one of the long tables in the common room, talking to Jimmy the Finder.

"Sean! Nice surprise."

Jimmy stopped talking and slumped into a shy pose as Sean approached. He responded with a slight smile when Sean said hello. Then Sean and Father Nick went to the big window overlooking the Bowery.

"Nick, did you know that Matt was into fighting dogs?"

"No. I had no idea."

"You were his friend first. Both of you were three grades ahead of me in school. You must have known something."

"What makes you think that he is participating in dog fights?"

"That's where he was the night our dad was shot. Not at the restaurant, waiting tables."

"How do you know that?"

"I know."

Nick looked away from Sean. Out the window.

"His cruel streak showed itself from time to time," the priest said. "Not often. Most of the time he professed to be a pacifist. A gentle soul. He berated you for joining the Marines, you know. At other times, he could kick dogs and torment your neighbors' cats."

"Did you ever see him hurt an animal?"

"Yes."

"Didn't you stop him?"

"No."

Nick turned back to Sean.

"I didn't stop him when he beat up the weaker kids, either," Father Nick said. "Those moods didn't come often. And they passed quickly. Most of the time, he was fine."

Sean was relieved when his cell phone rang. He didn't care who was calling, as long as he could break from his conversation with Sneaky Nick. Another conversation he wished he had never had.

It was Dexter Birmingham.

"Sean, we need to talk. Tonight."

"What's up, Dex?"

"I can't tell you. It's something you have to see for yourself."

"Yeah. I'm at the Bowery Mission now. Where are you?"

"You know where Moonstone is, right? I can be there in about half an hour."

"Right."

Sean and Nick went to one of the long tables. The phone call had broken the thread of their words at the big window, and they sat and had cups of coffee and moved on to thoughts of better times. They were both laughing when Sean got up to go see Dex.

He left the Mission by the back door. Was walking along the brick wall in the alley when the first shot hit the bricks at his shoulder. The sudden crack of exploding gunpowder and the impact of lead sent a splatter of brick fragments against his cheek. Sean was as helpless as a deer in the headlights when he heard the second shot.

———

The shot landed somewhere behind him, and higher on the wall.

Sean! Do something! he heard his father say. Perfectly clearly. As if Ted was standing next to him in the line of fire.

He dove for the only cover within reach. Garbage cans. They were empty. Galvanized steel scattered with a hollow sound as he scrambled to get between the cans and the brick wall. He unholstered his 9mm. When he looked up, there were only shadows.

Somebody was still shooting at him. Again. And again.

Sean saw the flash of a muzzle in the darkness and put the front sight of his Glock on that spot and squeezed the trigger. He had both hands on the pistol's grip. The Glock barked and kicked in his hands. He returned fire over the tumbled garbage cans, until he realized that the other guy was no longer shooting.

He waited for what seemed like an eternity, compressed into a few seconds. Then he stood up. Moving slowly. Still looking over the sights of his pistol.

Son of a bitch! Sean thought. Suddenly angry.

He advanced towards the shadows, holding his piece in both hands. Driven by pure adrenalin. He remembered that his flashlight was in his duty bag. Somewhere on the ground behind him. Too late to go back and get it.

Sean wanted to see the face of the shooter.

And then he wanted to kill him.

"Sean! What's going on out here? Are you okay? Sean!"

Father Nick had come outside. Sean turned from the shadows. Lowered the muzzle of his piece towards the ground.

"Son of a bitch," Sean muttered. He felt his body tingling with high voltage electricity. It seemed that if he touched metal, a spark of nervous energy would arc off his fingertips.

Sean turned back towards the shadows. He kept the muzzle of his piece down. He wanted to reach for his cell phone. But he couldn't take one hand off his piece. Just then, that 9mm Glock was the most important thing in his world.

"My cell phone," he said to Father Nick. "In my pocket. Call 911."

The third watch rolled up and blue lights and a blur of blue uniforms filled the alley. The cops advanced with guns drawn. Flashlight beams probed every nook and cranny.

Captain Tom Sweeney arrived moments after the first units. He strode into the alley, standing tall in his white shirt and took charge of the situation.

"Get that civilian to a safe location," was the first thing he said, pointing at Father Nick as he walked by.

"Are you okay, Lamont?"

"Yes, sir."

"How many shots fired?"

"I … don't know."

"You better know, next time. Did you see the perp?"

"No, sir. Just a muzzle flash and some movement over there."

The captain said a few words into his radio, making sure that the perimeter was secured. Tightening the noose on the shooter.

"Christ, Lamont!" Captain Sweeney bellowed when he saw Sean standing idly. "Go sit in a unit and get your shit together, rookie!"

Rhoda Abernathy grabbed Sean's arm and dragged him out of the alley. Until that moment, he hadn't realized that she was one of the cops backing him up.

"I guess I'm not going to be much help here," Sean muttered, still in a state of shock.

"You already did your job, Sean," Rhoda said as she sat him in her RMP.

"I can't believe I made some dumb mistakes," Sean muttered. "Shooting at shadows."

"You did great," Rhoda shrugged. "You returned fire and survived. You'll get the bad guy next time."

———

Whenever a member of the service comes under fire, the NYPD initiates two parallel investigations. One is concerned with satisfying the law. The other is all about keeping cops alive.

For the latter, two veteran officers from the Training Division responded to the alley behind the Bowery Mission that night. They took photographs and videos and measured distances. They talked to Sean at the Fifth Precinct, recording every detail, with assurances that nothing he said would ever be used against him in a courtroom or a disciplinary action.

They would make a detailed study of the incident. When each member of the service reported to Rikers Island for quarterly tactical training, they would recreate the shooting under controlled conditions. Every cop in the city would learn from Sean Lamont's close call, as well as every other recent incident.

Except for one detail.

"I can't explain it," Sean told the training officers in a hushed tone. "I feel goofy even mentioning this. But I swear ... I heard my father's voice. Clear as can be. I think I would have died there if he hadn't told me to *do something*."

The training officers looked at each other. Actually smiled. Each of them wore the Combat Cross above their shields.

"We hear that a lot," they said. "With slight variations. You're not alone."

The Internal Affairs Division was not quite so understanding.

Frick and Frack confronted Sean in an interrogation room.

There was a Smith & Wesson .38 caliber revolver on the table when he walked towards it. Blued finish. Two-inch barrel. Walnut grips.

Sean knew it was his father's off-duty piece right away. And he didn't doubt that the ballistics tests would show that the gun that killed his dad was on the table in front of him at that moment.

It sent a chill up his spine. Which Detectives Dick Francis and Frank Capella had to notice.

"How do you explain this, Lamont?"

"What do I need to explain?"

"This .38 snubby was found at the scene. How did it get there?"

"That's my dad's off-duty piece, isn't it?"

"Absolutely," Frick nodded. "The numbers match."

"As if you didn't know," Frack stated, more than asked.

"Are you always the asshole?" Sean said to Frank Capella. "Or do you guys take turns?"

"Funny, Lamont. You'll need to take a gunpowder residue test."

"I fired my piece seven times. It will be positive."

"Okay. How many times did you fire the .38?"

"What?"

"This .38 was found exactly where you said the shots came from. Which seems unlikely, since you were spraying ammo at shadows all over the alley with your service weapon. Maybe you knew exactly where this .38 was … because you left it there?"

"I don't like the direction you're heading," Sean said. "Why don't you just lay it out for me?"

"Sean," Frick took over. "We have to cover all the bases. You've been unable to produce Ted's off-duty piece for almost a month. Then it shows up in the alley where you were in a shootout. With no witnesses. Except your best friend, who just happened to come along after the fact. Doesn't that sound like a sour note?"

"You think I had the .38 all along? That I was carrying it as a backup?"

"No," Frack leaned onto the table. "I think you were the only one in that alley, Lamont. I think that you fired some shots into a brick wall. Then you ran across the alley and fired your duty piece at nothing and nobody. That's what I think."

"That theory doesn't pass the laugh test," Sean chortled.

"Really? Somebody was a really terrible shot to miss you five times at close range. Who are you covering for, Lamont."

"I'm not covering for anyone. I'm telling the truth."

Dick Francis lowered the heat on Sean's interrogation.

"Help us out here, Sean. Who else even knew you would be in that alley?"

"I don't know," Sean shrugged. "Other than Father Nick. And my wife. She knew that I was going to the Mission before my watch."

"How about your brother?"

"I suppose he heard me tell my wife where I was going."

"Nobody else?"

Except Dexter Birmingham, Sean thought but did not say. *I'll deal with him myself. When the odds are in my favor. Son of a bitch.*

———

Sean didn't have to wait long to confront Dex. Helen had driven into Manhattan to give him a ride home. She was waiting in the muster room after Frick and Frack finished their interrogation. When Sean stepped outside onto Elizabeth Street with her, Detective First Grade Dexter Birmingham, NYPD Retired, was sitting alone in his Land Rover.

Sean pushed Helen aside and stood on the curb outside the passenger side window. Legs spread in a wide stance. Hands at his side. Fists clenched.

"You son of a bitch."

"Easy, Sean," Dex held up both hands in surrender. "Be cool. Just be cool, son."

"Dex, you set me up, didn't you?"

"Sean, it's me. Dex. Dex Birmingham. Be cool."

"Nobody else knew where I was, Dex. And where I was going."

"Sean," Helen pleaded. "What is going on?"

"Someone set me up, Helen. Some bastard teed me up in a big way. Someone who knew all about the investigations. Someone like a retired detective."

"Sean, listen to me," Dex said as he handed him a manila envelope out the window, speaking and moving very slowly. "Take these pictures. Take a good look at them. Pay close attention to the dates. And times. That's all I ask."

Sean took the envelope.

"Next time I see you Dex, look out."

"Don't do anything foolish, son. This thing is almost over. God help us, it is almost over. Just look at the pictures. Then call Sy Levinson if you still don't trust me."

"It's still on," Sean pointed at Dex as he backed away from the black Land Rover.

When he turned to walk to the car with Helen, Sean realized that half a dozen cops were standing on the front steps of the Fifth Precinct. Frozen in their tracks. They had seen everything.

I don't care if they heard the whole thing, Sean thought. *I really don't. Son of a bitch.*

Helen drove. She didn't say a word until they were up on FDR Drive.

"Sean, I'm scared."

"You should be."

"Tell me what's going on. It's because of the money, isn't it?"

"Of course it is," he barked. "It's always money. Or sex."

"Let's just give them the money," Helen offered. "They can have it. Just leave us alone."

"It's too late for that. Dad is dead. Somebody has to pay for that."

"Sean, you're scaring me."

He didn't have an answer for her. Instead, Sean opened the manila envelope in his lap.

He had crumpled the envelope without noticing it. So he smoothed the pictures flat. Grainy black-and-white photographs. Images from surveillance cameras. Cars running the tolls without paying.

"Helen, stop the car."

"What? I can't. There's no place to pull over."

"Then turn on the dome light. And the map lights."

With better light, Sean studied the pictures while Helen drove.

An old Cadillac. North Carolina plates.

Jake Morrow behind the wheel.

"What have you got?" Helen pleaded.

"Wait … this is important."

The time stamp: *9/9/12 @ 23:42 hours.*

Jake Morrow had run the tolls on the Verrazano–Narrows Bridge, outbound from Brooklyn, towards the New Jersey Turnpike. Twenty-seven minutes after the time of Ted Lamont's murder.

"Lucky me," Rhoda Abernathy said as she climbed into the patrol car with Erik Ramos. "I get to work a double shift, thanks to Sean Lamont."

"Just think of all the OT you're making," Erik said.

"So, what do you think?" Rhoda shrugged and looked out the window. "Was there another shooter tonight? Or did Sean just make up that whole scenario in the alley?"

"There was a shooter."

"Who?"

"I hate to say it, but I think it was his brother. Rumor has it, the .38 they found tonight belonged to Sean's father. Who else would have had access to it, besides Matt? He lived in the same house as Ted Lamont."

"Erik, how well do you know Sean?"

"I've met his family. And I was with him the night his father was shot."

"Yeah. I guess if you trust him ... I do, too."

"With my life," Erik said.

Their first call was to see a man at the Faith Bowery Mission. When they rolled up, a young man in a dark suit stepped up to the car and leaned into the passenger side window.

"I was hoping you were on duty. I asked them send you, Erik. I'm glad they did."

Erik spoke past Rhoda, who was riding shotgun.

"What's the deal, Father Nick?"

"It's about Jimmy."

"Jimmy the Finder?" Rhoda asked.

"Yes," Nick nodded. "He saw the whole thing."

"What?" Erik was amazed. And very interested.

"Jimmy was outside when Sean left here tonight. He saw everything in the alley."

"Where is Jimmy now?"

"He hid in the Mission until the officers finished their investigation. I didn't even know that he was in there. He took off about an hour ago. One of the volunteers just now told me his story."

"Did he say where he was going?"

"No idea," Nick shrugged. "I was hoping you would know."

"What color shirt did he have on?" Rhoda wanted to know.

"A denim shirt. And a dungaree jacket."

"God bless you, Father Nick," Erik said, already pulling into the traffic. "This could be a big break. We'll let you know."

"Are you thinking what I'm thinking?" Rhoda asked as Erik turned the car around and headed towards the Battery.

"You know I am."

"I'll call for the Transit Bureau to meet us there."

"No, wait. He might not have gotten that far. We might find him above ground."

"Okay."

"Anyway," Erik added. "We should be the first ones to talk to him. He's afraid of cops, but he knows us. He'll remember that we saved him from drowning in the subway."

Rhoda transmitted a description of Jimmy as a possible witness to the shooting in the alley, with the hope that some unit would spot him on the street. But no sightings were reported before they arrived at One New York Plaza.

"Let's take a look," Erik said when he parked their RMP near the ramp to the subterranean parking garage. In front of the green stairs leading to the subway platform, where they had pulled Jimmy the Finder to safety, at the height of the hurricane.

"Are you crazy?" Rhoda laughed. "Our radios won't work in the Hole. The Transit Bureau is on a totally different frequency."

"Just a quick look. Don't forget your flashlight."

The green railings around the stairway leading down to the platform were wrapped in yellow tape. *Police Line – Do Not Cross.* Erik stepped over it.

Since the flood, the Blue Line was shut down, south of 36th Street. The platform was eerily dark. Dank. They shined their flashlights on the tile walls and across the dark void of the tracks. They could see the vapor of their breaths when the beams crossed their own faces.

"Okay," Rhoda said, after a cursory look around. "He's not here."

Erik stood with his toes on the edge of the platform. Across the yellow suicide line, and aimed the beam of his flashlight down the tracks.

"Let's just walk down that way a little bit."

"On the tracks? You really are nuts, Erik."

"Everything is shut down. We'll be okay."

"Right. If you say so. But stay away from the third rail. Just in case."

The tunnel itself was quiet, but they could hear the sounds of Underground New York seeping through the walls. Ventilators churning somewhere nearby. The throb of traffic on FDR Drive. Steam hissed from a leaky pipe connection. Away from the platform, massive concrete pillars separated the uptown and downtown tracks.

"What's that?" Erik asked, shining his light across both sets of tracks.

"Some kind of access shaft," Rhoda said. "With a ladder. And don't you even think about it!"

"Right," Erik laughed. "We've come this far. Let's just take a look."

They stepped over the wooden planks above the third rails and shined their lights into the narrow iron shaft. The entrance was guarded by a heavy metal door, which was open. Rungs were built into the side. Warm air rose up, driven by the churning of distant machinery.

"Do you believe in hell, Erik?"

"Yes. I do," he said, putting a foot on the rungs leading down. "But this isn't it."

Rhoda Abernathy followed Erik down the access shaft. It was longer than either of them had anticipated. When they reached the bottom, they stood in a lower level of tracks, which were dimly lit by a string of overhead lights.

"Where is this?" Rhoda asked, shining her light around.

"Must be the tunnel to Brooklyn. Under the river."

"Okay. That's enough for me. Let's get out of here."

Except that—no sooner than the words were out of her mouth—her flashlight beam caught a figure slinking away down the tunnel.

"There he is!" Rhoda said. And took off running.

"Jimmy!" she shouted. "Jimmy the Finder! It's me, Rhoda. Don't run!"

Erik followed as Jimmy led Rhoda down the tracks. It was suddenly very noisy in the tunnel. She caught up when Jimmy suddenly stopped. Erik was right there. And he realized that a train was coming behind them at the same moment that Jimmy pulled Rhoda into a small alcove.

The big headlamp of the lead subway car was an angry eye probing through the tunnel. The alcove was a dark shadow. A tiny space dedicated to wiring and plumbing. Erik hoped there was room for a third. The train was bearing down on them when he squeezed behind Rhoda, who was facing Jimmy the Finder.

"Hi, Jimmy," Erik said over Rhoda's shoulder as the Brooklyn Express missed them all by inches. "What's new?"

"You shouldn't be down here," Jimmy solemnly said.

"No kidding. We came to find you."

"Jimmy," Rhoda asked after the train passed. "Is there a better place to talk?"

"The place where you came in. Hurry, before another train comes."

The trio made their way quickly back to the access tube to the upper level of tracks. They huddled in the larger alcove there. Rhoda started the questions.

"Jimmy, do you remember Sean?"

"Sure. Father Nick likes him."

"Do you like him?"

"I don't know. He's a cop."

"So am I."

Jimmy seemed surprised. *You are?*

"Listen," Erik said. "We need your help. Did you see Sean in the alley behind the Mission tonight?"

"Is it still tonight?"

Rhoda shined her flashlight on her wristwatch.

"It's a quarter past one in the morning, right now."

"Oh."

"Jimmy," Erik asked, "what did you see in the alley?"

"A big man. He ran funny. With a limp. He was shooting at Sean."

"Did you get a good look at this man? Could you identify him if you saw him again?"

"No. I don't want to see him again."

"What else can you tell us about him?" Rhoda wanted to know. "Did he get into a car?"

"A big car. Red, with tail fins."

"Did you see the license plate numbers? Can you remember?"

"No. But it said, *First in Flight*."

"North Carolina," Erik muttered. "That's all we need. Damn. Jake Morrow."

"Do you want to go up with us, Jimmy?" Rhoda asked. "You need to talk to some nice detectives."

"I don't think so," Jimmy shrugged.

"Listen," Erik offered. "How about if we have the detectives meet you at the Mission? Father Nick will be right there. They won't hurt you."

"Promise?"

"We promise," Rhoda smiled. "We'll be there, too."

"Can I get breakfast?"

"Sure," Erik said. "In the morning. At breakfast. Father Nick will call us, and we'll come with the detectives. Deal?"

Rhoda and Erik climbed the rungs up the tube. At the gravel floor of the upper level, they were looking at the shoes of cops. Flashlights were beamed on them.

"What the hell," the transit cops said. "Who are you guys?"

"Ramos and Abernathy. First Precinct. Tom Sweeney is our captain."

"You know you're not supposed to be down here. This is our beat."

"We needed to talk to a witness to the shootout at the Faith Mission earlier tonight."

"Did you find him?"

"Yes. Jimmy the Finder, he calls himself."

"Right. We know him. We'll go roust him out if you want."

"No," Rhoda said. "We've set up an interview with the detectives in the morning. One of our guys is all jammed up with Internal Affairs. Big trouble. Jimmy could be the one who clears him."

"Okay," the transit cops agreed. "That's another story. If he doesn't show, call us. Lewiston and Blanco. We'll get him. Gently."

"But this meeting never happened," the other transit officer added. "Not down here, anyway. Our captain goes berserk when he hears about street cops down in the deep tunnels. It's a thing with him."

Back on the sidewalk, Erik and Rhoda both filled their lungs with fresh air. Rhoda checked in with dispatch on her radio but didn't mention having spoken with Jimmy the Finder.

"Are you calling Sweeney?" she asked when Erik pulled out his cell phone.

"He's next," Erik said. "First, I have to take a chance. And I pray to heaven that my cop instincts are working tonight."

———————◆———————

Beverly Lamont was alone in the apartment, watching an English mystery on PBS Channel 13. Smoky in her lap. A good book in her hands. A steaming cup of tea nearby.

She was calm on the outside. Years of waiting for Ted to come home had taught her that a tranquil exterior might allow serenity to seep into her pores. That the panic might be mitigated by the book and the tea and the cat purring in her lap. But the fear that gnawed at her insides that evening was testing her mettle.

Sean had been in a shootout, and the only thing that mattered was that he would soon come through that door. He would have surrendered his service weapon and would have been told to stay at home until the investigation was completed. Until he decompressed.

She had been through it with Ted too many times. The one blessing was—ironically—that her house was unlivable. So that she could be here with her baby. If only briefly.

She heard the key in the lock.

"Where is Matt?" Sean demanded as he came in the door and swept through his apartment.

"Hello, Sean." Beverly calmly put her book down. *He shouldn't be so agitated.* "Are you okay?"

"I'm fine. Where is Matt?"

Something is terribly wrong, Beverly realized. *Ted had always been so drained after action. Exhausted, when he arrived home. Physically spent. Emotionally bankrupt.*

It was always *over*, when Ted came in the door.

Beverly was on her feet by then. Sweeping towards Sean with open arms. When he pulled away, her panic was complete.

"Matt is fine. He went out for a beer with Jake Morrow. Please come sit with me, Sean."

"It's no use talking to him," Helen said, tossing the car keys in the basket near the front door. Her anger was up. "He's made up his mind."

"Made up his mind about what? Sean, what is going on?"

He needs you now, Beverly wanted to say to Helen. *Don't push him away.*

"Jake Morrow was here?" Sean demanded. "Tonight?"

"Yes. He called not long after you left to see Nick at the Mission. Then he came by about two hours later. He took Matt out. Why does that matter, Sean?"

"Where did they go?"

"I'm not sure. Paddy's, I suppose." She looked at her watch. Sought comfort from the dial. "But it's after closing time now. Isn't it?"

"Damn it," Sean muttered, and stormed into the bedroom. Rummaged in the back of their closet.

"No, Sean!" Helen screeched behind him. "No!"

Beverly's heart sank when he emerged from the bedroom with Ted's old M1 carbine.

Sean stood at the kitchen table. Jammed the magazine of ammunition into the military weapon and pulled the bolt back. When he let the bolt slam forward, Beverly and Helen both knew that the gun was ready to fire.

He clicked on the safety.

"Sit here," Sean said, motioning to the table. "Both of you."

Beverly sat with Helen. The appearance of the weapon had them both transfixed. Sean held the carbine over the table between them.

"This is the safety," he demonstrated. "Click it off, and you're ready to shoot."

The women began their plea in unison. "Sean…" But he cut them short.

"Bolt the door behind me. Don't let anybody in. If Jake Morrow shows up, call 911. Don't hesitate. If Jake comes in that door, pick this gun up and flick the safety off. It will fire each time you pull the trigger. Understand?"

Sean put the carbine down on the table between the women. Then he went directly to the door and took the car keys from the basket and stormed out.

"Sean! Please!" Helen said, too late. "Don't go out there!"

"Helen," Beverly said. She felt Ted at her side. *Be calm.* "Bolt the door. Then come here and hold my hand."

Beverly Lamont held her hand out to Helen. With her other hand, she had already called Sy Levinson.

———

Dexter Birmingham's apartment on the Upper West Side featured a magnificent panorama of the Hudson River and the Palisades. The lights were low near the large windows. He sat at a baby grand piano, musing over the keys. Allowing the soft progressions of notes and chords unfurl their colors slowly.

There was more light on the lower level, where Joyce was reading a magazine on the settee. But Dex was of a mood for the shadows and the view. Which was more than he would ever have been able to afford on a cop's pension.

In the morning, he would be back on location with the television series, lending the credibility of his years as a real detective to the production. He could coach them on the lingo and the procedures. *Talk the talk.* But there was no way to teach the walk.

Am I an unwilling accomplice to a friend's murder? Dex wondered. *A man who trusted me, as I trusted him, with our very lives?*

When Erik Ramos called, he arranged the meeting with few words and put the cell phone in his pocket.

"It's going down," he told Joyce, putting on a black beret and a leather coat.

"Good luck."

"This is the end of it, Joyce. One way or the other."

"We'll be fine, Dex." They embraced. *My man.* "You know what you're doing."

He drove down the Henry Hudson Parkway. Took his pistol from under the seat and put it in his coat pocket. Erik and Rhoda were parked across from the Fifth Precinct. *The Fighting Fifth*, they used to call it, before political correctness.

Captain Sweeney came out to the cars.

"I need to borrow Erik," Dex said up front.

"What?" Sweeney squinted. The way his uncle Bill Sweeney used to, when he was perplexed. "He's already started the watch. I can't let him go."

"Send him on a wellness check for a member of the service. I'll ride along."

"Sean Lamont?"

"Right on."

"Something is going down, Dex. I don't like not knowing what it is."

"I wish I could tell you, Bill," Dex looked up Elizabeth Street. "Just know that it's unfinished business from one night on the Brooklyn Bridge."

"What do my officers have to do with that?"

"Right now, your officers are the only cops who Sean trusts."

"I don't like being the senior man with a secret," Sweeney said. "Especially when I don't know what the secret is."

"Sy Levinson is in this, all the way."

Bill Sweeney looked the other way on the street before he spoke.

"Don't leave the city," the captain said to his officers. "Come back before the end of watch. And you damn well better be able to account for your actions."

———

Sean pounded on the door to Paddy's until the barkeep couldn't ignore him any longer.

"My brother is in there. Open up!"

The bar was dark. Closed, supposedly.

"Don't forget to lock the door when you leave," the barkeep said when he let Sean in and himself out. "Use the back door."

They were in the back room, where the card games were held. Jake had his back against the wall. His left hand was under the table. Sean knew that he was holding his .357 revolver.

"Sean," Matt said. As if he were surprised to see him.

Jake didn't say anything for a long time. Then he smiled, and laughed as he put his revolver on the table.

"They took your piece, didn't they?"

"Stand up, Jake."

"Ha! What are you going to do, Sean?" Jake put his fleshy paw on the gun. "Sit down. Have a drink with me and your big brother."

Sean pulled a chair away from the table. Turned it around and sat with his arms folded across the backrest.

This was a dumb mistake, he thought. *I'll be lucky to get out of here alive. Much less settle the score with Jake.*

"Uncle Jake was telling me about the money," Matt said.

"Oh? What money is that?"

"Nearly a million," Matt slurred. Drunk already. "I can't believe it was in our basement, all these years. And we never knew."

"Not quite," Sean forced a guttural laugh. He still had a card to play. "More like a quarter of a million. And I knew it was there, Matt."

"Don't try that shit with me," Jake growled. "I know exactly how much is left. We all had to agree, every time Ted made a payout. So don't get cute with me."

"Apparently, most of it got spent while you weren't around," Sean lied.

"Bullshit," Jake muttered. "I'm going to get my share, and then some."

"You're losing it, Jake. How did you miss me in the alley?"

"Ha! I never miss. I was shooting over your head intentionally."

"So you could set up Matt to take the fall for killing Dad?"

"That was just to throw the detectives off," Matt answered for Jake.

"Why did you kill our father, Jake?" Sean wanted to know.

"It was an accident," Matt answered for him again. "Jake didn't mean to do it. They were fighting, and it just happened."

"That's the way it was," Jake moaned. He turned sideways and poured whiskey into Matt's glass as he spoke. Spilled about half of it. "I didn't go there with the intention … you know … it wasn't supposed to go down that way, Sean. I just wanted my share. But Ted never should have moved the money to the new house … without telling us."

"What makes you think it was in the new house, Jake?"

"Sean, don't play stupid with me. They were selling the old house. I went to check on the money that day, and it was gone."

"The day you shot our father? With his own gun? Did you steal the gun from our house when you were looking for the money, Jake?"

"It's my money, too. He shouldn't have moved it. Can't you get that through your thick skull?"

He's a drunk old man, Sean decided. *I can take him.*

"Yeah, I get it, Jake. So does the task force. They've figured it out. They're going to make a move on you. Soon."

"You're lying, Sean." Jake poured a glass of whiskey for himself and pushed another in front of Sean. Left the bottle between them. "You know how I know you're lying, Sean? You're a lousy liar. Just like your old man. He could keep a secret, I'll say that much. But Ted couldn't lie, for shit. Neither can you."

Now or never, Sean realized.

He reached for the glass of whiskey—grabbed the bottle instead—and leaped across the table in one motion. He brought the heavy bottle down on Jake Morrow's left hand just as the old cop reached for the shiny .357 Magnum. Jake struggled to stand as the younger cop threw his shoulder into his chest and tackled his shoulders—they both hit the wall—but he didn't go down.

Sean never saw the spring-leather blackjack when Jake slapped the side of his head with it.

———————

Sy Levinson drove from his house in Brooklyn, northbound on the Jackie Robinson Parkway, at full speed. Blue lights flashed under the grill and in the windshield of his unmarked city SUV, and the siren, when he used it to alert drivers who managed to ignore the blue lights in their rearview mirrors, sounded like Gabriel's Trumpet, summoning the angels.

Dex and Erik and Rhoda were waiting in front of Sean's apartment building.

"We're too late," Dex said, leaning into the window of Sy's vehicle. "Sean and Jake are both gone."

"Bring me up to speed," Sy said.

"Matt is up in the apartment, drunk. Babbling. He said that Sean confronted Jake at some after-hours joint, and got himself knocked out. When he came to, Jake was long gone. Sean came home and got Ted's old M1 carbine. Then he took off, too."

"Damn," Sy uttered. "This is a mess."

"Hopefully, Sean won't find him," Dex offered.

"That will buy us some time."

"Sy, maybe we should go straight with this. Call it in and have the patrol units pick up both of them, before something really bad happens."

The right thing to do, Sy Levinson set his jaw. *Except that…*

"I think I know where Jake is going, Dex. Don't you?"

"He wouldn't do that," Dex shook his head no. "He'd go to his daughter's house in Bellmore. Or to a hundred after-hours bars or whorehouses or all-night card games he knows of. But he wouldn't go there."

"Jake will ditch the car and lay low until he can get out of the city," Sy said. "There's only one place where he'll go."

CHAPTER

14

OLD SLIP

S ean didn't see Jake's car near the abandoned precinct at Old Slip. The stone facade looked cold and foreboding with no lights in the windows and the green lanterns flanking the front doors extinguished.

No matter, he thought. *Jake must know a hundred places to stash his Caddy. He would lay low until one of his cronies could pick him up. Then he would make a run to get out of the city.*

Sean Lamont parked in front and went to the trunk of the car for the carbine. Checked that there was a round in the chamber and a full magazine, ready to fire. Took his flashlight and handcuffs from his watch bag. Then he threw the handcuffs back into the bag.

No prisoners, Sean thought. *If Jake is in there, only one of us is coming out alive.*

When he went up the stairs, he found the padlock and chain hanging limp on the heavy bronze doors. A link had been cut.

This is it, he thought as he pushed the one side of the double door open. *Jake Morrow is here.*

Sean used the other side of the metal door for cover as he scanned the muster room with the beam of his flashlight. The room looked enormous. Abandoned. Peeling paint and plaster. High ceilings. The large booking desk still spanned the far wall.

He tried to make his leg take the first step into the precinct. But his limbs wouldn't obey.

Damn it, Sean doubted himself.

He needed Erik and Rhoda and Captain Sweeney and the rest of his watch. But they would stop him if they were present, and call in the ESU.

He needed Sy Levinson and Dex Birmingham. But he wasn't sure if he could trust them.

He needed his father. But...

The English driving hats. The way he could drive a nail with two swings of a hammer and make a perfectly square cut with a handsaw. Bait a hook and steer a boat. Standing at the sink with a razor. Old Spice aftershave.

Sean! Do something!

He stepped quickly through the door. Sidestepped out of the backlight from the street, with the flashlight under the barrel of the carbine. Safety off, finger on the trigger.

The big man came out of the shadows fast, limping on a bad leg. The carbine spit blue flame and a bullet into the floor when Jake knocked it out of Sean's hands. Then it clattered to the floor in the middle of the muster room with the flashlight.

Jake's calloused knuckles landed on his jaw and Sean went down. He was barely aware of the big man closing the door to the street. Dragging him to the holding cell. Tossing him on the floor behind the bars.

In the half-light of the streetlamps coming through the windows—and the beam of his flashlight lying in the middle of the floor—Sean saw Jake limp to the booking desk. He sat there, with his feet up, and lit a cigar.

"Bad mistake, Sean. I thought you were a better cop than that. Walking in the front door. No backup. It's a shame you didn't learn from your old man."

Sean regained his senses. Stood up and held the bars. A chill went up his spine when he saw that Jake had a 12-gauge pump gun on the desk. Nervous energy coursed through his body in waves. He clenched his fists and set his jaw and flexed his shoulders to tamp it down. *No fear.* "You won't get away. My car is out front. Someone will figure out that we're in here."

Jake sat motionless in the shadows at the booking desk and blew smoke from his cigar. "Your car will be at the bottom of the East River in a few minutes."

Sean noticed that the door to the holding cell wasn't locked. Not even closed all the way. *No key,* Sean realized. It took a big jailer's key to lock the holding cell, and Jake didn't seem to have one.

"You won't be able to hide in here," Sean said, matter-of-factly. "The workmen are coming in the morning."

"Take a look around," Jake laughed. "Nobody has been in here in weeks. They've given up on this place."

"ESU will respond," Sean found his cell phone in his pocket. Held it out of sight, and waited for a chance to dial 911. "They'll use sharpshooters and automatic weapons. Flashbangs and tear gas."

Jake tossed a gas mask on the desk.

"I won't go down without a fight, Sean."

It startled both men when one of the big front doors creaked open ever so slightly. A crack of light from the street. A scrawny figure peered in.

Jimmy the Finder, Sean instantly knew. *Never one to pass on an unlocked door.*

"Get in here!" Jake bellowed, and stood up. "Come all the way in right now and close that damn door!"

"Jimmy," Sean's voice broke up an octave. "Run!"

Jake fired the shotgun. Deafening noise. Lead pellets splattering on the door and the wall. Sean was out of the holding cell by then. He threw his cell phone at Jake's head, totally frustrated. Jake ducked. Sean didn't see if Jimmy was hit or not. He only saw the carbine and his flashlight on the floor, and he dove for them.

The second explosion from the shotgun was even more deafening. Mind-numbing. A boom and a miss, right over Sean's head. He slid across the floor—slick with plaster dust—and grabbed the carbine. He clutched the butt in his chest when he fired. Right hand on the trigger, almost under his chin. The carbine kicked and the muzzle flashed and the spent shell casings ejected into his face, but he ignored the hot brass hitting his forehead and cheek.

Jake dove behind the booking desk. Most of Sean's rounds only splintered mahogany. Sean scrambled for cover behind some old, steel filing cabinets before Jake fired the shotgun again. When he next saw Jake, he was climbing the stairway to the second floor. And firing the shotgun to where Sean had been moments before.

Sean felt strong. Confident. Jake Morrow was on the run. He grabbed his flashlight and sprinted to the stairs. He propped the light on the banister with the beam aimed up. Then he stepped to the other side of the bottom step and waited for Jake to show himself with a look back.

Just give me one shot, Sean prayed, with the carbine's sights trained on the top of the stairway.

———

When Deputy Chief Sy Levinson's unmarked SUV and Erik's patrol car arrived at Old Slip, the officers saw Sean's car out front. As soon as they dismounted, they instinctively took cover behind their vehicles and watched the doors and windows of the abandoned precinct. Sy Levinson pulled on a blue NYPD windbreaker.

"Jake will have a 12-gauge," Dex said as he checked his Colt .45 Combat Commander.

"It's not the first time we've been outgunned." Sy Levinson unholstered his service Glock. "If we're not too late, maybe we can keep Sean alive until ESU arrives."

Sy turned to the uniformed officers, who were also behind their car, pistols drawn.

"Call it in," he said. "Tom Sweeney will know what to do."

"I'm going with you," Erik Ramos stated, at the same time that Rhoda Abernathy spoke into her portable radio.

"Listen, no offense," Dex said to Erik. "This is old-school business. You might not be ready for how we roll."

"My partner is in there. I'm with you."

"Okay," Sy nodded. "Follow me."

Rhoda tossed her flashlight to Dex, and the trio went up the stairs in front of the precinct. Sy held his finger up to his lips as a signal to Erik. *Quiet.* Then Dex held the door and Sy made entry. After all three were inside, they swept the muster room with their flashlight beams. Dex went left, and Sy and Erik went right. They started to clear the first floor.

Until they heard voices from upstairs.

Sy led the way to the top of the stairs, moving cautiously. The tableau which greeted them on the second floor was gristly. A discarded pump shotgun and a trail of blood, leading deeper into the dark recesses of Old Slip.

———

Jake Morrow was behind the last row of filing cabinets in the old pistol range. A cornered animal. Sean had him pinned down from behind some other steel filing cabinets. But he couldn't advance on the big man, either. Not without exposing himself to Jake's line of fire.

The old pistol range was a windowless alley of connected offices. There was only one way in, and one way out. And that was behind Sean.

He'll bleed to death, Sean thought, looking at the trail of blood in the alley between the filing cabinets. *All I have to do is wait.*

But Sean's heart sank when he saw Sy Levinson and Dexter Birmingham approaching from behind his barricade. Pistols drawn. He didn't know who he could trust. Were they co-conspirators? Were they there to help him, or Jake?

He readied the carbine to return their fire if it came to that. But Sean relaxed when he saw Erik Ramos with the older cops.

The trio crouched behind the metal cabinets on the other side of the former pistol range.

Sy motioned to Sean, *Let me do the talking.*

"Jake! It's Sy and Dex. Let's talk."

"Hey, you two," Jake laughed. "The kid winged me. Can you believe it?"

"Jake, you're bleeding all over the place," Dex said. "Time to end this."

Sean saw Sy motion for Erik to move to his position across the room while Dex was talking.

"Hey," Sean whispered when Erik hit the deck at his side. "Sorry about this mess."

"Are you okay?"

"Yeah. Better keep your head down. This guy means business."

"So do I," Erik said.

"Jake," they heard Sy Levinson ask. "Where are you hit?"

"In my bum leg. Again! Can you believe that shit?"

"Jake, let us help you," Sy said. "We don't want you to bleed to death. Toss out your piece so we can end this."

"Oh, I intend to end it." He fired a shot their way. The crack of a .357 revolver passed over their heads.

"Man!" Dex yelled. "Don't be like that!"

"Listen to me, Jake," Sy tried. "You're not thinking straight. It shouldn't be like this. We always trusted each other with our lives. Remember?"

Sean listened closely. A slobbering sound. Wet breathing. Could that be sobbing?

"You have to see it my way," Jake said. The words came unsteadily. "What have I got? What did I get out of it? A bum leg and a lousy pension?"

"We can help you," Sy said.

"No. You guys don't care. You're a big wheel, Sy. Deputy chief. Hobnobbing with the mayor and the governor. And Dex, you're all Hollywood now. Living on the Upper West Side with the television stars. What have I got? My used car lot went bust. I'm living in the sales shack until they evict me from there, too."

"This isn't the way to end it, Jake," Dex said.

Sy looked at Sean and tapped his fist on the side of his 9mm Glock. Then held his palm up. *Hold your fire.*

"Listen, Jake," Sy said. "Just stand up. Show yourself. We won't fire if you don't."

"I can't look at you guys," Jake's tone wavered. "How did this get so messed up?"

"Think about the way it was," Dex said. "Think about the old days."

"No," Jake's voice heaved with emotion. "It's all over. It's a mess."

They could all hear the chatter on Erik's portable radio. ESU was arriving at Old Slip.

"Jake, we're going to have to back out," Sy was clear. "We don't want to leave you behind."

"You know what ESU will do," Dex added.

While they waited for a response, the sobbing stopped.

"Hey, Sean," Jake's voice was firm again. "What's the worst way for a cop to die?"

"By his own gun, Jake. The way you killed Ted."

"It was an accident, son. Do you believe me?"

"Yeah. I believe you, Jake. But he didn't deserve that."

"You're right. But ... I guess ... I deserve this."

The cops flinched at the muffled report of a muzzle pressed against flesh. The last shot ever fired on the old pistol range echoed down to the muster room of the abandoned First Precinct at Old Slip and took Jake Morrow's soul with it.

———

When Sean Lamont stepped out of the old precinct, he was blinded by the flashing lights of a dozen patrol units. ESU, CSI, and the Bomb Squad had responded. At the end of the street, the antenna mast of a mobile command post was raised to the night sky. At the other end, paramedics and the Fire Department were standing ready.

It was cold.

Sean realized for the first time that he wasn't nearly well dressed enough for the night. He crossed his arms against his chest. Raised his eyes above the buildings and the squawking of radios and a hundred responders and saw stars. He took deep breaths. He wanted to hold Helen. He wondered when he would see her again. Detectives from the Major Crimes Squad separated them and began the questioning immediately. Their stories jived. Then the old cops and the young officers regrouped and stood across the street while CSI worked the scene inside Old Slip.

They asked Sean if he was okay. Not much else was said. The training officers arrived, shaking their heads in disbelief when they saw Sean.

"You again? Two shootouts in twenty-four hours? This never happened before."

"Yeah," Sean sighed. "Listen, I'm really tired. Beat. Maybe we could do this tomorrow?"

"Sure. We'll do our thing with the crime scene, and talk later."

When Frick and Frack rolled up—Detectives Dick Francis and Frank Capella—it was apparent that they had been roused out of their homes and beds.

"Okay," Dick Francis said. "Who wants to bring us up to speed?"

The group circled the Internal Affairs detectives and looked at each other. Sean and Erik and Rhoda and Sy Levinson. It was Dex Birmingham who finally spoke.

"Jake Morrow killed Ted Lamont. We all heard him confess. Just before he shot himself."

"No kidding?" Frack looked surprised. "I didn't see that coming. But why?"

A long silence followed.

"It was a personal matter," Sy Levinson finally mumbled.

"Okay," Frick offered. "Would you care to expound on that, Deputy Chief Levinson? Sir."

"Sean," Sy said. "Would you leave Dex and me alone with the Internal Affairs detectives for a moment?"

"I don't think I will, sir," Sean braced himself. The East River Trust was certainly about to be exposed. "I'm involved in this, as much as anyone."

"Okay," Sy shrugged and turned to Frick and Frack. "Jake Morrow is Matt Lamont's father."

What? Sean's head began a slow spiral as his mind attempted to reach around Sy Levinson's words. *What did he just say? My brother Matt was … is …*

"We all knew it," Dex Birmingham shrugged. "Although I can't remember ever saying it out loud. Until this very moment. It was always in the looks and pauses between our words."

"It's true," Sy Levinson looked at Sean. "You have to understand how things were, in the old days, Sean. We were always together, on duty and off duty. Things got mixed up sometimes. When your mother got pregnant … well … Ted always did the right thing. But we all sort of knew. Especially as Matt got older."

"I need to sit down," Sean reached behind himself. Erik and Rhoda grabbed his arms. Half held him up.

"You're okay," Erik said.

And Rhoda added, "Chill, Sean."

In a moment, Sean had recovered. He looked at Sy and Dex.

"We don't know why it boiled over that night in Brooklyn," Dex said. "I guess we'll never know. They were best friends. Something made that unspoken old grudge flash up, I suppose."

"Christ almighty," Dick Francis muttered. "A crime of passion."

"Which brings us to tonight," Frank Capella looked squarely at Sean. "Police Officer Lamont, when you entered Old Slip tonight, what was your intention?"

Sean moved his lips to speak. His handcuffs were still in the trunk of his car. He came to kill Jake Morrow, and he didn't care anymore. The words were almost out when Dex moved.

"He went in to arrest Jake Morrow," Dex said, stepping half between the Internal Affairs detectives and Sean. "For the crime of murder."

"Let the officer talk. You didn't intend to kill him?"

Sy stepped alongside Dex. Closing the gap between Sean and the detectives. "My officer was attempting to arrest a felon."

The detectives seemed lost in thought. They looked at Sean, between Dex Birmingham and Sy Levinson.

"That's what I saw, too," Erik voiced.

"Me too," Rhoda raised her hand.

"Okay," the detectives looked at each other. "I guess that settles it."

"But we're going to have a hell of a time writing this up for the grand jury," Frack said to Sy Levinson. "It will have to be very carefully presented."

"My daughter is an ADA in Brooklyn. Maybe she can help with the verbiage."

"You're on, Deputy Chief. Thanks for the help."

Frick shook Sean's hand as the detectives departed.

"You're a good cop, Sean," Dick Francis said. "Just like your old man. A cop's cop."

Then Frack—Detective Frank Capella—surprised Sean when he reached for his hand.

"If I'm ever in a tough spot, I hope they send you as my backup, Sean."

FINAL CUT

They all got together one last time on the West Lido Promenade. Sean, with Sy Levinson, Dex Birmingham, Beverly, Rebecca, and Matt. And Helen, of course.

This was the middle of December and it had snowed the night before. Just a dusting. Beverly's house was coming along. It was almost back to normal.

They all went to Beverly's bedroom when Becca got on Sean's shoulders and went into the attic. She came down with a cardboard box and they took it to the kitchen. Beverly had coffee cake and a fresh pot brewing when they sat down at the kitchen table.

Becca and Helen took the bundles of cash from the box and laid them on the table in six equal stacks.

Matt took his thirty thousand dollars and left right away. Bernadette was waiting in her car in the driveway. Motor running. They were going straight to Atlantic City to double their money, he said.

"Do you think he'll be a problem?" Dex asked, after Matt left.

"He'll talk about his big score the rest of his life," Sean shrugged. "His friends will get tired of hearing the story. They won't believe it, any more than any of the others."

"Yeah, man," Dex smiled.

Beverly was the first one to put her cut of the cash back in the box. She was looking at Sy Levinson as she did so.

Then Dex Birmingham put his thirty thousand dollars back in. So did Sy and Becca. Sean put his in last and asked Helen to go to the oven.

It took her a few trips to bring the other sixty-five bundles of cash to the table. Becca finally got up to help her. The group put the rest of the money from the oven—the $650,000 they hadn't told Matt about—back into the cardboard box. Sean closed the top on $810,000 and folded the tabs under to keep it shut.

For a long time, nothing was said. Until Sy broke the silence.

"I'm done with the East Side Trust, Sean. I don't care what you do with this money. But I never want to hear about it again."

"Same here," Dex smiled. "You're on your own, son."

Beverly took a sip of coffee. Sean thought that she had been looking at Sy for a long time.

"It seems that my generation has spoken," she said to Sean. "Be careful. And be kind. And never again mention it to me, either."

Sean was sitting between Becca and Helen. "We have a plan," he told the old folks.

"Yes sir-ee, bobcat-tail," Becca whispered.

"Well, good for you!" Dex slapped his hands together and rubbed his palms. "I have a hot date with a Nubian princess at our cottage in the Hamptons. So if you'll excuse me…"

"I should be going, too," Sy said. "They decided that I should retire after the end of the year. But I'm still responsible for Manhattan South for a few weeks."

"I would have a beer with you on the way out," Dex said. "But I might not be able to handle Joyce if I leave her motor running too long," he laughed.

Sean never did meet a cat half as cool as Dexter Birmingham.

"Sure," Sy muttered.

Then Beverly totally surprised Sean.

"I'll go and have a beer," she said. "If you buy me dinner, too. I don't feel like cooking for myself again tonight."

"Sure," Sy's face lit up. They all saw color there nobody had seen since Hoda passed away. "That would be great, Beverly. We'll go someplace nice."

"I'd like that a lot, Sy."

"Where are you going, Sean?" Beverly asked as he and Helen left.

"No place," Sean answered, feeling like a teenager again.

———

Sean could see Sneaky Nick in the vault with an employee of the institution. He was waiting in one of the bank's private counting rooms, right outside the massive steel door. Beverly, Sy and Dex did not know which bank Sean had gone to, only that it was somewhere in the city.

Helen was waiting outside, in the car. Nick had come on the subway and taken the safe deposit box in his name. Nobody would suspect a priest, right?

Nick put the safe deposit box on the little table between him and Sean. Nick had no idea what was in the cardboard box, which Sean had carried in, until he peeled the top back.

Sean laughed when Nick's jaw dropped.

"I'll need you to get small amounts of this over time," Sean told his oldest friend as he shoveled the bundles of cash into the metal box. "Unfortunately, you'll hear from me every time a cop gets killed in the city. Other than that, this is our deepest secret. We won't talk about it. We'll pretend this never happened."

"Sean, I don't know what to say."

"Say nothing, Nick. If something happens to me, Becca and Helen will take over. Becca will have the other key to this safe deposit box."

"Sean, why me?"

"Because you're my best friend, Nick."

"This is a big secret to keep. A mystery…"

"We can keep secrets. Can't we, Nick?"

His eyes fell to the floor.

"Thanks for never telling, Sean. I was drunk, you know."

"We're friends, Nick. Nobody else needs to know."

"It's embarrassing…" His eyes came back up.

"No need to be embarrassed. That's the way your God made you, I guess. I don't care one bit. Anyway, let's not talk about it." Then he laughed, "It was damn embarrassing for me too, you know."

"May I bless this box before we put it away?"

"Sure. Not that I believe in that stuff. But it can't hurt."

Nick said a little thing and then the door was open and Sean could see him putting the money away in the vault. He went home on the subway and Sean went out to the car.

"You drive," he told Helen.

"So that's it?" she said as they left the parking lot. "You lied to your brother. You took the money that your mother and sister need. And you're going to give it away? A little bit at a time?"

"Yeah. But let's not talk about it."

"We're not exactly rich. In case you haven't noticed."

"A teacher and a cop can do okay."

"Why Nick?"

"Because I can trust him. And he's not a member of the service."

"Neither am I."

"Yes, you are. We have a family membership, kitten."

She drove. Sean spoke softly.

"I can't do this alone, you know."

She looked at him. One of those rare moments when he couldn't read her eyes.

"We're not moving out of the city, are we?"

"It's the greatest show on Earth. You don't want me to miss it, do you?"

She sighed. Resigned.

"Close your window, Sean. It's freezing."

"I've got to be able to hear the streets."

"They talk to you, don't they?"

"Yeah."

They drove. Sean saw a drug dealer in front of a convenience store.

Even the fat old cops in this sleepy part of the city will spot him, sooner or later, he thought.

He looked at her.

"Helen, did I ever tell you what Ted said the first time he met you?"

"No."

"He said that you were a keeper, right off the bat. He thought you'd make a fine wife for a cop. He told me that when we were first dating. Before I even got accepted to the Police Academy."

"I love you, Sean. But I don't know if I can go on like this."

"Sure you can. I love you, Helen. I need you."

She was crying.

"Damn it, I could never leave you," she said. "But at least promise me that you'll retire the day you are eligible?"

"I can't make that promise. Let's call it a working understanding that I'll leave the service when the time is right."

"Sean…"

"I need to know that you are at home waiting for me. That's the only way I can get through a watch. That's what will keep me alive, kitten."

"I know, Sean."

He looked at her. She sighed. Words were failing her.

Sean held her hand and looked out the window. Towards the streets.

She's a good kid. She'll come around.

AUTHOR'S NOTE:

The First Precinct at Old Slip was decommissioned in 1977. The structure later served as the NYPD Museum until it was damaged in Hurricane Sandy. The house on West Lido Promenade, the Roebling tugboat pier, and the East River Trust exist only on these pages.

www.dscooperbooks.com